MY NOT-SO-SUPER BLIND DATE

SUBPARHEROES

ALLISON TEMPLE

I'm Morgan Murray. You probably haven't heard of me. With a raft of allergies and powers that won't do more than charge a phone, I never lived up to my super family's super expectations. It's okay. I'm used to being overlooked.

But there's only so much disappointment one man can take, and finding out the cute guy on my blind date is a henchman for the city's most notorious crime boss? That's one letdown too many. This date is over before it even starts.

Or is it?

In the meet-cute that won't end, Jasper and I are stuck in a time loop, and the only way out is deadly. Good and evil may be relative terms, but if we can't escape, we may find out that love is forever . . . and ever.

Cover Design: Jo Clement, Covers by Jo
Developmental Editing: Jennifer Graybeal
Copy Editing: Adam Mongaya, Tessera Editorial
Proofreading: Lori Parks, LesCourt Author Services

❀ Created with Vellum

For Russ, the superest partner ever

CONTENT WARNINGS

This book includes death. A lot of it. It's like the movie *Groundhog Day,* except sleep won't cut it. Death is the only way out. Stabbings, gunshots, vehicular accidents, death by supervillain. Even a few self-inflicted ones to get out of a sticky situation. There are no falling anvils or pianos, but that's about the limit of it.

Also, there's the usual raft of superhero tropes. Deceased parents. Violence. You get the idea.

For more information, use the contact form at AllisonTemple.com/contact-us.

CHAPTER 1

I may not be able to leap tall buildings in a single bound or read minds, but there's one thing I know for sure: any blind date that starts with a painting of your mother staring down at you can't go well. Especially if your mother is dead.

Another bad sign: my mystery man is late. Six whole minutes. Anything after five and I get anxious. Is it me? Did I get the day mixed up? Am I in the wrong place? But I check my phone and the details in Clarissa's text are clear. *Wench. 7:00 pm. Thursday. Have fun!* She wrapped it up with several kissy emojis, which seems optimistic. I'm not the kind of guy who has rules about these things. You can kiss on the first date if you want to. But I've never been that lucky. The best I've ever managed was a handshake and a "This was fun." Then a string of unanswered text messages that indicate maybe it wasn't so fun after all. Which is probably how I wound up on a blind date arranged by my BFF and her girlfriend in the first place.

A blind date. I sigh, trying not to dwell on how pathetic this feels. Who even goes on blind dates anymore? Isn't it supposed to be all *swipe left* and *swipe right* and "Hey, how you doin'? Here's a picture of my penis you didn't ask for."

And yet . . . the answer to that question is me. I go on blind dates because my love life needs a jump start. Or at least I need Clarissa to stop bugging me about when I'm going to meet someone so we can double date with her and Alyssa.

Yes. Clarissa and Alyssa. You love who you love, right?

Eight minutes late.

"You sure you don't want anything to eat? I could cook you up something." Vee comes to stand at my table. She's been hovering since I arrived. She probably thinks she's being subtle, pretending to be on her way to other tables but always making sure to walk past mine. When she first came over, I faked a phone call rather than speak to her. Childish? Maybe. But either she'll make small talk like we're strangers, which would be awful given she basically raised me, or she'll ask me earnest questions about how I've been for the last two years, which would be worse. This time, though, she catches me unawares, and I have no choice but to answer her.

"I'm fine. I'm waiting for someone."

Her eyebrows shoot up. "A friend? Or someone else?" The quirk of her lips is probably meant to be friendly. I know what she's trying to do, but somehow I can't make myself return her smile. We aren't friendly, not anymore, and opening myself up to that risks feeling too many other things I can't deal with, especially not while I wait for my mystery man.

"He'll be here soon," I say.

Vee's smile falters. She looks the same as she always did. Tanned skin. Dark hair in a long braid. Though as she turns, the streaks in her hair I thought were a reflection of the overhead lights might actually be silver strands. A silent reminder of the passing of time.

Speaking of time, we're at eleven minutes now. I got here twenty minutes ago. Punctuality is the most basic form of respect. Since I was early, I pulled out my laptop to do some work. And now I've got the warning notification that if I don't charge it soon, it'll go into hibernation. Not like there's an electrical outlet in the middle of this superhero-themed diner. Fortunately, I have a way to fix that. I put a finger to the computer, just over where the battery is located. I take a deep breath. It's hard to perform when Mother is watching me from overhead. She's midfight with Indigo, the shadow assassin. The expression on her face is probably intended to be one of fierce determination as she saves the world yet again, but all I can see is the way one eyebrow is arched in scorn over the band across her eyes. She's daring me to charge this laptop without frying it.

Superpowers are meant to be used for the greater good, Morgan. Not for your convenience.

It's a great philosophy for someone like her. The Legendary Flame. She could incinerate the bad guys with a thought. Melt the Great Lakes in February by sneezing. I focus on the laptop, but all I manage is a little spark that makes the display flicker and sends a faint smell of burning into the air. I shut it down and toast my mother with my tea. Our family line of superheroes started with my great-grandfather and ends with me. I'm not a black sheep so much as a dud. At least there's no one left to remind me about things like responsibility and wasted potential.

God, I'm getting maudlin and I'm not even drinking. Time to go. I'll tell Clarissa her mystery man stood me up, and hopefully she'll be distracted with sympathy enough to leave my love life alone for a few weeks.

The front door flies open. A guy in a green toque bustles through the bar. When his gaze lands on me, he slumps.

Oh no.

Watching him rally is physically painful. I know I'm not boyfriend material. Not at first glance, at least. A little too short. A little too soft around the edges. Gay guys can be so judgy. If you don't have a paint roller six-pack and a bubble butt, half the time they won't give you a second look. For a while, I thought my future was a normal human life with a normal human man. That went about as well as you would expect when your childhood was anything but normal and your idea of small talk is differential equations and the physics of climate change.

This is a disaster and we haven't even spoken. Why did I think I could do this? Years of motherly admonitions to "work on myself" echo in my head. And she didn't only mean the superpowers that never quite kicked in. It was everything. My poor social skills. My lack of athleticism. I'm pretty sure she even resented having to pay for braces when I was twelve, like it was somehow my fault my teeth wouldn't straighten themselves.

I have to fight back the urge to flip the image of Mother off as my would-be date comes toward me. I've arrived straight from work, so I'm in a button-down and sweater, along with a pair of khakis that only have one ink stain on the pocket. As he approaches, though, I still feel overdressed. My ears go hot.

He's kind of cute. No, more like really cute, though I could give him some fashion tips. The hat on his head is so old and worn it looks like something infected crawled up there and died. Bits of sandy brown hair stick out beneath it, and his pale skin is freckled over the nose. When he pulls himself up straight and smiles, he's the kind of guy you want to know. Maybe you see him at work or at a party, and the twinkle in his eye and the width of his shoulders say he'll be a good friend. Someone to lean on.

This will never work. Clarissa said we'd have a lot in common, but unless he has a mountain of insecurities and mommy issues, I can't see how this handsome lumberjack is the right partner for me. He's going to want to do things like hike and make organic trail mix. I want to stay up late running data sets and I'm allergic to mosquito bites. And nuts. And some dried fruits.

Still, while I failed crime fighting 101, my mother did manage to teach me manners, so I stand as he approaches and say, "You must be Jasper."

His eyelids flutter for a second and his jaw tightens. Is he already disappointed? But he nods like he's made a decision— maybe to stick this out for a minimally polite amount of time— and sits down with a bright smile.

"Jasper Jackson, at your service."

There's a joke on the tip of my tongue about how I really would like him to service me, but I'm not brave enough to let it out. Things get worse when Vee returns to the table. She smiles at me and I flinch, my gaze darting from her to Mother on the ceiling to Jasper before finally settling on my lap. Vee probably thinks the mural overhead is a touching tribute to a dead friend. I think it's gaudy.

"You're here," she says to Jasper like she knows him.

"I am." His smile is polite. He probably rocks small talk too.

"Can I get you something?" she asks.

Jasper says, "I'll have whatever he's having."

"Iced tea." She writes it down on a stained notepad. I expect her to walk away, but instead she says, "Anything else?"

"Want something to eat?" He's speaking to me. I shake my head. This date isn't going to last very long. Not with the easy way he's smiling up at Vee. I'm going to say something rude or boring, and he's going to realize that we are not meant to be. Also, me ordering food in a restaurant is complicated since I'm allergic to half the menu. Of course, Vee would make something special for me if I'd let her, but I'm not a child. That's not the first impression I want to make.

When Vee finally leaves, Jasper drums his fingers on the tabletop in a happy little rhythm. He dips his head, trying to catch my gaze.

"You look familiar," he says. "Have we met before?"

I meet a lot of people. Travel a lot with the research team at the Ziro Foundation. It's possible I met Jasper somewhere before, but his face doesn't ring any bells. I'd remember the gold flecks in his eyes and the way one of his front teeth is just crooked enough to be endearing.

Maybe it's better if I cut this short. If I'm already cataloguing his features, it's only a matter of time before he notices me staring and I embarrass myself.

"I think I'd remember if we'd met before," I say. I check the time. I've been here for a half hour. Never mind that he just got here. Forty-five minutes is long enough for a first date, right? If I stick it out for fifteen minutes, I can tell Clarissa I tried and save myself from the hurt of waiting to hear from Jasper when he's never going to talk to me again.

"You're probably right." He makes a disheartened noise. See? Doomed to failure.

But Vee returns with his iced tea and also a basket of tortilla chips with salsa and queso we didn't ask for. When I go to point it out, she gives me a wink and says, "There's onion in the salsa, but you should be good with the queso."

It was Vee who was there for my first allergic reaction. Mother was chasing a dehydrated supervillain causing droughts in East Africa. Vee was left behind to make sure little Morgan did basic things like putting his shoes on the right feet and getting proper meals. Except it turned out my aversion to onions wasn't only childish picky eating. When I finally choked down that first spoonful of French onion soup, I started to choke for real, sending us on a panicky ambulance ride to the ER. Thus began my lifelong fear of eating things I shouldn't and making sure I was always armed with a trusty EpiPen in case my careful planning wasn't careful enough.

"Don't like salsa?" Jasper asks when she goes. He dips a chip into the salsa and sure enough, a big glob of it splashes onto the others, contaminating the whole thing.

Well, that's just great.

"So, Jasper," I say quickly, turning the subject away from myself. "Clarissa says you and Alyssa went to med school together. Are you a doctor too?"

He works a mouthful around until he can talk past it. Still, the words are garbled when he says, "I'm a henchman."

My stomach drops. I can't have heard that right. "A what?"

Jasper shrugs as he fishes around for another chip. "A hench-man. I hench. If you need henching, I'm your man."

I glance up at Mother, like she might be listening. Did her eyebrow arch get a little higher?

"You're a criminal?" I ask. "Does Clarissa know about this?"

He sticks out his bottom lip like he's considering this. The skin is chapped. His stubble is dark and scruffy against his cheek. Suddenly, I'm annoyed he didn't have the consideration to shave. What about that first kiss? Just because we won't see each other again doesn't mean we can't have one little kiss.

"I guess," he says. "Technically."

"Technically?" Not that there will be a first kiss. Not with someone like him. Henching? I didn't even know that was a verb.

And yet, he doesn't notice my mounting incredulity. Instead, he stuffs another chip into his mouth and says, "Good and evil are relative terms, don't you think? You sure you don't want some of these? The queso is awesome. I wonder if she has guacamole too."

Relative terms? They most definitely are not. You don't need to be a superhero to know some actions help people and others hurt. I clench my fists under the table.

Jasper licks melted cheese off his fingers. Like he's having a conversation with himself, he says, "I mean, my employers are certainly criminals."

"Employers? You have many?" I do my best to look casual as I reach for my drink, but my hand shakes with growing rage.

He shrugs, like we're talking about the news. Stocks are up. War is ongoing. What can you do?

"The economy is tough. Hard to find full-time henchwork these days. I've got a few freelance henchgigs. Mostly, though, I work for Walter Wolfe. You've heard of him?"

I'm gripping my iced tea so tightly the plastic cup creaks. I consider throwing it at Jasper. Who confesses to criminal activities on a first date? Walter Wolfe claims to be a businessman, and maybe he was once. He made a fortune in industrial chemical manufacturing over a decade ago, and now he owns real estate all over the city. But the common wisdom back at SPAM was it's all a front for more illegal activities. He's just very good at covering his tracks, and technically his most obvious crimes are the sort that can be handled by regular human law enforcement, so we never got involved.

Also, I don't work at SPAM anymore, so he's not my problem. But if Jasper's involved in any part of Wolfe's operation, then our rosy future together is officially over. Doesn't matter about his charming crooked teeth or his flecky eyes. I have standards, and they involve not running from the law.

"You sure we haven't met before?" he asks, those same eyes sparkling like we're sharing a good joke. He's the only one who's laughing, though.

"I don't consort with criminals," I say as I stuff the laptop into my bag. My heart is pounding with embarrassment, and I can't say why. I've done nothing wrong here. My jacket sleeve is twisted as I pull it off my chair, and I can't get it undone gracefully, so I stash that too. I give Jasper a frosty smile. "Goodbye. Good luck with your . . . endeavors."

"See you soon," he says, which is not the response I expect, but whatever. He's a smart-ass. I'm a law-abiding citizen. It was never going to work.

"I highly doubt that," I say.

He winks at me. Winks! "Call it a feeling."

Well, he's wrong. As soon as I'm outside, I call Clarissa. She has so much explaining to do. The phone rings and rings. Around me, the street is empty, and I've already wasted too much time tonight, so I cross against the light.

"Hello?" Clarissa says just as I'm about to hang up. She sounds far too pleased with herself. "Are you in looooove yet?"

"You don't know me at all, do you?" I growl.

"Sure I do. What's wrong?" She coos, and unlike my all-too human growl, her sound has a distinct edge of pigeon to it that only irritates me.

"What's wrong?" I ask. "You said he was a doctor."

"Right. Jasper and Alyssa—"

I don't find out what she says. Instead, I'm blinded as headlights swing around the corner. Too high off the ground to be a car. The telltale hum of one of the city's new fleet of electric busses is my final warning before body meets grill and my world goes flying.

Surprisingly, the act of getting hit by a bus doesn't hurt nearly as much as you might expect. The problem isn't the moment of impact. It's the part where you hit the concrete. The resulting trauma is unpredictable. Some people get up and walk away. Others land a fraction of an inch in another position and everything goes to hell. In my case, I bounce off the curb while bus tires screech. Pretty sure my pelvis is broken. Probably one if not both my legs. It's hard to see out of my right eye, and my hair feels wet against the back of my head. It's only been a few seconds, but already every breath is getting harder than the last. The wheeze says I've punctured a lung. Basic field medicine is one of those things I learned while I waited for my superness to reveal itself. If you can't be part of the solution, you can be there to treat the collateral damage.

Passengers rush out of the bus where it's come to a halt. One of them says they're calling an ambulance. I can't see who is speaking, though, because suddenly my field of vision is filled with Jasper. I try to tell him to go away, but the words don't come out right and they're punctuated by a goobery cough that is undoubtedly bloody.

He bats my hand away as I try to push him back, and his voice is oddly calm. He wipes my face with a cloth.

"It's okay. It's okay." His gaze swings up like he's talking to someone, though everything goes quiet and dark for a second, so I don't hear what he says. It really is too bad he's not a doctor. We aren't going to have a torrid love affair, but someone with some more extensive medical knowledge than how to dress a wound would be really handy right now.

When my vision clears again, I realize his hair is uncovered.

The cloth against my cheek is his toque. There's no way that's hygienic. I go to tell him to leave me alone—people like him don't get to hurt others one minute and help them the next—but all I can do is cough and gasp.

"I'll see you soon," he says, which makes me laugh at least. God, that hurts. Soon I won't be seeing anyone. But he leans over me and whispers urgently. "Morgan. Listen. Tomorrow. Please. I need you to remember me tomorrow, okay?"

Why is he still here? We don't know each other. And if he sticks around much longer, the police will arrive. They won't be able to save me, but at least they can arrest him for all his henching. Odds are good I won't be here to witness it, and that's a shame.

I wonder if I'll get to see my mother again.

CHAPTER 2

My mother stares down at me from the ceiling with her eyebrow arched halfway up to her hairline. Is that even physically possible? I try to do the same, and the headache that pounds inside my skull nearly makes me pass out. Oh god, it hurts. Everything does. My head. My hips. My legs.

"You sure you don't want something to eat? I could cook you up something." Vee is standing at the edge of my table and I practically jump out of my skin, which only makes the pain worse. The idea of eating anything makes me want to throw up.

"I'm good," I say, swallowing hard. She cocks her head like she's about to ask more questions, so I frown down at my laptop screen. The battery is almost drained, but she doesn't know that. I type something. It might be gibberish. My vision doubles as I try to focus so I can read it anyway. When Vee walks away, I breathe an unsteady sigh of relief.

The chair across from me scrapes back. I didn't even hear someone approach. For a second, I think it's Vee, but it's not. It's a hipster lumberjack. My vision swims again. Is he my date? Clarissa said he was cute. Too cute for someone like me, though by the way it feels inside my skull, the aneurysm that's about to burst will probably kill me before he comes to that realization.

He smiles, showing one crooked tooth, and my head spins. For a second, the feeling is more like déjà vu, but it recedes quickly, overwhelmed by the burning nausea in my throat.

"Am I late?" he asks, pulling the toque from his head. It's the same colour green as his eyes. He holds out his hand to shake. "Jasper Jackson, at your service."

Whatever he's offering, I don't want it, unless it's a few ibuprofens and maybe a ride to the hospital.

"I'm sorry," I say, pushing up on wobbly legs. There's a good chance I won't make it to the door without collapsing, but I have to try. "I need to leave."

"Oh, cool." He rises too. "Where are we headed?"

We? Who said anything about us going together? We just met. I haven't even introduced myself, and if I try now, I'm probably going to throw up on his shoes.

"Leaving already?" Vee comes to our table as I try to put my laptop in my bag, and I can't help the way I shrink back from her. When Clarissa said she'd arranged for my mystery man to meet me at Wench, I was immediately uncomfortable. I haven't spoken to Vee since Mom died, much less stopped at her super-hero-themed diner. When Mother was alive, Wench seemed quirky. Since her death, the whole place feels like a gratuitous memorial that I want no part of. All I want right now is an ice pick to stab the living thing that has to be currently clawing its way outside my cheekbone.

I pitch forward and strong arms wrap around me, helping me slump back down to my chair.

"Can we get a couple of fresh iced teas?" Jasper's voice is surprisingly close. Oh. He's the one who caught me.

I push him away as I burp down some puke. "I'm okay."

Vee chuckles. "He always was stubborn. Runs in the family."

She's not allowed to talk about my mother. Not after everything. I point a finger in her direction as I try to work up the gumption to tell her so, but she's already walking away, long braid swinging down her back.

"I have to go home," I say, at the same time Jasper says, "Three more minutes."

"What?" Seriously, why are the lights so bright in here?

He leans toward me, face serious. It's a cute face. Stubble and one crooked tooth. If I saw him on a bus, I'd hope it was the kind of face I'd see regularly on my commute.

"Three more minutes," he says. "Can't have a repeat of yesterday. Looks like you're still feeling it. Three more minutes and it's safe to go. Trust me, you'll thank me later."

Excuse me? Lumber Jasper has no right to tell me what to do. Clarissa said he was a doctor or something, but we don't know each other. I struggle out of his hold, even though I'm shivering. My jacket. I should put on my jacket. But when I pull it from the chair, I can't even find the sleeve, so I stuff it into my bag along with the laptop.

"Morgan. Wait."

"Let me leave or I'll vomit all over your shirt." I stagger toward the door. Hopefully the cool air outside will settle me.

It doesn't.

The scuff of a shoe on the pavement means Jasper's followed me. "Morgan. At least let me call someone for you. You really don't look good. Is there someone who can come get you? Clarissa?"

Clarissa. She can pick me up. She should, actually. This is all her fault.

I fumble for my phone. I'm going to give her a piece of my mind. The streetlight overhead hurts my eyes, but I stumble on.

Oh, wait. Not the streetlight. It's not shining down at me, it's shining at me. Too high to be a car. The grill of a bus shines chrome fangs at me as it comes around the corner, moving too fast.

Here we go again, a voice says inside my head, but before I can ask what it means by "again," it gets swallowed up in the pain as I trip and—

Something pulls me back. The bus blares its horn as it rumbles into the dark. I'm sprawled on my back. An immovable weight holds me down on the damp sidewalk and hot breath pants in my ear.

"It's okay. It's okay. Morgan, you're okay. You're alive." The tips of Jasper's fingers are rough as he brushes hair out of my eyes. The gesture is weirdly tender considering we've just met.

But despite his words and kind touch, adrenaline is coursing through me. Something is very wrong. The bus. The concrete. I try to breathe, and it's so painful, my vision fades in and out.

"No, no, no. Morgan. Hey." Jasper grabs hold of my shoulders and shakes. I flinch at the pain. So much pain. "Hey. Look at me. Look. You're okay. It's a panic attack. Look at me."

My gaze meets his. The streetlight shines around him like a halo. Is this heaven? Did the bus hit us both? Are we both dead? I'm the only one who should be dead. I'm the only one who—

No. That's not right. Is it? Memories ping around in my brain. It feels like trying to focus on a picture being held too close to my face. I back up, retracing my steps. The bar. Jasper was late. I left. I walked outside. There was a bus. Pain. People.

I glance around. The street is empty.

"The bus," I say slowly, pushing up on my elbows.

"Yes." He helps me all the way up to sitting. "Yes, the bus. Do you remember what happened?"

"You . . . pulled me out of the way. You saved me. I think."

"Yes. Yes. And?" His voice rises excitedly. He probably wants thanks. Hard to give it, though, when my palms are scraped and there's dirt on my knees. I take a deep breath and exhale slowly until I feel calmer.

"Usually when one saves someone else's life," I say, straightening my glasses, "they do it out of compassion, not for the thanks. I'm sure I'd have managed to get out of the way on my own, but if you insist, thank you."

He blinks, confusion flickering over his face. A car slows down, and the driver rolls down the window as they pass.

"You two okay?"

I wave them off. "Fine, thanks. I tripped. No big deal."

Jasper slumps until he's sitting next to me on the curb. He puts his face in his hands, scrubbing at the skin before he pulls off his hat and tugs at his hair.

"Why do I remember and you don't?"

"Remember what?" While this date hasn't been great, I guess it's technically been memorable, what with the near vomit and even nearer near-death experience.

Tomorrow. I need you to remember me, okay?

My brain's still doing that magic eye optical illusion thing, and the question—more like a plea—sticks out like a hangnail I can't cut away. In my mind, Jasper leans over me, brown hair exposed. There are other people too. Someone calls an ambulance. There's blood on Jasper's shirt, but when I glance at him next to me, the flannel is clean.

What is this memory? When is it from? He said I looked familiar. Have we actually met before and I'm only remembering now?

Wait. When did he say I looked familiar? Our date lasted all of about thirty seconds before I had to run for the door.

He sighs as he pulls himself to his feet. Jasper doesn't look at me as he brushes his palms on his jeans.

"See you tomorrow, I guess," he says.

Suddenly, I need him to stay. I don't know why. Ten minutes ago, I wanted to get away as fast as possible, and now as he turns his back to me, I'm scared. The things in my head don't match what I know to be true. The sequence of events. The bus. The lingering pain is more than can be explained by a scraped hand and a few bruises when Jasper pulled me to safety. I bend my leg as I sit up, afraid that they'll give out under the slightest pressure or that my pieces won't hold me together. But I'm fine.

"Jasper."

He glances over his shoulder. "Yeah?"

Impossible. The words that come out of my mouth are impossible, but I can't stop them.

"Did I die yesterday?"

We stare at each other. The evening air is cool, and my breath swirls in a white puff in front of my face. Unexpectedly, Jasper drops to the sidewalk. Scrambles to me and puts his hand on my cheek again, in a way that is too familiar for people who just met on a blind date. He says, "What do you remember? Don't worry if it seems far-fetched. Tell me."

It's not just far-fetched. It's unthinkable. Beyond the laws of reality. Still, I sound out the words as I try to get the memories straight. "The bus. But you didn't stop me. Someone calling an ambulance. Pain." His hat on my face like he was trying to take care of me, a stranger who didn't want him. "I think I died after I walked out of our date. Except it was our date yesterday. Not the one today. I don't know how that works."

Panic flickers as my brain tries to make sense of something that doesn't fit in a three-dimensional puzzle. Squeezing the pieces together brings my headache back.

But Jasper sinks back onto his heels again and covers his face with his hat. He makes soft gasping sounds that might be sobs, but soon they deepen and round out until he's clearly laughing. His smile, when he lowers his hands, is electric. Cool relief on a face that is suddenly younger than it was a minute ago. He launches himself at me and pulls me into a hug, shaking as he holds me too close.

"Thank you," he says breathlessly, kissing the side of my head. I'm too shocked to push him away. "Thank you so much. This is the sixtieth time we've been on this date. We're stuck here, and I was starting to think you were never going to remember."

CHAPTER 3

Sixty? That's like two months. I don't remember what I had for breakfast this morning. Trying to remember where I was two months ago . . .

That's a really long time. And we've . . . what? Been going on dates that I don't remember, except for the one time I got hit by a bus?

My laugh is thin, tinged with nervous desperation. "You're joking."

He shakes his head sadly. "I'm not that funny."

"You expect me to believe you?" A muscle jumps behind my eyebrow. Is this what they mean by a brain cramp?

"Morgan, I'm sorry. I don't have any other way to tell you and—"

"You're lying." Am I dreaming? I fell asleep at the lab and my anxiety about Clarissa's ridiculous blind date has manifested itself as this strange person who thinks he can get me to believe that this is not even our second date, but our sixtieth.

"I'm not lying." His fists clench on the cement. "Please, you have to—"

"I don't have to do anything." Certainly nothing he says. Brush my teeth, drink more water, look both ways—now more than ever, apparently—when crossing the street. Those are things I *have* to do. Listen to a stranger spouting impossible nonsense? Doesn't even make my list. Travel through time? I can't even charge a laptop.

"Morgan. Wait." He scrambles to his feet as I try to march off. "You remember. You just said. The bus. You said you remembered."

"I don't know what I remember, but it's not that. That would be impossible. How can I be here now if I were dead?" How many times did I wish for my mother to come back when we all knew that she was gone?

"I know it's a lot. If you would just come with me, we could talk." He reaches for my hand, but I yank it away. The door to the diner opens, and a bunch of people stumble out.

Good. Witnesses.

"Get lost. I'm not going anywhere with you."

"No." His face turns anguished, and if I knew him or liked him better, I'd feel bad about it. But I don't, on either front. The only thing recommending him is he did save me from a second horrible death by bus—though the very idea it's happened twice makes my brain spasm. I shake it off. Saving my life doesn't make up for his career choices. He works for Walter Wolfe.

Though if he's a criminal, why did he save me? Maybe I'm making that up. Clarissa said he and Alyssa met in med school. So he's a doctor, right?

If you need henching.

Woah, where did that come from? We hadn't even gotten to the "so what do you do for a living?" part of our supposed date. Trying to make sense of it only leaves me with a twisting, nauseous feeling.

"Please. You're the only one who can get me out of this." He grabs for me again. I step out of his way, and he crashes into the group who just exited Wench.

"What the hell?" someone asks.

"He's drunk," I say. "And an asshole."

"Watch where you're going." A big guy in a leather jacket shoves at Jasper, pushing him farther away from me. The big guy folds his arms over his chest like he's expecting a fight, but when Jasper rights himself, his gaze is on me and his smile is cold.

"You've tried this before," he says. "It won't help. I give you two hours tops before we do it all over again."

Is that a threat? I take an unconscious step back before I gather myself and say, "Thanks for coming tonight, but I don't think this date—"

"Is worth repeating," he says, overlapping the end of my sentence. My cheeks heat, either in fury or from the rush of fear that comes with the little voice in my head that says he might be telling the truth. Either way, my erstwhile bodyguard is holding his ground, and Jasper doesn't push it. I blow Jasper a gentle kiss, then hurry across the intersection—after checking for oncoming vehicles—to the lot where my car is parked.

The last time I see Jasper Jackson, he's staring after me as I drive down the street, leaving him in my rearview mirror.

I call Clarissa on the road home.

"So?" Her voice is full of anticipation.

"You're in so much trouble."

"It didn't go well?"

I can't even begin to describe the levels of fucked up still rattling around in my head. So instead, I sigh. "It didn't go well."

She makes a noise of sympathy. "Did you try? I know you were nervous, but Alyssa said he's a really nice guy. But if it wasn't a fit, that's okay. There's this guy from the Toronto office I want to introduce you to. He'll be at the board meeting next week."

Ugh. The idea of the board meeting is exhausting, as is the idea of meeting more guys like Jasper. It's been a long day, regardless of how many times I've supposedly lived it.

But at least the mention of work grounds me in something

normal. No time loops. No lying bloody on the sidewalk while Jasper asks me not to forget him again.

"Did you send me the updated slides?" I ask.

She growls. Really growls. Clarissa's superpower at SPAM was the ability to mimic animal noises. Her range is impressive, and today's sound is either a pissed-off Doberman or Rottweiler. They're very similar, and over the phone it's hard to make the distinction. And fortunately, there's not a lot of call for animal noises in crime fighting, even minor crime fighting, so when I jumped ship and went to the Ziro Foundation, she was more than happy to go with me.

"Morgan," she says. "The slides are fine."

"They can't only be fine. They have to be impeccable. Ezekiel is counting on us."

In four days, we're presenting the Ziro Foundation's research. The findings will change the world. It's going to be a massive paradigm shift, and I've been at the centre of it for the last two years. It has to be perfect.

"The slides aren't ready," I say.

"They are," she says. "It's all ready. You're ready. It'll be great."

The annoying thing about best friends is they know what you need to hear. That I'm enough. That I'm ready. It's taken a lot of therapy to realize being unsuper in a super family has left me with a pathological fear of letting others down. And since I can't walk on water or hit a target from a mile away in a strong head-wind, I've had to dedicate myself to more earthly pursuits. It's been a lot of work, and it's culminating in something amazing.

"Did I tell you April's going to be there?" Clarissa asks.

My skin crawls at the name, and I have to adjust my grip on the steering wheel where my palms tingle. April was my boss when I worked at SPAM. She was a tyrant with a minuscule tolerance for bullshit, though she can't really be blamed for that when she's wrangling subpar superheroes around the world. I haven't heard from her since the day I turned in my resignation, though. The fact she's resurfacing now only makes me uneasy.

"Why would April be coming to the presentation?" I ask.

"Moral support?" Clarissa asks hopefully.

April is not one for pep talks. She's much more of the "pull yourself together and get back out there" type. In another life, she'd make a killer high school football coach. In this life, she helps catch other kinds of killers. And her two-year silence is all the confirmation I need to know she wasn't sorry to see me go. The superhero life was never for me. I thought SPAM was a reasonable compromise, but I never got promoted beyond filing and phone answering, and after Mother died, there didn't seem to be much point in trying to prove myself that way.

"So it really went badly?" Clarissa asks.

"The presentation? My job? My life? You'll have to be more specific."

She laughs. The sound is like a parrot mocking me, but I know it's unintentional.

"The date, silly."

We're not talking about the date. For once, I was the one let down, because no one can blame me for not wanting to go on a second date with a man who claims we've already been on sixty first dates. There are weirdo stalkers, and then there's whatever Jasper was.

If you need henching, I'm your man.

I shake my head. That didn't happen. He's a friend of Alyssa's with a weird sense of humour. I never have to see him again.

But before I can make up some half truth that won't lead to more questions, Clarissa says, "I have to go. IT is calling. Get some sleep and stop looking at the slides." Then the call ends, and I'm left to my own thoughts about Jasper and his wild theories as I drive down the darkening road toward home.

When I pull into the curved driveway at Ziro Hall—yes, it's cheesy, Ezekiel's grandfather named it—the lights are all on. The

BMW iX is parked in the garage, but as I walk into the foyer, Ezekiel's still in his coat.

"Are you just getting in too?" I ask. "Have you eaten?" Since my stomach is no longer turning itself inside out, I'm ravenous.

He shakes his head. There's a tightness to his jaw that says he's not popping out to the store for snacks.

"I'm on my way back to work, actually. Make yourself something. I'll eat at the lab."

Ezekiel is a creature of habit—and also my stepfather, so I've had years to learn his patterns—and going out after dark is not one of them. For a while after my mother died, he hardly went out at all, even in daylight. It was only when we started working on the Ziro Machine that his routine finally returned to normal, and both our schedules have mapped a loop between the lab and the house without much deviation for the last two years.

"Everything all right?"

He rolls his eyes. Even on a late-night errand, he's immaculately dressed. Pressed shirt, silk tie, charcoal suit that sets off his salt-and-pepper hair. Clarissa told me a few months ago he'd be on top of several Most Eligible Bachelor lists in a heartbeat if it wasn't for the fact he's still not over Mother. Then Clarissa realized what a shitty thing that was to say and changed the subject.

Either way, he's good-looking, and it's easy to see how he swept Mother off her feet, even when she swore she was married to her job—or jobs, really. Together, they were the ultimate power couple. Ezekiel Ziro and Farah Field. They wined and dined. They didn't go places; they made appearances. But the couple I knew—Ezekiel and the Legendary Flame—were even more powerful. They were going to save the world. Ezekiel, through patronage and scientific discovery. My mother, by taking down the criminals human agencies wouldn't mess with. They were unstoppable, until they came face-to-face with Indigo.

"There was an attempted data breach at the lab," Ezekiel says.

I clench my keys. I may not have super speed, but I'm ready to leap into action.

"Let's go. I'll drive."

"No." He puts a hand on my shoulder. "They didn't get very far. Nowhere near the machine. We don't have to both go. Take it easy. You look tired."

Why does "You look tired" always sound like an insult? The passive aggressive way of saying "You look like shit." But I really must be tired, because I know he doesn't mean it that way. When Mother was killed, we probably both needed some looking after, but neither of us was in a place to do it for the other. So instead, we drifted through the halls and around the grounds for a few months like living ghosts. Eventually, though, the silence turned to stilted conversations, which then became a slow exchange of ideas. We never talked about Mother, but late at night, we devised the concept for the Ziro Machine. It was a far cry from grief counselling, but it's given us a purpose and drawn us closer than the stepfather/stepson label might make one believe.

All this to say, he doesn't mean I look like shit. He means I look tired. Hard not to be. The conversation with Jasper—the many conversations?—rattles back to life in my head, along with visions that can't possibly have happened, since I'm here to tell the tale.

After Ezekiel leaves, I make a plate of cheese and crackers and settle into bed with my laptop. As I take notes on final adjustments for the slides, my eyes grow heavy. My headache still hangs like an echo inside my skull, as does the memory of Jasper's face as he asked what I remembered. Sandwiched between these is the crushing sensation of being flung through the air as the bus hit me. But when I hold up my arms, they're straight and unmarked. I kick at the blankets, and my legs work exactly as they should and without any pain.

If Clarissa wants to set me up again, we're going to have another conversation about who does and does not qualify as proper boyfriend material first. Men with criminal connections—even ones with broad shoulders and charming smiles—and dubious fashion sense shouldn't make the cut in the first place. But if they manage to sneak through, wild stories about living the same day over and over are an automatic disqualification.

I don't think this date is worth repeating.

Did I say that or did Jasper? Doesn't matter. He also said it would only be a few hours until we saw each other again, but here I am, safe at home.

I know I fall asleep because soon enough I'm in the dream. The same dream I've had almost every night since my mother died. It feels like a memory, but it can't be, because I wasn't there. I am now, though, watching it all. My mother on the roof of the hotel, a bright ball of orange and red as she chases after Indigo's long shadow. They'd been adversaries for years. Indigo was the assassin's assassin. Leaving no trace, a perfect kill every time. Mother pursued him, but Indigo was always one step ahead of her. Tonight, though, they're finally in the same place, and it's time to settle the score.

I'm in the van, watching the whole thing unfold on the monitor. Vee is beside me. She says something like "You have to get up there. I don't know what went wrong" and suddenly I am running across the roof. My mother tells me to stop, but the split second of her distraction is all it takes for Indigo to break free of the light box that Ezekiel and Vee have been building for the last ten months. I try to shout a warning, but it's too late. Indigo engulfs her. He's like an eclipse, swallowing her light whole. I rush for her as her face disappears into darkness, then they both fall over the edge of the building, tumbling down. Sometimes, that's the end of the dream; tonight, I tumble after them, falling and falling into nothing.

My whole body jerks against the mattress as I wake up. I've been drooling on my pillow and the laptop screen has gone black. When I check my phone, it's almost one in the morning.

I hate that dream. Hate the falling feeling and the powerlessness of it all. The therapist said there was nothing I could do. Only Ezekiel was on-site. April, Clarissa, and I watched from a bunker several hours away as my mother fell to her death. Vee was in the hospital after a lab accident. Rationally, I know none of it is my fault or anyone else's beside Indigo's, but my subconscious has other opinions.

Hopefully that's it for the night, though. Between Jasper's whacky time loop ideas and my endless guilt for not saving the world's greatest superhero when she finally met her match, I'm tapping out.

But just as I pull the blankets back up around my ears, a noise makes me freeze. No. Not really a noise. The idea of one. Maybe the squeak of the bed frame as I roll over. Like the memory of being struck by a bus, it's very possible I imagined it.

Except then the sound happens again, and it's clearly a real sound. Like a cabinet door being closed. I sigh as I wrestle my way back out of bed. Probably Ezekiel. I didn't hear him get home, but he could have come in while I was asleep. So much for well-rested, but the data breach at the lab is more important.

My feet are quiet as I go down the stairs. When I get back down to the main floor, the door to his office is open and a light is on inside. See? He's back and finishing up a few things before he calls it a night.

"Everything okay at the lab? I thought—"

The rest of my question dies in my throat.

The man at the desk is not Ezekiel. His size and bulk are all wrong, as is the way he basically sucks up all the light in the room. His form is entirely a deep opaque blue, like the sky at twilight, despite the glow of the desk lamp. There aren't even any shadows in the folds of his clothes, and while he's wearing a brimmed hat, like a fedora, the void where a face should be is too absolute to be a function of his headwear.

My breath turns short and frightened. I blink, trying to clear my head. Surely I'm still dreaming.

"Indigo."

Who knows if I say the word out loud? Everything is screaming at me to run. I am staring into the empty face of the monster who killed my mother. The murderer who has haunted my dreams for the last two years, even though no one has seen so much as his shadow since the night he killed the Legendary Flame.

He lifts his hand toward me. I flinch, but I can't move. There's a rushing sensation beneath my skin, like all my blood has reversed course. The wrongness of it burns inside me. Then he snaps his fingers—though the gesture makes no sound—and he might as well have shoved a hand into my chest and stopped my heart, because the stabbing pain behind my sternum is blinding.

"Why?" I say, but it's already getting hard to breathe. He brushes past me like I'm not even there as I drop to my knees.

My last thought as the room goes dark is that Jasper better be right.

CHAPTER 4

Any blind date that starts with a painting of your mother staring down at you can't go well. Especially if your mother is—

I blink as I take in the sight of Wench around me. Same patrons at the bar, same lukewarm tea on the table in front of me. Same painting of Mother dearest mocking me above the bar.

How?

Vee is approaching me, no doubt so she can make sure I don't want anything to eat while I wait for my mystery man. Instinct tells me to run. We should all run.

Indigo. He's back.

The door swings open, and Jasper stumbles through. He's looking right at me, and he sits down with breathless anticipation.

"Morgan?"

I stab a finger at him. "You asshole." Whether he's right or not, I'm not feeling very charitable toward him right now.

"Do you remember?" He leans in.

"Can I get you something to drink?" Vee stands above us.

"We're leaving," I say, pushing up from my seat. Jasper's with me in a heartbeat as I hurry toward the door.

"What about your laptop?" Vee says. I spin on one heel and stride back to grab my computer, along with my coat hung over the back of the chair. I don't make eye contact. Jasper is waiting by the entrance, and he follows wordlessly as I step out into the street.

I wait at the intersection until the bus rumbles by. When Jasper goes to speak, I hold up my hand, silently telling him to wait. When the illuminated man says walk, we do. Safely.

As we approach the parking lot, Jasper is walking ahead of me, making a beeline for my SUV.

"How do you know which one is mine?" I ask.

"Date fourteen," he says. "I tried to explain then, but you wouldn't listen. Nearly ran me over with your car trying to get away."

"That's still an option now," I say, but I press the fob and unlock all the doors. My fully electric Range Rover has flush door handles that the average person struggles to find on the first try, but Jasper doesn't even hesitate. He swings it open, slides inside, and is shutting the door again before I'm halfway in.

"You remember?" he says into the dark interior once I've closed my door too.

I remember the horror of finding Indigo in Ezekiel's office. The pain of my body shutting down. Again. The further pain of the bus accident. But now is not the time for breathless confessions. It's time for questions.

"What the fuck is going on?"

His eyes widen. "Did you die? How? I'm never sure—"

I press my palm to his mouth. "No. No. My turn for answers. Tell me what is happening."

The interior of the car gets quiet. A few guys—the same ones I used to fend off Jasper yesterday (today? How do you tell time like this?) stumble out of the diner.

Behind my hand, Jasper smiles widely, and I realize what I've done. In another life, he might kiss my hand. Oh my god. What if he *has* kissed my hand already? If you can kiss on the first date, surely we've kissed on the sixtieth? And I don't remember?

I can't cope with that. It's too much. To have kissed someone who looks like Jasper and not remember it is worse than—Well, okay, that's not true. Getting killed in quick succession by an environmentally friendly transit vehicle and a supervillain are worse than forgetting about kissing a cute guy. So much worse.

"Start at the beginning." I say, trying to slow my breathing.

"Alyssa said we should meet."

"Alyssa? What does she have to do with any of this?"

"You said to start at the beginning. Alyssa and I went to medical school together. She and your friend Clarissa thought—"

"This is about the date?" My voice rises. "I don't care about who thought we would be good together. I care about the fact that I died last night and the night before, and yet here we are. And anyway, medical school? I thought you were some kind of goon, not a doctor?"

His lips thin. "I dropped out."

Great, so he's a slacker as well as a criminal. What a waste of a cute face.

"Jasper. Focus." I may be talking to myself on that last part. "Why is this happening?"

"I don't know!" For the first time, his boyish enthusiasm cracks. He balls his fists up on the dash, and I shrink away, waiting for him to punch something, but instead he turns to me, eyes desperate. "Why would I know any more than you do? Alyssa said I should meet you. I did. It was fine. Eventually you said you had to get back to work. I stuck around, had a couple more drinks. Then I went home and fell asleep, and when I woke up, I was on the sidewalk outside the diner again."

"And?" I say, ignoring the bit about how our first date— whenever that was—was only fine. Of course it was. That's the best I could hope for. Right up until the time loop kicked in. No one could predict that part.

Jasper shakes his head. "And you were inside. And you left again. And I went home again. And then it happened . . . again. It always happens."

"Sixty times?" I ask.

"Sixty-one now."

I glare at him because now that I am once more alive and breathing, what he's saying sounds too implausible to be true.

I say, "Have you ever considered standing me up? Maybe if we don't meet then—"

His laugh is dark. Angry. "Oh, trust me. I tried that. Repeatedly. It didn't help. I'd get on with my life—"

"Henching around? Terrorizing women and children?" I say sweetly, which earns me a narrow squint that gets my blood pumping. Maybe the "good dude" persona he puts out only goes so far. I always do love an argument. If Jasper could give as good as he gets, maybe we would have had a shot if it weren't for all of . . . this. I want to fight about whether paper straws were ever going to do anything to stop climate change. Not who is responsible for a date that won't end.

"I get on with my life," he says again slowly. "And then at some point, whether I'm awake or asleep, at home or at . . . somewhere else—"

I snort. "Don't sanitize it for my sake." When the world goes back to normal, making sure he pays for his crimes is first on my to-do list. I may not work at SPAM anymore, but I still have connections. Jasper will be sorry we ever met.

"Whatever I'm doing, suddenly I'm on the sidewalk again, heading toward the diner."

It's a lie. Has to be. The last two months, I've been working. The only people I've seen are the board members, the engineering team, Ezekiel, and Clarissa. And while some days no doubt blend together, they've all been different.

"If what you're saying is true, then why do you remember and I don't?"

The anger drains out of him. He's back to being the guy I saw coming through the diner. He'd make a charming bartender or an appealing stranger at a party. Too bad about his career choices. As a doctor, his powers would be unstoppable. Even if he dropped out of med school, he could at least play a convincing doctor on TV. He'd have a funny nickname like Doctor Steamy. Mister McSexy.

Focus, Morgan. The alluring henchman doesn't get sexy nicknames. He gets evil ones. McSneaky. McStab-You-While-You're-Sleeping.

In fact, what he gets is a pained look on his face. Jasper says, "It has to be you. Every time you die, the day starts over."

My fingers slide to my chest. It still aches. My other hand goes to my ribs, then my hip, snapped from the impact of the bus. They don't hurt much today, but yesterday I could barely think from the pain. What pains and injuries have I already forgotten? Never mind forgotten kisses. This is a far more important question.

On a shaky breath, I say, "Are you telling me I've died sixty times?"

His cocky grin is back, a little more sheepish than before. "I think so? I wasn't there for a lot of them. You really don't seem to like me."

I jab a finger into his chest. "You knew what was happening and you didn't do anything?"

He blinks. "I saved you from the bus yesterday."

But not from Indigo. And how many busses before that?

I nearly tell Jasper to get out of my car, but he has more information than I do, and it's not like I can go home and search "How do I stay alive so I can escape a blind date that's really a time loop?" on the internet.

Jasper's picking imaginary lint off his jeans and pretending not to look at me. He's about as subtle as a bag of hammers, but I guess we're a team now. The fastest way to extricate ourselves is to use what Jasper knows and to do my best not to die anymore.

Easy peasy, right?

"So, what else have you figured out?" I say with a heavy sigh.

He squirms. "Not much. The day's not always the same length. Sometimes it's fast."

"Because of the bus," I say.

"Yeah. And sometimes it takes longer. Once I made it all the way to noon tomorrow before everything started all over. Whatever you did that day, I really thought we were going to make it."

"But you don't know what happened . . . or will happen . . ." Seriously, thinking about time this way is hard. "Tomorrow if we split up?"

"Well, obviously, you die." He gives me an apologetic smile. Somehow, I keep having to remind myself about the whole henchman thing. Jasper really seems more like the kind of guy who holds your hand during the sad part in movies than the kind who slaps it away and tells you to give him all your money. "But no. No. Sorry. I don't know how or where. The only time I ever see it is when it's here with the bus."

That's really not very helpful at all. All those data points lost. We could have used those to map something better going forward.

"What about you?" I ask.

"What about me?"

"Do you die?"

He looks away uncomfortably for a second, which gives me the answer I was expecting even before he says, "No."

"Have you tried?" The question comes out meaner than I intend. His eyes get big. Has he really never considered this? Jasper scrabbles for the handle on the door. On instinct, I bang the lock down on my side. He goes pale.

"I—" He swallows. "What if I don't come back?"

Oh, for fuck's sake. "I'm not going to murder you in my car in the name of scientific inquiry, Jasper. I only want to know what we're dealing with. And I'll have you know that, even though I come back, it still hurts like a son of a bitch. After Indigo obliterated my—"

"What?"

The car goes quiet. Shit, I wasn't ready to bring that part into this. Not yet. I still want to understand how this works—the limitations, the variables—before I introduced new factors.

"Indigo?" Jasper says slowly. For a guy who was so cavalier about his underworld connections earlier—yesterday? Damn, this really is hard—he suddenly looks nervous, maybe even more than when he thought he was about to meet his demise in the front seat of a luxury SUV.

I stare up through the moonroof. Full moon. That wouldn't be relevant, would it? Of course not. The moon causes tides, but it doesn't alter the course of time. Whatever is going on, there's a person causing it. If it were a natural phenomenon, it would have been documented. Studied. Even the parting of the Red Sea has a plausible scientific explanation. And if someone is doing this, they can be found and be made to stop it. Maybe knowing a henchman will prove valuable after all. We just need to follow the clues.

I try again, without the insinuation of murder.

"After I left our date . . . yesterday? Last night? The one before this. Ugh, what's the best way to talk about this?"

Jasper relaxes. "Yeah. Yesterday. That's the easiest way, I've found. Even if today only lasts a few hours, it's easier if you think about each one as its own day. I never know how much time I'm going to have, so stitching it together to make a twenty-four-hour period is an exercise in frustration."

"When I left yesterday, I went home. I went to bed and I woke up later, and I heard a noise downstairs. When I went to check it out—"

"Were you in your underwear?" He shows off his crooked

tooth again as he grins, but I'm not in the mood for his leering, even if he's clearly joking. I punch him—hard—on the shoulder.

"Ow." His amusement turns to a plaintive pout. It should not be as endearing as it is.

"Not so tough for a henchman, are you?" I ask, watching the way he rubs his arm. Despite the fact he's dressed super casually, he fits his flannel very well. In another timeline, I wouldn't mind rubbing his shoulder for him.

"Why did you punch me?" he asks.

"Where do you get off asking questions about my underwear? Just because we've been on sixty dates doesn't mean we're a couple. That was rude."

"It's such a horror movie cliche. All alone at night. You hear a sound. You go to investigate, usually wearing only—"

I jab a finger in his face. "You don't get to ask about what I wear to bed. We don't even know each other."

His mouth works like he's going to argue. I almost want to make him feel better, but then I think about sixty days where he knew me and I didn't know him and my sense of reality gets fuzzy all over again. Finally, he says, "So you heard a strange noise."

Right. Answering feels risky. There's still a chance I'm a rat in Jasper's maze. Maybe he's wearing a wire and some researcher somewhere is listening to my answers going "Hmm. Yes. Very interesting. The simulation is progressing as expected."

But not telling him means we're more likely to continue to repeat the same mistakes over and over, and somehow those always seem to result in me bleeding from an important artery or trying not to move as my bones puncture an organ. So I'll have to give him this much.

"Indigo was there. In my stepfather's office." My eyes widen as a terrible thought occurs to me. "Ezekiel! Where is he? If Indigo got me, then—" I fumble for my phone, getting ready to type a text. Only what am I supposed to say? Don't go home? I can't tell him how I know what I know. We've got too much riding on the presentation for Ezekiel to start worrying about my mental well-being, and he absolutely will if I start texting him impossible stories about blind dates that never end.

"Indigo?" Jasper's still hung up on other revelations. "Like, *the* Indigo?"

I nod. I guess it doesn't matter what happened to Ezekiel last night? We're back at the beginning, which means even if Indigo killed him too, he's alive again, just like me. Right? My fingers still itch to message him, but Jasper whistles softly and says, "And then?"

Even though I technically lived to tell the tale, talking about it is still hard. "He . . ." I snap my fingers, then make a gagging sound and wrap my hands around my throat when Jasper looks like he doesn't understand.

"But I thought he was dead."

That theory did get floated around. They never found Mother's or Indigo's bodies after the night at the hotel, so no one could ever say for sure. Yet, when there was no further sign of him, some of the media outlets reported that Indigo must have been buried under the hotel when it collapsed too.

"Dead and alive are relative terms right now," I say.

"Like good and evil!" Jasper's grin returns once more, but dims when I give him my best flat stare. I can't believe this is happening. And of all the people I could get stuck with, it had to be this guy.

His stomach growls, and he pats the front of his jacket. "Have you eaten?"

"Excuse me?"

"I haven't eaten. The first time, on our first date, I was hoping maybe we'd hit it off and drinks would become dinner, so I haven't eaten. And no matter how much I eat before the day starts over, I'm always hungry again."

That sucks. I don't eat much. Don't have time. We've been so busy at the lab that if Clarissa didn't order lunch in for me, I'd probably eat breakfast and subsist on coffee for the rest of the day.

I stare out the windshield at Wench. With everything, I can't face going back in there.

"We can't go to my place," I say. "Indigo will be there."

Jasper twists his mouth. If he suggests we go to his place, I'll say no. That sounds like a surefire way to wind up in some abandoned warehouse or dungeon somewhere, chained up to the wall and with no way to escape.

Instead, he says, "I know somewhere. They've got good food, and they might be able to answer some questions."

"About time loops?" Is that what this is even called?

"About Indigo."

The idea of going after Indigo makes me go cold. "Oh no. I don't want to find him again. I want to stay very far away from him at all costs." If my mother, Vee, and Ezekiel couldn't stop him, what hope do I have, especially with only Jasper as a sidekick? Indigo can kill with the snap of a finger. Mother believed there was a proximity element to it, that he couldn't kill someone unless he was close enough. But he could be captured, at least temporarily. That was what their light box was for . . . until it failed, that is. But I have neither the powers nor the technology to test these theories on my own, and who else is going to believe me besides Jasper?

Speaking of the devil, Jasper spins toward me, and this time he does reach for my hand. His palms are warm, even though the evening is cool. "But isn't it weird that we get stuck in a time loop and Indigo is suddenly back?"

"You need both those things to happen at once before it gets weird?"

Jasper sighs impatiently. "Do you have a better idea? We'll get food and ask around. If you want to do something else, I'm all ears."

I'm seriously thinking about buying a one-way ticket to a remote resort deep in the jungles of Belize, but since it sounds like that plan would only end in a fiery plane crash, I have to admit I've got nothing.

"Then let's see what we can find out." Jasper squeezes my hand. "Trust me."

Trusting him can only be the start of a very bad and very fatal string of decisions, but I put the car in gear.

"Let's go."

CHAPTER 5

We drive across town, Jasper giving me directions. It's still early enough in the evening the city streets are busy. Everyone goes about their business like nothing weird is happening. Does anyone else know? The thought that this all hinges on me and my death—my *deaths*—weighs uneasily on my mind.

"Are you worried about your presentation?" Jasper asks.

I shoot him a glance as we drive through an intersection. "How do you know about my presentation?"

"You told me about it. A few times, actually. It's the sort of thing people talk about on a first date, you know? Work. Movies."

"So, I told you about how I'm going to change the world and you followed up with 'my boss uses his real estate holdings as a front to launder drug money'?" My hands tighten on the steering wheel. I'm not usually such a jerk. People have called me blunt. Direct. Small talk is never my strong suit. The snark coming out of my mouth right now is fuelled by the ticking clock in my head that says I'm about to die for the sixty-somethingth time in a row, and so far, Jasper's done nothing to stop it.

He doesn't answer my question. Instead, he points through the windshield. "That way. Park anywhere past the second light."

The second light is the intersection of Mill Street and Key Boulevard. My throat goes dry. This is not a part of town I come to very often. Or ever, really. We stop in front of a bar called Kicks. Pounding music thumps behind the door. If I thought Wench was tacky, this place is flat-out seedy. Darkened windows. A poster promising *Girls Every Night!*

Also, the name is a shortened version of the word *sidekicks*. It was well known at SPAM that Kicks was a popular spot for low-level criminals in town. If you needed information about someone's dastardly plan or to start working relationships with informants, Kicks was where you went.

Not that I ever did. When I went to work at SPAM, they immediately saw that my strengths lay in administration. Ideally in ways that didn't involve talking to people.

Still, if anyone inside gets even a whiff that I worked at SPAM—or worse, finds out who my mother was—we're in big trouble.

Speaking of which, it appears that even after so many first dates, even Jasper doesn't know any of those details either. Or at least he hasn't mentioned them. Probably better to not let him in on those little tidbits until I'm more certain he isn't going to drag me into the bar's back freezer and leave me there until Mr. Wolfe is ready to speak with me or whatever.

The street is illuminated by the glowing Kicks sign. Something shaped like a large rat scurries across the sidewalk. I sigh as I watch from behind the steering wheel. "I guess the upside to living the same day over and over is I don't need to worry about a rabies shot."

Jasper shoots me a look. "You're not going to be weird here, right?"

Suddenly he doesn't want my help?

"What do you mean by weird?"

He shifts uneasily, looking out at the bar. "You're kind of . . . fussy. You know that, right? If you look at everyone in there like you're better than them, no one will tell us anything."

My mouth drops open. I have to remind myself he thinks I'm a lab nerd who has no idea where he's taken us. In fact, I can use his worry to my advantage. Let him think I'm exactly who he believes me to be.

"Fussy?" I ask, making the very suggestion sound offensive. "That's pretty judgy, considering we just met."

He holds up his hands between us, counting off the fingers in multiple rounds. "Sixty dates, remember? I know a lot more than you think."

Fear ripples down my spine.

Where's a bus to step in front of when you need it?

I wave him off as I undo my seat belt and open the door. "I'll be fine. There's sanitizer in the glove compartment. I'll bathe in it when we get back."

The second we walk inside Kicks, it's like a scene from an old Western movie. Heads turn, and everyone might as well be peering out from under the brim of a black cowboy hat for all they appear to be having a good time. Even the music seems to get quiet for a second.

But if my chosen cover story is a nervous nerd out of his depth, Jasper puts on this cloak of sunny confidence that means he walks assuredly through the room, though he doesn't make eye contact with a single person as we go. I make eye contact with lots. None look friendly. A few narrow their eyes. One goes so far as to crack his knuckles.

"Nice place," I say as a man with a face tattoo of a knife runs his thumb over his throat.

If Jasper hears me, he doesn't reply. He takes a seat at an open table near the back and flags down a server. He orders a beer and a plate of nachos, then looks expectantly at me.

"Soda water. Two lime wedges."

"Oh, come on," he says, sighing heavily.

"What? I have a lot of allergies, and E. coli is an equal-opportunity pathogen. You can't tell me the health inspector has been here recently."

Jasper pinches the bridge of his nose, so I drive the point home by smiling up at the server and saying, "Wedge salad. Hold the blue cheese. I'm allergic to that too."

"We don't have a wedge salad," the server says, looking confused. "Or any kind of salad."

Jasper's toe finds my shin under the table. I gasp.

"We'll share the nachos," he says. The server looks like he's going to forget our order before he ever gets back to the kitchen.

"You didn't have to kick me," I say, making sure to pout.

"What did I tell you about not standing out?" His jaw is tense, and he may not be aware of the way his knee is bouncing nervously as he surveys the room.

I lean into Fussy Morgan even harder. "Why are you being so bossy?"

He glances around. "Do you even know where we are?"

Yup. When I worked at SPAM, April once sent a team here to do some recon on a rumoured neurotoxin that was being trafficked through the city. Eight SPAM agents went in. They came back out with twelve black eyes, five broken noses, six broken legs, and twenty-nine broken fingers between them. Also some missing teeth. No neurotoxin. No desire to ever go back in.

But Jasper doesn't know I know any of that, so I say, "Yeah, it's some shitty dive bar where I'm more likely to get a staph infection than I am to get a salad." I wriggle my fingers in disgust. I don't even want to touch the table we're sitting at. It looks like it hasn't been wiped in months, and the empty stage in the back corner holds only a microphone stand and some shredded silver fringe that are a sad attempt to add some sparkle to the grime.

But Jasper throws a nervous glance at the people around us before he gets even closer and lowers his voice. "This is *Kicks*."

I study the faded menu. It's the kind in the little plastic stand on the side of the table. I pretend to study it. "I could swear this font is Times New Roman. Clearly no one put any thought into graphic design. I could give them some tips. Everyone comes to me for help with their PowerPoint presentations at work."

If laughing wouldn't draw attention we don't need, I would laugh at the dawning horror in Jasper's face. He's obviously beginning to question if bringing me here was a good idea. Fantastic. Let him underestimate me.

The server brings our order. I suck on my straw and make a big show of looking around the room. All those disgruntled SPAM agents who were stuck on desk duty after the neurotoxin incident make sense now. The bar is full of a lot of unshaven faces and shifty eyes. People hunched over phones, which isn't uncommon, but the ones here seem extra paranoid that someone might peek over their shoulder and glimpse which criminal mastermind they're texting. One guy even has an eyepatch, and the scar that runs from his hairline to his lip says it isn't a frivolous accessory.

"We should go," Jasper says. "This was a bad call." But before he can get out of his seat, we're interrupted as a flurry of feathers and sequins takes the chair next to his. For a moment, Jasper is engulfed. He squawks, but the sound is drowned out by a smacking kiss, and when he reemerges, shaking a feather out of the collar of his shirt, a large and sparkly lipstick print is smeared on his face.

"Jasper Jackson," the new arrival says. "Where the hell have you been keeping yourself?"

"Oh, you know, Max." He gives the woman his charming smile, now looking even more lopsided thanks to the lipstick. "Been staying busy."

"And out of trouble?" She takes his chin between manicured nails that must be four inches long.

It's fair to say I have not met a lot of drag queens in my life. In college, Clarissa used to . . . well . . . drag me to drag queen brunch from time to time. She'd hoot and cheer and wave her dollar bills in the air. I'd pretend like I recognized any of the songs the performers sang. When you spend your childhood in perpetual superhero bootcamp, you don't get a lot of time for pop culture.

But the woman in front of me is not only the most beautiful drag queen I've ever seen, she's possibly the most beautiful person. Her skin is flawless, her hair is basically a sculpture, her dress must weigh sixty pounds, and despite the grimy surroundings, she looks perfectly put together.

And she's watching me like I'm gum on the heel of her reinforced Louboutins.

"I'm Maximum Shade," she says. "Welcome to my establishment."

"Nice to meet you," I say. "Morgan Murray."

"Pleasure." She may have kissed Jasper, but her lips are still perfectly painted as she gives me a thin smile. "I think I met your mother once."

Whatever I was going to say dies in my throat. I glance at Jasper, but his gaze is on the front door.

"She knew many people," I say. "When you run your own company, you make a lot of contacts."

Mother came up in the era where superheroes were still treated suspiciously and secret identities were commonplace. Her life as Farah Field, CEO of Field Security, a contractor that provided private security services to dignitaries and VIPs, was a great cover for the Legendary Flame's travels around the world fighting crime. But I can't imagine someone like Maximum Shade ever going to Mom for security.

"You seen Ravensburger lately?" Jasper asks.

Max lets her gaze linger on me for one last long second before she snorts and turns her attention back to Jasper. "Ravensburger? What do you want with that kind of bad news?"

"We're. . ." He shoots me a nervous glance. "He used to work with Indigo, right?"

Now, Max's immaculate composure cracks the barest amount. You'd have to be watching her closely to notice, but not even the two-inch-deep eye shadow is enough to hide the way her eyes tighten and her mouth goes white at the corners, contrasting starkly with her plum lipstick.

But her voice is still calm when she says, "Now why would you go chasing after ghosts like Indigo?"

"Jasper!" Across the bar, a mountain stands up from a table. Okay, it's not a mountain, but it might as well be. The man is as wide as he is tall, and he's really tall.

Jasper goes pale, and he pushes slowly up from his seat. "Oh boy. That's not good. Excuse me while I go clear up a . . . misunderstanding."

I half rise, like I might follow him, but a pair of talons wraps around my wrist, and the way Max clears her throat very clearly says "I wouldn't if I were you."

Jasper calls a casual greeting to the mountain as he moves across the bar, and he gets a grumble that puts erupting volcanoes to shame in return.

"Don't worry," Max says. "He can talk his way out of any situation."

"If you say so," I say. The upside is, if the mountain man crushes him into powder, we'll know if the time loop resets for Jasper's death too or if it's only for mine.

Though if he doesn't come back, I'll be alone in this thing, and the idea is surprisingly upsetting.

"So how long have you two known each other?" Max asks conversationally, and I drag my attention off Jasper.

"We only met today."

"He's a good boy. Sweet."

"Sure," I say, not really listening. Jasper's speaking with the giant man. He puts a friendly hand on the massive shoulder, then slowly pulls it away when the man's tennis ball–size eyes narrow in warning.

"I really am sorry about your mother. She was a great woman."

Why is she harping on Mother? It's been two years.

"She was," I say, looking around for that server with our drinks.

"The Legendary Flame got me out of a few jams in our day."

It takes a long time before her words settle in my brain. Out of all the shocks that have come at me today, somehow this one is the most horrifying. Time loops and repeated shocking and horrific deaths? These are problems to solve and issues to avoid. But someone who knows my mother's real identity, even now after she's dead?

That's a serious failure. Outside of Vee, Ezekiel, and a few select agents at SPAM like April, no one should know who she really was.

Max is examining her nails, but she gives me a sly grin. "I won't tell anyone, honey. But if I were you, as soon as Jasper's done with Krusher over there, I'd make your way out. Your mother was very good at what she did, but I'm not the only one who knew her secrets. Dead or not, some people hold grudges a long time." Max stands, tapping one nail on the table. "My lips are sealed. And stick with Jasper. He'll keep you safe."

I bristle on reflex. "I can take care of myself."

Max's smile turns wistful. "I'm sure you can, honey. I'm only saying that Jasper is—"

Whatever Jasper is, I'll have to find out some other time, because a roar sounds across the bar, and suddenly Jasper is flying through the air toward the darkened stage as the mountain bellows. Several other patrons have darted out of the way, but Jasper's trajectory knocks over a few drinks, along with a few more drinkers, and they don't seem very happy about it.

"Oh no, not again," Max mutters next to me before she wades into the fray, sequins flashing.

But "again" is exactly what's going on. The bar dissolves into chaos as a full-on brawl breaks out in a second. Fists fly, curses are shouted. I can't see Jasper through the silver fringe where he landed, so I skirt along the edge of the room, ducking as a stray pint glass soars past where my head was a second ago. As I round the second table, Jasper is lying in a crumpled heap at the rear of the stage.

Great. Maybe we really will find out what happens if he dies.

I scramble along, keeping low. The fight around me is getting louder, like this whole place was a powder keg waiting for an excuse to blow. As I finally reach Jasper, he lifts his head. A cocktail napkin is stuck to his cheek, and his nose is bloody as he pulls the square of paper away.

"Safe to say Krusher and I did not come to an understanding." His charming smile is less charming when his lip is split.

I roll my eyes. "Can we get out of here?"

"Thought you'd never ask."

I go to lead him back the way I came, but he takes my hand and starts to pull me toward the seething throng of warring henchmen.

"It's faster this way," he says.

"It's safer that way." I point toward the door that must lead to the kitchen.

Jasper shakes his head. "You haven't met Max's cook. He doesn't take kindly to unexpected visitors in his workspace."

Fine. Sure. Whatever. We can't be more than fifty feet to the door. If we stay down and avoid Krusher, we can get out of this, right?

Surprisingly, people mostly leave us alone. We get jostled around, but as long as we don't make eye contact, people seem more intent on fighting the people in front of them than us.

"What about Indigo?" I ask as we approach the exit.

"We'll have to find him some other way," Jasper says over his shoulder.

Great. So we've made zero progress.

Or less. Just as Jasper's at the door and I'm two steps behind him, something heavy collides with my back, and I tumble to the floor. Actually, it's two heavy somethings. Two bodies, engaged in some furious combat, and I get tangled up in their fight. They may not even notice I'm there as I get slammed against a table leg, caught up in their momentum.

"Jasper!" I call out, though a little bit of me dies—though better than all of me dying, I guess?—inside at the idea of needing to ask him for help. He's the reason we're in this mess in the first place.

One of the two fighting bodies grabs hold of my arm, twisting until I have to roll to avoid snapping the bone. My fingers scrabble on the sticky floor. Tetanus, here I come. But I freeze when white-hot pain buries itself in my side.

What is it Max said?

Oh no. Not again.

The tearing of a blade slicing into organs gets worse as I push to my feet. The fight has moved away from me, and Jasper is there in a second.

"Morgan?"

"It's fine, I'm fine," I say, even though I know I'm not. The pain in my back is excruciating, and my whole body is going numb. Jasper pulls me out through the door and onto the street, but we're only a step away from the bar when the world goes sideways.

Oh. I fell.

Hello, concrete. Nice to see you again.

"Morgan."

I wonder how many people can say they've had legitimate déjà vu involving their own death.

"I think he hit a kidney," I say.

"You can't die from a knife to the kidney. Not this quickly."

I laugh as the streetlights dim in a way that is already becoming familiar. "We can talk about it tomorrow."

"No, wait. Morgan. I'll call an ambulance, hang on."

"Tomorrow," I say.

"You'll remember me tomorrow?" he asks. "Promise?"

Oh god, I hope so. He's clearly terrible at plans, so he can't be the one in charge. At the very least, I have to remember that part.

"Tomorrow, you get to die for a change, because this seriously sucks," I say as my voice fades and the world goes black.

CHAPTER 6

Any blind date that starts with—

I'm so glad Jasper's the one who's always late to this thing. I am never late. I get sweaty if I'm not fifteen minutes early for important meetings and appointments. If I had to be late to the blind date from hell in perpetuity, I'd lose my mind.

Also, hi again, Mother. I glance up at the mural on the wall. Nice to see you. Did you know there's a drag queen on the south side of town who knows who we are? Who else does?

Yes, I know it's pretentious to always call my mother "Mother." It was her decision, not mine. She said moms were women who baked cookies and went to soccer games, and she did none of that. We can talk about what her insistent distinction between herself and "those other moms" meant for her own sense of femininity on a day when I don't die for the sixty-third time in a row.

"You sure you don't want something to eat? I could cook you up something." Vee comes up to the table.

"Who else knew about Mother?" I ask, not bothering with her question.

She blinks a few times, clearly not expecting me to go right for the heavy stuff.

"Who else . . ." She frowns.

"Who else knew the Legendary Flame was Farah Field?" I ask.

"Morgan!" she says, shushing me. We get a few curious looks from the other patrons in the diner. Vee turns her head like it's on a swivel, no doubt doing the same thing I did at Kicks when Max said she knew my mother. We don't talk about this. Ever. And considering Vee and I haven't talked since the night my mother died, she can't even begin to guess where I'm going with this.

If she only knew.

"It doesn't matter," I say, leaning back in my chair. "I'll be dead by the end of the night, anyway."

Also, holy shit, my back is killing me. I shift, and something like a scar tugs along the side of my spine. My hands are halfway to lifting my shirt to check if I can see anything before I remember I'm in a public place.

"What? Morgan, are you okay?" Vee's voice rises even louder than mine did a minute ago.

Jasper crashes through the door, rushing toward me.

"Oh, look," I say. "My date is here."

This time, instead of taking the seat across from me, he throws my laptop bag on the ground and sits next to me, eyes intent on mine.

"You're okay?" he says.

I tuck my shirt back into my pants. "I've been better."

"Can I get you anything to drink?" Vee's looking nervously between us, and I give her what I hope is an insouciant smile. Let her wonder if I really am dying. Or why I suddenly don't care about protecting my mother's secret identity. Not like I can give her a straight answer about either, anyway. I've died, but I'm not dead. I'll probably die again soon, but I can't say I'm actively dying now. Surely a massage is all I'd need to sort out this massive kink in my back. Wait until the masseuse hears how I got it.

"Just water," Jasper says distractedly.

"Two beers," I say. "And do you have any nachos?"

"Chips and salsa," she says with a soft smile as she writes the order down. "Though there's onion in the salsa. You don't want that."

I roll my eyes. "We'll have the chips. Put queso on the side too." I need Jasper well-fed while I yell at him for getting me killed in a villain dive bar brawl.

"Just the water," Jasper says. "We're not staying."

"We aren't?"

"Two waters it is." Vee stuffs her pad into the front of her apron and walks away.

When she's gone, we stare at each other for a long time before Jasper says, "So, how are you feeling?" The way he wrinkles his nose says even he knows it's an awkward question.

"Oh, you know. Just died again, then got sucked back in time. The usual." I wince as I lean in and the scar—or the memory of the stab wound, whatever the hell it is I'm feeling—pulls.

"You're okay, though?" He sounds so hopeful. His golden retriever vibe would be irresistible in so many other circumstances. If I'd met him in an undergraduate chemistry class, I'd have offered to be his study buddy for the semester while secretly hoping he might teach me to do way more than study.

"It's not something you bounce back from." I shift again, trying to relieve the ache in my back, but I can't quite find the right spot to sit. "But it hasn't killed me yet. Not permanently, anyway."

"Did you see who stabbed you?" Jasper reaches for my arm, like he might be trying to turn me to check for wounds. I pretend not to notice, even though some small part of me would really like him to touch me. Maybe pat my shoulder and tell me it's going to be okay. Maybe more. But the portrait of Mother on the ceiling is still watching, and I can practically hear her tell me now is not the time to be soft.

"No," I say, pulling clear of his grasp. "That's kind of the point of stabbing someone in the back. So you don't see them. Anyway, what does it matter who stabbed me?"

"It would be useful to know for when we go back to Kicks. We'd be able to keep an eye out for them and—"

"Absolutely not." I bang on the table to punctuate the point and Vee, who is arriving with water glasses, jumps. "We're not going back there."

"I think we should at least—"

My casual act is over. I don't need to repeat this experiment to know what the outcome would be. We walked into the lion's den and got eaten for dinner.

"Look, we tried it your way. You got thrown across a room, and I got stabbed. Why would we do that again?"

But Jasper's not listening. He's nodding like he agrees with me but then says, "We'll be better prepared. We can get some disguises."

"Disguises? People there knew who I was. Who my mother was. Do you think a funny hat and a pair of sunglasses is—"

"Wait." Jasper holds up a hand. "Your mother? Who's your mother?"

Shit. I shouldn't have said that out loud. Dying so many times has scrambled my brain, and I'm letting secrets that I've been protecting my whole life slip. I don't care if the other people at Wench know who my mother was because they'll all forget with the next stabbing or bus accident. But Jasper won't forget, and he works for someone who would be *very* interested in this information.

"Nothing. Never mind." I grab my jacket and laptop bag. "We're not going back there."

Jasper follows after me as I head to the door. "Then where are we going?"

"We tried it your way, now we're going to try it mine." No

more diving in headfirst. We're taking the careful approach. The scientific one. We are consulting experts instead of devising our own methodology when we clearly have no idea what's happening.

"Then what are we waiting for?" he asks, glancing around. We're standing on the street corner. I didn't even realize I had stopped.

"We're, uh . . . we're waiting for the bus."

"We're taking the bus?"

"No." My feet feel like they're glued to the concrete. "I'm just . . . waiting for it to pass so I know it's safe to cross."

Jasper checks his watch. It's an old one with a gold face and a worn brown leather strap. "The bus came three minutes ago."

"You're sure?"

"Yeah. I had lots of time to figure out the timing of things before you started remembering." He laughs softly and takes my hand. This time, I don't shake him off because I'm honestly not sure how I'll get my feet to move otherwise.

I try not to think about that too hard. It's like someone experiencing something while you were asleep. He could have done anything to me those first sixty times. Told me anything. He could have been all "come with me if you want to live," then pushed me off a cliff for shits and giggles, and I wouldn't know.

But true to his word, there's no sign of the bus. We cross the street and through the parking lot to my car and wow—this is a head spinner. We were here two hours ago, where I lectured Jasper and demanded answers, and now we're here again and I've died yet again and it's a different day, but the same day.

Jasper gives me a sympathetic smile. "Don't hurt yourself."

"Excuse me?"

His consideration is so at odds with the imaginary Jasper in my head who is still yeeting me off a cliff to pass the time. So much of him is at odds with what I know. He doesn't seem to have a mean bone in his body, yet somehow he works for Walter Wolfe.

"That's the face you make when you're trying to solve a tough problem, like how to tell me you've had a really nice time but you don't think this relationship has a future. I've seen it enough to know." He raises a finger to my forehead, and I jerk my head back. He doesn't look hurt by the action. "You're thinking about it. Time. Truth."

"Truth is relative," I say. "It's really not much more than consensus in the face of empirical evidence."

He laughs, even while I still feel way too vulnerable. "It's still better if you don't strain yourself trying to make sense of something that doesn't make sense."

"This is a man-made phenomenon. Someone is doing this to us. We just have to figure out who it is, how they're doing it, and get them to stop." I unlock the car and motion for Jasper to get in before we have any more squishy feelings between us.

Jasper rolls his eyes as he slides into the front seat. "Oh, is that all? Why didn't I think of that before?"

I have to fight to keep from smiling. It's the first snarky thing Jasper's said, and the frustration in his tone makes me feel a little better. He's not operating with more information than I am. Despite his ambiguous views of good and evil, he needs me as much as I need him.

I say, "And if we can't figure it out on our own, we'll have to ask for help."

"Help?" Jasper asks as we pull out of the lot. "Who could possibly help us with this?"

"We're going to see the smartest person I know."

I only hope he's smart enough to know what to do.

———

I actually start driving us home before I remember Ezekiel has gone to the lab for the data breach. We do the same.

Ziro Labs is a white ultramodern complex built into the hillside at the edge of town. It's basically the complete opposite of

Ziro Hall and its gothic architecture, but with the same imposing sense of scale. I skip my usual spot near the front of the cylindrical main building and go around to the back. With the story I'm about to tell Ezekiel, I want as few witnesses as possible. I have an image to maintain here. These people are my colleagues, and while their first impression when I started working here was some trust fund baby riding his stepfather's coat tails, I've worked hard to earn their respect. I can't show up now with a wild story about time travel and blind dates.

"Wow. Alyssa said this place was big, but it's *big*," Jasper says as I scan my thumb on the reader at the back door.

I frown at him. "When was Alyssa here?"

"She must have come with Clarissa. I didn't—"

"Prestidigitator," I say when the screen prompts me for the password.

"Prestidigitator?" Jasper laughs. "What kind of place is this?"

"It's just a lab, but the password is set up to require a random word with five or more syllables." The lock clicks and I pull it open.

"Metamorphosis was already taken?" Jasper says as we head inside.

"I used that one last week." Honestly, as we've finalized our research, I lobbied hard to increase security. Changing passwords once a week isn't nearly enough, though the real security is inside, on our servers protecting the data and engineering models. "So, what did Alyssa say?" We typically don't have visitors in the building, not even spouses.

"What?" Jasper's walking around with his mouth open and his eyes wide, like he's never been anywhere like this before. It occurred to me on the way over that bringing someone who works for Walter Wolfe into Ziro Labs was probably a bad idea, but desperate times and all that.

"Alyssa said this place was big and what else?"

"Oh. She said you were . . ." He glances around like he's trying to find an escape, but we're waiting for the private elevator that takes us up to the executive level, so there isn't anywhere to go.

"I was . . . ?" I ask, mostly to watch him squirm. And maybe a little for my own ego, because I really need him to finish that sentence. Clarissa always framed my date with Jasper like she was doing me a huge favour. Like I couldn't be trusted to meet someone on my own. So what if I've been locked up in the lab the last few years? When I was ready, I would have found someone. Look how well her plan to set me up with Jasper has gone. But I'm curious to hear what Alyssa said that convinced him to go out with me. "Morgan's a nerdy shut-in with mommy issues and a boatload of emotional baggage" isn't exactly a great sales pitch.

But Jasper's still got his friendly, relaxed smile on as his gaze meets mine. Not a shred of pity. I'm already blushing before he says, "Alyssa also said you were funny and really good-looking, and well, I guess she was right."

Jesus, how pathetic can I be? A guy I don't know who works for a criminal organization called me pretty, and suddenly I'm out of words and my shoes have become very, very interesting.

"Sorry," he says. "That was weird, wasn't it?"

I should say yes. I should tell him this isn't really a date anymore. It's a survival mission. But my face is on fire, and what I actually want to do is tell him to keep talking. I might as well rub myself against his ankles like a cat.

Fortunately, before I have to confirm or deny, the elevator arrives. The distraction means the moment is gone by the time we start rising toward the top floor.

"What exactly do you do here?" Jasper asks.

"We're saving the world." My answer is immediate. A reflex. It's the same answer I give at press conferences and cocktail parties. Everyone loves a good sound bite. For the first while, I wasn't sure I believed it. The statement felt incomplete, knowing that we only had very human methods to accomplish the goals Ezekiel and I set out for ourselves. But over time, we made progress and came to understand how much we could do with the Ziro Machine. We're going save the world. No superpowers required.

"Save it in general or in a specific way?" Jasper asks with a laugh.

"Didn't we talk about this any of the first sixty times?"

He shrugs. "You said you had a presentation for work. Something about climate change. It feels more real, though, now that we're here."

I glance at him, but he doesn't appear to be laughing at me specifically, so I humour him. "It's basically impossible for industry and personal mitigation measures to achieve the carbon reduction targets world governments have set. We don't need a better light bulb, we need a complete technological shift on how we illuminate the planet."

"Sure." He stuffs his hands in his pockets, which says to me this isn't something he thinks about day and night the way I do.

"Ezekiel has designed a machine that captures excess energy from warming oceans."

"But then what?" Jasper asks. "He beams it back to space?" The way he asks, he's not being sarcastic. It's a genuine request for more information. And yet, the question surprises me. Hardly anyone wants this much detail. Most people don't ask anything at all. Despite decades of warnings, humanity continues to think of global warming as a future problem. They certainly don't ask what happens to the energy we remove, which has always been the issue. Storing that much energy is like building a giant bomb. A world killer. And we did consider the space launch option for about half a minute, but the risks were huge, and we ran into the continued issue of traversing the greenhouse gas layer.

"We repurpose it. The Ziro Machine essentially functions as a power conversion and transmission plant. Like a heat pump for your house but with additions and on a scale to power whole cities. Industries can access it the way they would power from a fossil fuel–fired system, but it basically becomes a closed loop. We're recycling power."

It's a work of art, honestly. It took forever to come up with something that would actually do what we needed it to. The technology to efficiently convert trapped heat in the seas into useable electricity doesn't exist. Or it didn't, until Ezekiel finally had his idea for the converter. I'd started to give up hope that our vision would only ever be theoretical. But one night, he burst into my office, face flushed and eyes bright with excitement. It was such a stark contrast after his daily persona of exhausted grief that I knew he'd finally broken through. He showed me a sketch of what would become the Ziro Machine, and the rest is history. One that will be responsible for shaping the future.

"But if you're cutting back on fossil fuel emissions, doesn't that mean eventually you won't need to be recycling the energy because it'll be escaping the way it's supposed to?"

My pulse is racing. Not in fear or annoyance like it has so many times since I met Jasper. More like excitement. I never get to have these conversations with people outside work. Never mind that we're in the lab. He's a henchman, but a pretty smart one. The concept turns me on more than it has any right to. I love a good argument with a well-matched opponent, but I love an intelligent conversation even more.

"Even if we stopped burning fossil fuels right now, it will take centuries for temperatures to go back to where they should be. It's only by collecting some of the excess heat that's already out there that we stop the temperature rises and changing weather patterns. So the system is sustainable and helps us stabilize and back us down faster from the tipping point than we would otherwise."

"You sound really proud of it," he says, and there I go, looking at my shoes again.

"It's going to be amazing," I say. It has to be. When my mother died, I swore I was done with superheroes. The last two years, I've given everything to the Ziro Machine. I was never going to save the world like my mother. This is the best way I know how.

The elevator slows and the doors slide open. We stand for a second, neither one of us moving. Finally, Jasper says, "I don't know where we're going, remember?"

His voice is soft and gently teasing, and he's standing so close to me his breath puffs over my neck, making the hairs at my nape stand on end. I flush. Right. Time to find a solution to this. The ice caps are melting, and so am I, apparently. The sooner we get out of this loop, the better.

"Let's go see Ezekiel."

CHAPTER 7

zekiel's office is just past mine, and as we go by the door to my office, a voice calls out.

"Morgan?"

Jasper and I both stop short as a head pops into the hallway.

"Clarissa?" I say.

Shit. In other versions of this day, I'd have called her to talk about the presentation. I assumed she left the office when I did, but has she been working late this whole time? It's a good thing she doesn't remember, because that is seriously unfair.

"What are you doing here?" she asks.

Yeah, how to explain that.

"We're looking for Ezekiel. The data breach," I say. "I was worried."

"Who's this?" she points at Jasper, though the quirk of her lips says she knows exactly who he is and is reading *way* too much into the fact he's here with me.

Right. "This is . . . this is Jasper. You know. My date. The one you set me up with."

"You're Jasper?" She screeches like an excited macaw and rushes forward to hug him. Despite her wide array of animal noises, in my mind, Clarissa really does look most like a bird.

Her dark hair curls in tight coils that always tend to stick out at odd angles, no matter how hard she tries to style it. And today's choice of a fluffy lavender sweater gives the impression of a tropical bird drying out after a rainstorm.

As she coos and squeezes Jasper tight, he gives me a surprised glance over her shoulder, but all I can do is shrug. She says, "It's so great to meet you. Alyssa's told me so much about you."

"Yeah, likewise." His gaze turns pleading. No doubt silently asking me not to start going on about his career path. I roll my eyes. No way am I bringing that up here. What if we actually succeed in escaping the time loop this time? The rest of my workdays would be filled with "Hey, Morgan! Remember that time you dated a criminal?" No thank you. Let them all believe he's still a med student with a heart of gold.

Clarissa—oblivious to all this—claps her hands excitedly. She squeals with the delight of a chimpanzee being handed a perfect banana, then collects herself as she puts a hand over her mouth. But it's impossible to ignore the sheer joy in her eyes, even though Jasper looks startled by her primate impression.

She says, "And the date must be going well if Morgan's bringing you to the lab. Getting him to go at all was like pulling teeth."

"It wasn't that bad," I say.

She nudges Jasper like two friends sharing an inside joke. "Morgan doesn't love anything as much as he loves his work."

Jesus, Clarissa, don't sugarcoat it. Not that I'm trying to make a good first impression on Jasper or anything. Hell, apparently, I've made sixty-three terrible first impressions. My chance was over before I even realized I had it. It sucks too. I was actually a little excited to meet him. Before I knew about the henching thing, anyway. But with the Ziro Machine launch coming up, it felt like I was coming to the end of something. And maybe that meant it was time to start something—maybe with some*one*— new too. Clarissa makes it sound like I'm an antisocial hermit, though. She could be a much better wingwoman and talk me up a bit.

"We're on our way to see Ezekiel," I say, taking Jasper's hand. I ignore the warm press of it against my palm and the calm feeling that washes over me at the contact. I'm expediting an awkward situation. Nothing more than that.

But Clarissa still doesn't take the hint. She coos and gives him a knowing look. "On your way to meet Dad already?"

Before Jasper can answer I say, "The data breach."

"Oh yeah," she says seriously. "He's been shouting on the phone for a while."

"Yeah," he says, surprising me with his quickness. "My specialty is cybersecurity. We got talking, and Morgan thought I could help."

Clarissa frowns. "I thought you were a doctor?"

Where Jasper has been lingering out of some sense of politeness, now his grip on my hand firms up, and he matches my pace as we head toward Ezekiel's office.

"It's kind of a hobby," he says.

"Medicine is a hobby?" she asks, bewildered.

I wince because Clarissa is going to have so many questions when I arrive at the lab tomorrow, and I don't have time for that right now. Though I guess if I do make it to the lab tomorrow, you could really say I have all the time in the world. But my track record on that front has not been awesome lately, so better to not get my hopes up.

Give me awkward dating debriefs or give me death.

When I push open the door to his office, Ezekiel's on the phone. His eyes widen when he sees me, and he promptly tells the person on the other end he'll call them back.

"What are you doing here?" he says.

"I, uh . . ." This isn't good. I didn't think this through. Ezekiel and I don't have many secrets. But he's an intelligent rational man of science, so how am I supposed to look him in the eye and tell him the very irrational thing that's happening?

"We're here about the data breach," Jasper says, walking confidently across the room, leaving me to trail after him.

"Who are you?" Then Ezekiel's gaze goes back to me. "How did you know about the data breach?"

Right. Because on this version of today, I didn't go home to find out this particular bit of information. But also, I didn't go home to have Indigo pulverize my insides, so I think I've come out ahead.

"Clarissa called me," I lie.

"I've got some experience in cybersecurity," Jasper says at the same time. "Have you managed to lock them out yet?"

Ezekiel still looks confused—and rightfully so—but he says, "We keep thinking we've closed the system, and then they find another way in. It's like Whack-A-Mole."

Jasper comes around the desk to look over Ezekiel's shoulder, and I swallow hard.

"We were on a date," I say, cobbling syllables together slowly. But I speak so softly and they're both so intent on Ezekiel's computer that neither of them hears me.

"So they got in. Did they get out? Did they take anything?" Jasper asks. Wait, when he said it was a hobby, did he mean hacking? Or is that part of what he does for Walter Wolfe? He's never said. Not specifically. I assumed henching meant driving the getaway car and terrorizing witnesses so they won't testify. But digital henching has to be a thing too.

"No, not that we can tell. But if we can't keep them out, it's only a matter of time." Ezekiel gazes at me pleadingly. "We're so close to launch, we can't have someone taking this from us."

Since we started the project, we've had a number of government agencies and tech companies offer to buy us, partner with us, or flat out take us over. They're threatened by what we can do and by how much Ezekiel doesn't care about making more money than he already has.

"Tell your IT team to run a search for a funhouse worm," Jasper says. My pulse is thumping again, but we're back to fear.

Maybe this is it. The why of the time loop. They've sent Jasper to steal the Ziro Machine. They duped Clarissa and suckered me into believing this handsome man had any interest in me so they could get inside the facility and take everything we've worked for.

"Funhouse?" Ezekiel asks Jasper, who is still frowning at the screen.

"It's like a hall of mirrors. Odds are good there aren't as many points of entry as you think. They're reflecting off each other, so it looks like more than it is. Really hard to tell which worms are genuine."

"Stop looking at that!" I finally blurt.

Ezekiel and Jasper both look up from the computer in surprise.

"What?" Ezekiel says.

Shit. Now what do I say? I just lead the Trojan horse through the gates?

"I . . . I realized he doesn't have security clearance."

Ezekiel's confusion deepens, and Jasper tilts his head like a confused German shepherd. His green hat flops to the same side.

"But you brought him here?" Ezekiel says slowly.

"We should go," I say, pushing back from my chair. It's like me fleeing Wench all over again. "Sorry, I wasn't thinking. Clarissa called and I panicked."

"Morgan," Jasper says, causing me to stop short as I back away from Ezekiel's desk. "Trust me. Let me help."

Trust him? Trust *him*? Why did I even bring Jasper here? Never mind the lapse in judgement. This scenario is impossible. Beyond comprehension. I should be at home reviewing slides. I should be double-checking the suit I plan to wear for our presentation doesn't have a stain on the lapel. I should be asleep without worrying that a supervillain is about to sublimate my guts. Instead, the safest option has become bringing a fucking henchman for Walter Wolfe right into my home territory.

"Morgan," Jasper says again.

I take a deep breath. All of me feels cold. My fingers twitch, and I have to plaster my palms to my sides. I can feel the chill against my thighs, even through the material. I hold Jasper's gaze. If my mother were here, she'd pin him down and demand to know what his intentions are. All I can do is silently beg him not to betray me the same way he did back in the hall with Clarissa.

But you know what? Fuck it. A kind of numb calm slips over me. What's the worst that can happen? He ruins the work I have dedicated myself to every day for the last two years and sells us out to his boss, who will then no doubt use it to hold the world hostage under threat of some kind of mega bomb. Ezekiel and I will shoulder the blame for building it in the first place, and we'll have to flee to a rapidly sinking island. That doesn't sound so bad. Better than sixty-three consecutive deaths.

Except it won't happen, because the second my worst fears come true, I'll fling myself off the top of Ziro Tower so we have to start all over again. If Jasper betrays me, I'll be sure to stab him as soon as he walks in the door at Wench, and then I'll get on with my life. I shudder at the thought of dying intentionally. So far my deaths—at least the ones I remember—have always been more or less accidental. But they don't have to be. I'm in charge. As grim as it is, I hold all the cards here.

I relax and nod at Jasper. He goes back to work with Ezekiel. They call down to the IT department and Ezekiel passes the phone to Jasper, who starts rattling off strings of questions and commands I don't understand in the slightest. His competence in this situation doesn't help my anxiety . . . and my attraction. I want so badly to brand him a criminal. Maybe a loser. But he knows what he's doing here and it's unsettling. Also a little sexy —okay, a lot sexy. Competence has always been my catnip. But if I can't trust him, I can't be attracted to him. There's no gray area that would allow that.

Eventually, Ezekiel comes to stand beside me as Jasper taps away at the keyboard.

"Who exactly is this guy?" he asks.

I glance up at him. "It's a long story."

Finally, Jasper leans back in the chair, arms over his head, looking for all the world like he's the CEO of Ziro Labs instead of Ezekiel, and says, "Done."

"Done?" Ezekiel rushes back to him.

"They're closed out, anyway. You'll have to wait for your team to confirm what information they got, but at the very least they won't get back in tonight."

Ezekiel breathes a huge sigh of relief, shaking Jasper's hand vigorously. "Thank you. Thank you so much . . . er . . . I'm sorry, I don't even know your name."

Jasper tips an imaginary brim on his hat. "Jasper Jackson, at your service."

"If you need henching . . ." I mutter under my breath. I'm still waiting for the other shoe to drop. For Walter Wolfe to burst through the door and say the machine is his now, or for Jasper to cackle and say he can't believe we fell into his trap. But none of it happens.

"What did you say?" Ezekiel asks me.

"Nothing," I answer quickly, but I don't miss the way Jasper throws a wink in my direction.

Ezekiel, of course, is oblivious. He doesn't concern himself with anything so mundane as his stepson flirting with a mysteriously charming and proficient computer genius who arrived uninvited in his office. Instead, he says, "I don't know if Morgan told you what we're trying to do here, but there are people who don't want to see us succeed. As long as there's oil, there's money to be made from it. If any of them can get their hands on our patents and figure out how to turn a profit on it—"

"Ezekiel," I say, because I know how passionate he can get when he starts talking about the Ziro Machine. "Jasper doesn't need the whole mission statement."

"He deserves something." Ezekiel's grin is broad. Standing together, he and Jasper couldn't be more different. Ezekiel in his suit looks like the kind of man who stands at the head of board-rooms and promises investors the world for a mere drop of their blood. Jasper, in his toque and flannel, looks like the kind of guy who asks if you need assistance picking out a Christmas tree. But he stands next to Ezekiel like an equal, and I still can't shake the feeling that I'm missing something about him.

"Actually," I say, "we need help."

"That sounds serious. Does it require a drink?" He goes to the bar cart he keeps near the window. I always tease him about how we're supposed to be an altruistic nonprofit, not a swanky law firm, but he insists hospitality is doubly important since we can't offer investors and shareholders an exponential return on their money.

"Does it ever," I say with a sigh.

"That's not good." He laughs as he pours whisky into three tumblers, passing me one and Jasper another. I spent so many nights like this back in the early days of the Ziro project. Ezekiel and I would sit here sipping on whisky and talking about what would happen if our plans were successful. It was exciting. Invigorating, following the months and months of silent sadness at Ziro Hall after Mother died. Now, though, there's no excite-ment. I'm so tired. I sink onto the leather sofa while Ezekiel takes the club chair across from me. Jasper pauses for an instant before he settles next to me, sitting at the edge of the cushion. I glance at him, hoping he'll speak first, but he tips his glass to me in a silent cheers. At the final second, so there's no confusion, he says, "I'll let you handle this one," then takes a drink.

Oh boy. I toss my whisky back, swallowing the fumes. I exhale slowly, running my palms over my thighs. Jasper nudges his knee with mine, and Ezekiel laughs softly to himself.

"Come on. Spit it out," he says.

Finally, I rip off the metaphorical Band-Aid and say, "We're stuck in a time loop where I keep dying over and over, and we don't know how to get out."

The office gets quiet. Ezekiel's face is blank, like maybe I didn't say anything after all. Jasper's knuckles brush mine and I go to swat him away because we're not holding hands in front of my stepfather, but instead he takes my glass and goes to the bar cart, where he refills both our drinks before returning to his spot next to me. We both sip a little more slowly this time. Mostly.

Ezekiel sets his drink down and rubs his eyes before saying, "It's possible you've been working too hard."

"No. No." I lean forward. "I'm not making this up."

"Morgan." His brow is creased with worry, which only sparks my anxiety because if he doesn't believe me, I don't know what I'll do.

"We need help." My voice rasps with desperation.

"What am I supposed to do? A time loop?" He sounds genuinely confused, and my heart feels like it cracks in two. He's supposed to help us. I wasn't expecting him to hop to it, but we've worked side by side for years. We trust each other, and I thought he'd trust me on this. Jasper's hand settles on the small of my back. I don't push him away this time. If I can't count on Ezekiel as an ally, Jasper's my last option.

"I know it sounds impossible," I say.

Ezekiel loosens his tie. "We've been busy, and there's still a lot to do, but you can't travel through time. You can't . . ." His voice fades as he stares out the window and frowns.

"I don't know why it's happening. It just is, and we're stuck, and . . ." My throat tightens, and I'm unprepared for the tears that form in the corners of my eyes. "And I don't want to die anymore."

Wow. There's the essential truth of it, isn't there? Never mind my brave words about holding all the cards. Dying three times is enough. Jasper pulls me a little closer, and I let him, but I keep my gaze locked on Ezekiel. He drags a finger around the rim of his glass, face pinched in thought.

"How long has this been going on?" he asks.

"About two months." My voice is soft.

His is not. "Two months!" The words echo off the walls, making me flinch.

"It's complicated," Jasper says, and relief washes over me that he jumps in. "They aren't like real days. Sometimes it's only an hour or two. But we've repeated it more than sixty times now."

Ezekiel watches me silently for a minute longer before he drags his gaze to Jasper. "And who are you again?"

If he goes with the "Jasper Jackson, at your service" thing one more time, I'll punch him, but instead Jasper sits up straight and says, "Morgan and I are on a blind date. It's our first date. Sir." He takes the last part on with a respectful dip of his chin that has my whole face going fiery. This isn't one of those sexy period dramas you see on streaming services now. He's not here to ask permission to court me and whisk me away to his country estate. He's a med school dropout turned henchman, and we're stuck together.

It gets worse when Ezekiel's eyes widen and he leans back in his chair. "Oh. Oh, that's, uh . . ." His lips quirk as he glances at me. "That's great, Morgan. Great that you're . . . uh . . . meeting new people."

Oh my god. I bury my face in my hands, feeling about fifteen years old. Ezekiel and I are close, but ours has never been the kind of relationship where we talk about my love life. Or his, for that matter. Mother didn't marry him until I was nearly done with high school, so Ezekiel and I bonded over college applications. And since it's been only the two of us, things have been entirely about the research. He never asks how I'm doing or if I'm meeting friends after work. And I've been fine with that, because apparently if he did, suddenly dying on the spot doesn't seem so bad after all.

"I know it's a lot," Jasper says as I wallow. "And we can't explain it. But Morgan said that you were the smartest person he knows and that if anyone can help us, it's you."

Ezekiel laughs softly. "That's very flattering, but my specialty is energy transfer, not time travel. I know about condensing mass and transferring energy forms from one state to another. I don't know what would be causing you to skip through time."

"But you have to know someone," I say, finally rejoining the land of the unembarrassed. "You know everyone. Someone who studies this?" Ezekiel has worked for think tanks, sat on panels. He's contributed to papers and generally hung around with some of the most educated people on the planet.

"Morgan," he says carefully, scratching at the back of his neck. His gaze is full of compassion, but his voice is the one people use when they have to break bad news. "You and I both know there are things that science can't explain. What you're going through—" He holds up a hand when I protest. "Yes, I believe it's happening. But I don't even know where to start with something like this."

Disappointment crashes into me like a grand piano falling off a building. We're on our own.

"There's something else," I say, because if I've told him this much, we might as well tell him everything.

"Besides you being stuck in this day for the last two months?" Ezekiel asks with a raised eyebrow. He lifts his whisky from the table again.

"You can't go back to the house tonight," I say.

"Oh no?" he says before he takes a drink.

Fear tightens my throat, but I need him to be safe. At least I can jump-start time and protect him properly. "Indigo. He's back."

You have to know Ezekiel to see his reaction. He's a master at the poker face. But his hand shakes slightly, and he holds the whisky in his mouth for a fraction of a second too long. When he swallows, his voice is a rasp as he says, "Indigo?"

"He was at the house . . . I mean, he'll be at the house. Later. You . . . I . . ." I squeeze my eyes tight and try to piece together the best way to explain this. "You asked how I knew about the data breach. It's because a few days ago . . . which is today, but not this version of today . . . instead of coming here, I went home. You were on your way out, coming back here to deal with the breach. I stayed home, fell asleep, and later a noise woke me up. It was—" I swallow. Sometime while I've been speaking, Jasper removed his hand, and now I miss it. "Indigo was in your office, and when he saw me, he . . ." I wave a hand as the remembered pain sweeps over me.

"Are you okay?" Ezekiel asks. He moves toward me, looking concerned, but I'm leaning against Jasper, so there's not much for him to do.

"I'm fine," I say, laughing weakly. "Just not an experience I care to repeat."

"Were you there too?" Ezekiel's gaze goes to Jasper, who shakes his head.

"No."

"Why not?" His voice trembles with barely controlled anger. It's a sign of how much Indigo's reappearance is shaking him. Ezekiel is poised in every situation. But we're talking about the monster who killed his wife. You can't expect him to hold it together.

"You can't go home," I say again quickly because Jasper doesn't need to defend himself. It's not his fault that I didn't believe him sooner. "Indigo will be there, and if something happened to you, I'd—"

Ezekiel looks between us. His eyes are worried, but whatever he sees pass from Jasper to me must be the reassurance he needs because he says, "I'll stay here. Won't be the first night I've slept at the office." He gives me a reassuring smile, and part of me wonders if maybe this has happened before. Maybe the reason he didn't come home the night Indigo was there was because somehow, another version of me had been able to warn him. If the day keeps repeating over and over, are there sixty different versions of me running around the city? Wouldn't that be wild? But no, that can't be right, because there's only ever one of me and one of Jasper when everything restarts at Wench.

"Thank you," I say.

"Why don't you stay here too?" Ezekiel says. "Both of you. That way I know you're safe."

I glance up at Jasper. It's tempting. My body is tired, though I don't know if it's from the stress of the situation or from the full day of work I put in "today"—whenever that was.

"We can't stay," I say.

"You can't?"

"We can't?" Jasper says, looking surprised.

"No. We need to find out what's going on. And I think . . ." I turn to Jasper. "What are the ways I have died? Sometimes I got hit by the bus, right?"

"Right."

"What bus?" Ezekiel asks, making me wince. He's had a lot of surprises tonight, and now he gets to relive my deaths.

"And sometimes I went home where Indigo showed up, right?"

"Probably," Jasper says.

"Were there any other nights? Any other things I did?"

He shrugs. "A few times you called the cops. We spent a lot of time talking to them and filling out reports."

"What did you tell them you do for a living?" I ask.

"It wouldn't have mattered." He smiles down at me, and I can't help my answering smile. Sitting this close to him is the calmest I've felt since this all started. Probably the whisky. Jasper says, "Even if they'd arrested me, I'd only be back at the date a few hours later."

"What do you do for a living? Why would they have arrested you?" Ezekiel asks. He's watching us with growing anxiety, no doubt trying to piece together answers from our shorthand. But I don't answer, and neither does Jasper. Someday I'll have to tell him about my date with the henchman, but right now, my priority is survival. If it has to be with Jasper, that's what I'll do.

"A couple times, I tried to follow you," Jasper says. "When

you'd leave, I'd call a cab and get it to follow you after you left Wench."

"And what did I do?"

"Most of the time you went home. The rest of the time you came here."

"And every time I died, right?" At my question, Ezekiel inhales sharply. Welcome to the club. It's a lot to wrap your head around, and when you do, the truth is pretty bleak.

Jasper isn't nearly as upset. All he says is, "As far as I know."

I turn back to Ezekiel, who is looking pale. "So I can't stay here," I say. "Because no matter what I do, I die, and whether it's a freak explosion in the lab or if Indigo is the cause here too, I can't put you at risk. So you'll be safer if you're not with me."

Ezekiel sighs, and I wish I could stay because at least here things feel normal. I've basically lived here for the last few months, and even before that I spent more time here at the lab than I did at home. But I can't put Ezekiel at risk.

He says, "You'll look out for him, right?" I realize he's speaking to Jasper.

And Jasper says, "I'll do my best."

We rise, the whisky leaving me feeling warm and a little floaty, which is nice. I hug Ezekiel, something I haven't done nearly enough since Mom died. He holds me a second longer than I expect, which tells me how worried he is.

As Jasper and I head to the door, Ezekiel says, "Walter Wolfe."

My blood freezes. Does he know who Jasper is after all?

"What about him?" I say, trying to stay casual.

Ezekiel scratches his chin. "It's probably nothing, but a few months ago, I was at a function, and Walter Wolfe was there." His gaze is somewhere up and to the left like he's remembering the evening. It's not uncommon for Wolfe to show up at these things. You see him in the paper sometimes making a donation to one organization or another. Helps him with plausible deniability that he's only a humble businessman trying to help his community.

"You spoke to him?" I ask. I can't imagine it, but the inevitable chitchat at those kinds of parties are exactly why I'm happy to let Ezekiel go to them while I stay at the lab.

He nods. "We got talking, and he told me that he thought our work was nobly intentioned but that it wouldn't even make the headlines because he was on the verge of finding a machine that would turn back time." Ezekiel drops his gaze to mine. "I didn't take him seriously, of course, but what if he meant it for real?"

I snort because even with everything, what he's suggesting is absurd. "You think Walter Wolfe built a time machine?"

He ducks his head, clearly understanding how ridiculous he sounds, but he says, "It would be quite the business opportunity. Think about what you could charge people to go back to the moment before a financial transaction went south, or"—his eyes soften—"before you lost a loved one."

Ouch. I know that feeling.

"But a time machine?" I question. "That's never been Wolfe's thing, has it?" Villains tend to fall into two categories. The first is the old-school guns and drugs kind, which is what I assumed Walter Wolfe was into. The other is more of the mind control, world subjugation, and travelling at the speed of light type of bad guy. I've never seen any indication that Wolfe has any interest or capabilities on that front, even when I worked at SPAM.

Ezekiel's phone rings on his desk. When he goes to answer it, Jasper catches my hand, tugging me close.

"We have to go," he says, speaking softly.

"Just a minute." But I can't very well walk out of Ezekiel's office without saying goodbye. Social graces are not my strong suit, but even I know to do that much.

Jasper has no such compunctions, apparently.

"No, I mean, we have to go because I think I know where the time machine is."

I inhale sharply. Ezekiel's on the phone with IT, getting an update on the data breach. He's got his back to us. Still, I turn a little closer into Jasper. He smells good. Does he always smell like this? Like freshly sawn pine. Maybe I will start calling him Lumber Jasper after all.

"Where?" I ask, balling my hands into nervous fists.

His lips are practically against my ear when he says, "Pretty sure I've seen the plans for a time machine in Walter Wolfe's office."

CHAPTER 8

We excuse ourselves after I get Ezekiel to promise a few more times that he really will stay at Ziro Labs tonight. I hold back my questions for Jasper until we're driving away from the lab.

"Your boss has a time machine and you didn't think to bring that up before?"

Jasper's back to looking sheepish. "I didn't *know* it was a time machine. I was in his office and saw some plans. It wasn't like they were labelled as 'Plans for Top Secret Time Machine, Don't Tell Morgan' or anything. Why would I think that was what it was?" He glares at me, and his expression is so hurt that I snort on a laugh that becomes a cough before it becomes laughter again. The sound is big and I lean into it. Jasper watches me with amusement in his eyes and for a minute I don't resent it.

"Ugh." I sigh as my laughter subsides. "Why can't everything have big labels like that? 'Top Secret Plot to Trap Jasper and Morgan on the Blind Date from Hell.' So much simpler."

He sticks his lower lip out. His eyes sparkle. My laughter starts all over again. Is this what having fun feels like? It's been a while since I've done anything besides work, which I would argue is its own kind of fun. But it's not the same as joking around with someone.

"It's not so bad, is it?" he asks.

"The company could be worse," I say, but I arch an eyebrow. "But that's like saying a funeral is a good time because you get to see long-lost relatives for the first time in years. It's fun for all but the guy who dies, and in this case the guy is me. You don't know what that's like."

"No." He folds his arms over his chest. "But I did have to do the first sixty days alone. I thought I was losing my mind. Nothing I did made a difference. I kept getting brought back to the beginning over and over and . . ." He glances out the window and the rest of his sentence is muffled.

"And what?" I prompt.

He glances at me before he drops his arms and says, "It was scary, okay? It was so fucking lonely. I tried everything I could think of to get you to remember me, but you never did."

Until I did remember him. There has to be a clue in the fact that we started remembering at different times. And yes, I could needle him. Solitude is still better than dying. But remembering three of those deaths is enough. Remembering all sixty-some dates and not having any control over when they end or how to get out of them would be a whole other thing. If the definition of insanity is doing the same thing over and over and expecting a different outcome, then what's defined as being forced to repeat something over and over with no control over the outcome at all?

So, because Clarissa reminds me frequently that some people respond better to empathy than they do to my usual "what are you going to do about it?" forthrightness, I say, "It must have been really hard."

Jasper gives me a sad smile that makes me want to say more kind things. "It's better now. I know you don't like me much, but I'm glad you're here."

Ouch. I bite back a bunch of protests because if I talk too fast,

I'll almost certainly say the wrong thing. It's not that I dislike him. In fact, I'm starting to like him more than I should given his career choices. I'm not completely oblivious of my own super-family and stepfatherly privileges. I know finding work can be tough, but he's clearly got real marketable skills. Ezekiel would probably give him a position at Ziro Labs if I asked, especially after Jasper wowed him with his IT wizardry tonight. Yet somehow Jasper chose Walter Wolfe. There have to be better ways to get a job after you flunk out of med school besides hitching your wagon to organized crime.

Speaking of which . . . "You know we're going to have to go check out that machine, right?"

He blanches so much it's visible, even in the dark car. "Maybe we don't?"

"No, we really do," I say. "If he's got a time machine so powerful you don't even need to be near it to move back hours, think about the scientific advancement he's achieved."

"That's what you want to see it for?" he asks, incredulous. I try not to feel hurt. There goes Morgan the nerd, all excited about science again.

"We need to know who built it," I explain patiently. "Whoever they are, they're the only one who can get us out of this."

"But what if they aren't?" Jasper says. "What if there's another way?"

"Like what?"

"Let's . . . let's lie low." He glances at me nervously. "Give me a few days to figure out how to do it safely. We've never really stayed together before. What if we see if we can keep you alive? If we hide out, we might—" The longer he talks, the faster the words come out until he's practically pleading, but the flaw in his thinking is evident.

"Jasper, we already covered this with Ezekiel. You think I wouldn't have accidentally stumbled onto a way to stay alive after sixty tries? It's statistically impossible to die randomly every single time. Someone is coming for me."

"But you don't . . ." He winces. "Look, if spending sixty days trapped in the same day was scary, Walter Wolfe is scarier. We can't just walk into his office and ask about his time machine."

"But you work for him, don't you?" I ask.

"Yeah, but we're not exactly buddies. Wolfe Tech isn't some family organization like what you and Ezekiel have going. I'm a henchman." His voice rises with frustration, seeming even louder in the confined space of my car. When I glance at him, he's torn off his toque and is clenching it so tightly in his lap that his knuckles are white. "Don't you get it? I look tough when he has business associates stop by and pick up bags of stuff I'm not supposed to know about but are almost definitely drugs or money. If I were in a comic book, I'd be a guy in a nondescript red shirt and a mask who was only on page to be cannon fodder."

"A red shirt would be better than your hat," I mutter.

That stops him halfway through his rant. "What's wrong with my hat?"

I stare at him. "Please. Do you think it's fashionable?"

"It keeps my head warm." He stretches the tattered wool between his hands.

"It's spring. It hasn't been below freezing in over a month." On a whim, I reach across the console and snatch the hat from him. His hair is sticking up in a million different directions, so I pat it down for a minute before he swats me away.

"Don't think you can cute your way out of this," he says.

"I'm not trying to be cute." The car jerks as I whip my head toward him again. "Wait. Do you actually think I'm cute? You weren't kidding before?"

He laughs. It's a big, open sound, and the tension in the vehicle dissipates. Before Jasper can answer my question, though, his stomach lets out a rumble that nearly shakes the car's windows.

"Jesus, I'm starving." He rubs a hand over his belly. "Look, whatever we do next, can we please go get something to eat first? If we're going to storm the castle at Wolfe Tech, at least don't make me do it on an empty stomach."

"Sure. Why not?" I say. "With my luck, I'll choke on a French fry."

"Don't say that." He shoots me a soft smile, and once again I'm annoyed by how much I don't dislike him. Yes, I need him, but he's not an awful person. At least in noncriminal settings. I don't know what to do with this information.

"I'm not going back to Kicks," I say.

His smile widens, which does fluttery things to my insides.

"No, probably not a good idea," he says.

"And we aren't going to Wench."

"Something about that place makes you uncomfortable, doesn't it?"

My soft feelings disappear because I don't like how much he sees. "It's fine," I say.

"No, it isn't."

I keep my eyes on the road. We aren't having that conversation. There are still some secrets I can't share.

Jasper must take the hint, because he says, "There are lots of great places to eat in town. Where do you want to go?"

"Wherever you want."

"You must have somewhere you like," Jasper says.

"I'm allergic to a lot of things," I say. "I usually eat at home. It's safer." At least it was before shadow-shaped enemies lurked in darkened corners.

"That's no fun." Jasper's practically pouting.

"Neither is anaphylaxis." But he's still waiting for an answer, and we're past me playing the fussy nerd, so I say, "What's your favourite?"

He sighs dreamily. "I like the deep-fried pickles at the Lazy Moose."

When I wrinkle my nose, he laughs.

"What?" I say.

"Not a fan of deep-fried pickles?"

"I honestly don't think I've ever had one."

His shout is so sharp, I almost jerk over the centre line a second time.

"What was that?" I ask.

"Morgan! You never had deep-fried pickles?"

If my hands were free, I'd put them over my ears. "Why are you yelling?"

He shouts again, then bumps his fist against the dash. "Take a left at the light."

And that's how we wind up sitting across from each other at yet another greasy spoon diner as Jasper gleefully orders a plate of fried dill pickles and an order of nachos. Why is it always nachos with him? The waitress pales as I give her my list of allergies. Onions, mustard, nuts—except almonds for no reason anyone's ever been able to explain to me—blue cheese, cilantro, raw eggs, raw peaches—but cooked ones are okay—and all cherries. She reassures me they use vegetable oil in the deep fryer and none of those other things are in the pickles, so I guess I'll have to take my chances.

And look, maybe the "prissy" act wasn't all pretend. It's not only the allergies. I'm professional. And careful. But I can honestly say the plastic chairs, the peeling forest animal wallpaper, and the way my shirt cuffs stick to the edge of the table every time I lift a hand do not recommend this place any more than the atmosphere at Kicks did.

"Are henchman only allowed to eat at places with less than three stars on Yelp?" I ask, making sure to smile enough that he knows I'm only half serious.

"No one gets into henching for the money. This place is cheap and tasty." He shrugs unapologetically. "I gave you a chance to pick. If you wanted linen tablecloths, you should have said something."

I so desperately want to ask him why he got into henching if it wasn't for the money, but I'm also afraid to hear the answer. Instead, I squeeze the limes into my ice water as I say, "Jasper, you seem to be under the misapprehension that I'm some kind of snob."

"Aren't you?"

"No. I . . . Maybe my mother was a bit of a snob?" Saying it feels wrong. Disloyal. But my mother's identity as Farah Field required her to mix and mingle with an elite tier of society. Those were the kinds of people who would hire a personal security firm. I travelled with her and her clients for a long time, since it took years before we finally gave up on me ever following in her footsteps. Field Security clients don't eat at places like the Lazy Moose, and so I never really got a chance to do it either.

"How long ago did she die?"

My gaze shoots up at his question. "What?"

But Jasper's looking down at the table and he shrugs. "My dad died when I was twelve. I know what it's like."

But he doesn't. He can't. Because he gets to reminisce with people about the good old days. I can never tell anyone the whole story.

"Two years ago," I say.

"That's hard. Was she sick?"

See? Here's where I have to lie, because how do I tell him that she was killed fighting Indigo? That when the light box failed, it set fire to the building they were in and the collateral damage meant my mother was branded a public menace after her own death? That the people who had been only too happy to bask in the safety the Legendary Flame offered while she was alive had refused to remember the good she had done in favour of the harm the final fight with Indigo had caused?

"Plane crash," I say, because that's the lie Ezekiel and I concocted. It took a lot of work to fake the traces of her private plane failing and forging everything needed to make it clear that Farah Field was dead.

Jasper whistles. "That's rough."

He doesn't even know the half of it.

"I think it was harder on Ezekiel. He and my mother weren't even married for ten years. That's not nearly long enough."

"What about your dad?"

That part is easier. "No clue. He died when I was a baby and Mother never talked about him much. All I got from him was a last name."

"So it was only you and your mom while you were growing up?"

I laugh because it sounds so cozy the way he says it when my childhood was more like a decades-long superhero tryout that ultimately came up empty. Mother always said her own powers had been notoriously unpredictable until she was well into her late teens. So public school was out of the question. We couldn't have me getting angry at the teacher and electrocuting her or blowing up all the computers in the building because I was thinking too hard about long division. So I was homeschooled, and I could speak four different languages by the time I was ten, thanks to our schedule of constant travel. In the end it amounted to nothing, though, since by the time I was eighteen, my powers had never advanced beyond making sure the flashlight always worked in case of a power outage.

"Something like that," I say.

"You must miss her," he says.

"It's complicated." I can't quite look at him. The longer he talks, the more I feel like I'm lying when I'm just not telling him everything.

"My dad was my hero. When I was a kid—"

I don't hear the rest of it. He doesn't know it, but the word sets me off. Jasper can't understand anything about having a parent who is a hero. It's not great. They don't take you to baseball games or teach you how to tie your shoes. They put the good of humankind ahead of everything else and email you gift cards on your birthday because they're halfway around the world chasing assassins most people have never even heard of.

"Can we not?" My skin tingles in irritation.

Jasper's sentimental smile freezes, as does his reminiscing. "What?"

"We're not going to bond over our dead parents," I say. "I can't right now. Every brain cell I have is swirled up in the time loop. I want to figure out how we get out of this damn thing, and then I'm getting on with my life. And you can go back to . . ." I wave a hand absently. "Scamming little old ladies out of their life savings, and holding up banks, or whatever it is you do."

He stops smiling and his gaze drops to the table. "It's not like that."

"I'm sure it isn't," I say. So much for empathy. I did my best, but there's a Walter Wolfe–shaped hurdle between us—and possibly a Legendary Flame–shaped one too—and I'm never going to get over it.

He exhales a long sigh and mutters something, but he pulls off his hat at the same time, so the words are muffled behind wool and I don't catch them.

"What?"

"Nothing." He runs his hands through his hair, but the gesture is rough and agitated.

"No, go on," I push, sensing the fight before it happens. "What did you say?"

"I asked why that was the date you decided to remember. You're such a pain in the ass sometimes."

I recoil at the unexpected declaration. I may be ruder than I should be, but Jasper's been nothing but consideration. I thought he'd call me weird. Awkward. Impolite. "Excuse me?"

He glares at me, lips thin, jaw tense. I should feel bad for upsetting him. We were almost getting along there for a second. But we're not friends. This isn't a teambuilding exercise. We're not forming a Dead Parents Club.

The server comes and deposits Jasper's nachos and a basket of what I can only assume is the magical deep-fried pickles. I grab one, consider swiping it through the little cup of brown sauce the server didn't bother identifying when she dropped it off, decide it's safer not to, and stuff it into my mouth. They must be fresh from the deep fryer, because the mound of food between my lips is an inferno. It's all I can do not to spit it back out, but I won't give Jasper the satisfaction. Instead, I suck a small stream of air, focusing on dropping the temperature at the point of entry as low as I can manage, until the tangy mush finally chills. My lips tingle, as do my fingers, so I take a long drink of water and force myself to swallow.

"How are they?" Jasper asks, giving me an uncertain look. "They're usually pretty hot."

"Delicious," I say with a grin before I grab a second one. I wince as the crispy breading hits my burned tongue, but what do I care? No doubt Indigo is lurking outside the door, waiting to jump me the second we go back outside. I'll have a whole new set of taste buds in no time.

"Look," Jasper says. He reaches for a pickle, but I snag the basket. If he wanted me to taste them, I'm going to eat the whole damn order. Let him ask for more. "Clearly I've upset you."

"No, I'm fine," I say as I swallow again. "I'm just really hungry."

"Morgan."

I eat another pickle. "Like you said. They're delicious."

"I'm really sorry."

"You have nothing to be sorry for." If anything, I should be apologizing for not telling him the whole truth. But let him think I'm a jerk. It's easier.

Also, the tingling in my lips is getting worse, even as the pickles cool. I suck down the rest of my water, hoping to rinse it away. I'm amazed I can feel anything at all, but for good measure I grab the last pickle and jam it into my mouth, chewing so fast I bite my tongue, but hey, what's a little blood on top of the dead epithelial cells?

Except the tingling grows. Actually, it's more like an itch. It's spreading over my scalded nerve endings and slowly making its way to the back of my throat and—

Oh no.

I glance up at Jasper, who's still watching me unhappily.

"What's in these pickles?"

His worried expression relaxes, his smile grows. "Do you really like them? I know it's not fancy, but—"

"Jasper, what's in the goddamn pickles?"

His fingers drum merrily on the table as the itching gets worse and adrenaline floods my nervous system, getting ready to do everything it can to keep me alive.

His smile fades. "It's pickles and—"

"Hey," the server appears, hurrying toward us from the direction of the kitchen. The worry on her face is unmistakable. "Did you say you were allergic to mustard or mayonnaise? Because I might have asked the cook if there was mayonnaise in the pickles and I think I got it wrong. It would definitely explain the look he gave me when—"

I don't hear the rest. What I thought was a symptom of burning all my taste buds off is actually the sensation of my tongue swelling as my autoimmune system goes into overdrive. I fumble, looking for my laptop bag, but of course it's not here because who brings a laptop on what must essentially be the worst second date they've ever been on? No, my laptop bag—along with the EpiPen inside—is in my car.

"Morgan?" Jasper says as I lean back, trying to find more room to breathe. "Morgan!"

Goddammit.

I haven't had an allergic reaction in close to ten years. I have been deathly careful my entire life, and all it took was one henchman with a greasy food craving to bring it all down.

As my lungs realize there's a problem and my chest aches, I glare at Jasper, whose face has gone white with terror.

"We'll talk about this tomorrow," I gasp.

Will we ever.

CHAPTER 9

He's late.

Honestly, who gets mustard and mayonnaise mixed up in a list of allergens?

"You sure you don't want something to eat? I could cook you up something." Vee comes to stand at my table.

"Have you ever heard of someone making deep-fried pickles with mayonnaise?" I ask, though the last three syllables are mangled with a cough. It's hard to get a full breath.

She wasn't expecting that question. "No? It would make the batter greasy. Unless you mean in the dipping sauce?"

The door bangs open and Jasper rushes in, his face etched with concern.

"We'll have two ice waters and a basket of chips and salsa," I say, mostly to get Vee to go away.

"Friend of yours?" she asks, watching Jasper make a beeline to our table.

"You wouldn't believe me if I told you."

Her lips quirk up in a smile, but she has to get out of the way as Jasper more or less throws himself into the chair next to me, and the distraction is enough to send her off to the kitchen.

"Are you okay?" Jasper asks. He's also breathing hard, and even his green hat looks a little more disheveled than usual.

"Never been better," I wheeze.

"That was super scary," he gasps. "She was really apologetic. I don't think she's ever had someone die in her restaurant before."

"Imagine that." I close my eyes, trying to focus on breathing instead of telling Jasper to shut up. It's nervous chatter born of adrenaline, but I have to take care of myself. Being the dying party means I'm not responsible for his feelings in the immediate aftermath.

"She said they put mustard powder in the breading," he continues when I open my eyes again, though the flush on his cheeks is subsiding. "Gives it a bite."

"Gives it more than that." I cough some more. Each breath rattles in my chest like a nest of tap-dancing spiders.

"You okay?" Vee asks, bringing our water and chips.

"Is there mustard in that?" Jasper asks, pointing at the salsa. He slings a protective arm around me, and that helps as much as anything.

She frowns in confusion. "What? No. Morgan's allergic to mustard." As I let loose another volley of chest-shattering coughs, her confusion changes to alarm. "Are you okay?"

"Peachy," I say. "Never felt better." Though, to contradict my point, my lungs constrict violently and I double over. Goddammit, the aftereffects of dying are the worst. Why does my body remember what happened but won't stay dead?

"We'll take this to go," Jasper says.

"You should eat something," I gasp.

"What? No, it's fine." He pats my back a few times. My eyes are watering, and I have to blot them with a napkin.

"You're only going to whine about it later." I blow my nose in the napkin. "Eat it, or order some soup or something so we can get to work."

Vee is watching us, pen poised over her notepad, eyes ping-ponging back and forth, and her shoulders finally relax when Jasper says, "Fine. We'll eat these and I'll have the burger. Extra tomatoes, no lettuce, pickle on the side."

Vee glances at me.

"I'm fine," I say.

"You need to eat," Jasper says.

"The plain chips are fine." Being under both their scrutiny is uncomfortable, though I'm finally starting to breathe easier.

"Morgan." He doesn't seem as reassured as I am.

"Jasper," I answer, mimicking his tone and trying for a smile.

"Wow," Vee says. "You two been together long?"

"We met tonight," I say at the same time Jasper says, "A couple months."

Vee backs away slowly. Just before she turns, I say, "Club sandwich, butter on the toast, not mayo."

She scribbles hastily as she retreats.

"Happy?" I say to Jasper.

He certainly doesn't look like it. His lips are pale and his frown makes it hard to see the sparkly shine of his pretty eyes. He says, "You have to take care of yourself. That cough doesn't sound good."

"It's no worse than anything else." I leave his hold long enough to twist my spine, but the restriction in my midback, the pain I felt yesterday from the stab wound, is still there. Not as bad, but it still feels like something in me is healing. I grimace.

"What?" Jasper says.

"Nothing."

The food is . . . Okay, actually the food is pretty good. I can't remember the last time I ate something before the murder pickles. And Jasper's burger is as big as his head, so it keeps him busy for a while, and we finally stop bickering.

I don't mean to argue with him. Not all the time like I have been, anyway. I learned a long time ago if you shoot fast, people don't realize you've got nothing in the chamber until they're already running away. But that tactic works best for finite things like a first date. Something like this? I'm not helping things. We'll never escape if we keep wasting time with pointless arguments.

I glance at the painting on the wall. Vee's memorial. When Mother died, I blamed her for it. She and Ezekiel built the light box that was meant to trap Indigo. In the last trial before that night, there was an accident. The room caught fire, and Vee was trapped. She wasn't anywhere near the building the night my mother died, no matter how my brain pieces fact and fiction together while I dream. She was in the ICU, half her torso and one leg covered in bandages as she recovered from the burns.

Vee never had any superpowers. She was handy with a gun and a power drill, better operating behind the scenes than on the front lines. That didn't stop me from blaming her, though. The box had been her idea. They'd all known the risks after the fire, but Mother said they couldn't wait for more trials. The time to catch Indigo was running out. So Vee wasn't there to help when my mother needed her, and I nursed that grudge for a long time. Indigo disappeared, I walked away from that world, and I guess Vee did too. She worked at Wench, where she could see my mother every day and nursed her grief. Maybe she's the one who created this time loop. Forcing me to come back here over and over until I'm finally ready to say what needs to be said.

"So I was thinking," Jasper says, but regardless of all my good intentions, I don't want to hear his idea. We're done with fact finding. It's time for action.

"We're going to Wolfe Tech."

He grimaces. "Was kind of hoping you'd forgotten about that."

"If he's behind this, I need to know." It's not really Vee, despite my musings. If she were that desperate to talk to me, she'd talk. No need for a time machine. Walter Wolfe, on the other hand . . . "And if you're not up for it, I understand. I'll find a way in myself. What's the worst that can happen? I'll meet you back here and we can try again." I give him a wry smile. "I'll try as many times as it takes." Do I want to die? No. Will I keep dying if it means eventually getting answers? I guess this is what it's come to.

"No." Jasper shakes his head emphatically.

"I don't think you actually get a say in this."

"No." He glances around, and when he speaks, his voice is urgent and hushed. "I mean, that's not the worst thing that could happen. If you do somehow succeed at finding a way in and Wolfe finds out, he won't only kill you." Jasper takes my hands in his and where before, in Ezekiel's office, his touch was comforting, now the way he clings to me is desperate. Scared. He may work for Walter Wolfe, but he's afraid of him too. "It won't be some tidy headshot that you die too fast to feel and then you meet me here so I can say I told you so."

I flinch at the casual way he talks about executing someone, but that's not the point. "Jasper, I can take care—"

"No." This time he raises his voice loud enough that a few heads turn, but he doesn't seem to care. "Listen. Walter Wolfe is a paranoid bastard. If he catches you—"

"He won't." I have to believe we can succeed at this, though I wish I'd paid more attention in Mother's Superhero 101 lessons about how to get in and out of places unnoticed.

Jasper won't be persuaded, though. His grip on my hand tightens as he tries to convey how serious he is about this. "He'll hurt you because that's what he does. He'll want to know what you know, and who else knows it too, and he won't stop until he gets answers. He'll go after your family. Ezekiel. Maybe Clarissa. Trust me. I know. I've—"

My throat goes dry as his warning cuts out and his face goes pale. There's real fear in his expression—and shame.

"Because you've hurt people?" I ask.

He shakes his head violently. "No. Never. But I've seen . . . after. I've helped . . . get rid of the evidence. Morgan. It can't be you. Even if you come back after. I couldn't—"

I pull my hand from his, shoving away from the table,

because I don't want to hear what he has to say. I don't want to hear that he cares what happens to me, not in the same breath that he says he's helped it happen to others . . . or at least hasn't interfered.

"Look, you don't have to get your hands any dirtier than they already are," I say. "I can go in myself. If it means finding out if he's the one trapping us here, I have to know. But you don't have to go. Take the night off or whatever. Go . . . hang out with your hench friends."

I pack up the laptop bag, checking the inside pocket for the EpiPen I no longer need, grab my coat, and head to the door.

No bus to avoid. It's later now, and the street is quieter. The crosswalk signal is green, so I march straight to my car, throw my stuff in the trunk, and get in.

The passenger-side door swings open as I press the ignition, and Jasper slides wordlessly into the seat next to me.

"I'm not changing my mind on this," I say.

"I know." He's staring out the window, and even if he sounds resolved, he's clearly not happy about the situation.

"So if you're here, you're coming to Wolfe Tech with me."

He takes in a big breath and holds it. "I am," he says on the exhale.

"And you don't get to sit in the parking lot like I've run in for a pint of milk and will be right back."

He laughs softly, but his expression is bleak. "I'll be there with you the whole way."

Jasper's obvious nervousness is making me jumpy when I have zero room to second-guess myself. I say, "And if this is part of some scheme to double-cross me and—"

"Morgan." He's gripping his hands between his knees, and the pop of his knuckles is audible. "Would you please put the car in gear before I change my mind?"

I wait a second longer, but when his next lecture on putting myself in harm's way doesn't come, I reverse out of the parking spot and head out onto the street.

Time for a little breaking and entering. Not exactly model superhero behaviour, but I never was much of a superhero. Mother always said there was no room for nuance between good and evil, but the longer Jasper and I are stuck together, the more I wonder if that's really true. The normal rules don't apply when you're stuck in a time loop. What's the worst that could happen?

CHAPTER 10

"Absolutely not."

We get about a block and a half before we have our next disagreement. Now we're pulled over in a pharmacy parking lot while Jasper puts forth his most absurd idea yet.

"Morgan, think about it."

I'm learning that when Jasper gets really annoyed, he yanks the hat off and pulls at it between his hands. Maybe that's why I can't stop picking fights with him. He looks so much better without the green monstrosity on his head. I have to stop myself from smoothing his hair down again because it will only upset him more.

"I have thought about it." I pet my dashboard instead. "This is my baby. There's no way you can drive it."

He lets out a heavy sigh. "Right. Because there will be nothing at all suspicious about you driving up to Wolfe Tech with me in the passenger seat. At least if I'm driving, we have a shot at getting past the gate. Come on, Morgan. You're a smart guy. If we're going to do this, we have to give it the best shot we can."

I feel weirdly proud that he calls me smart, then annoyed with myself at my momentary preening.

The thing is, I wasn't going to drive up to the front door. There has to be a back way in, like I took Jasper to the back at Ziro Labs. So maybe I'm arguing because he's poking holes in my thinking. Acting on the fly isn't my specialty. I'm a scientist, after all. But if there's one thing I've learned over the last few days, it's that time is not on my side. If I can die via deep-fried pickle, everything is on the table. Acting like I have days to strategize an assault on Wolfe Tech is naïve. If past performance is an indicator of future behaviour, even if I locked myself in a padded room, it would probably turn out I have an allergy to the insulation material and asphyxiate in minutes. So we're going in.

I glance at Jasper. He's got his mouth pressed shut tight and his nostrils are flared. I really love the flash of anger in his eyes.

Also, he's right.

"Fine." I pop my seat belt.

The Wolfe Tech complex—and it's definitely a complex—is on the far side of town. It's a sprawling gated compound, and Jasper fumbles to find the button for the window before he throws a cheery "Hey, Bobby, how's your wife doing?" to the man in the guardhouse, like we're popping by to visit Grandma at the retirement village.

Speaking of the man in the gatehouse, he stares at Jasper with a flat gaze like a rattlesnake. He's older. White with whiter hair. There's tinny country music coming from a battered wireless speaker in his booth, and he's got what looks like half a ham sandwich in one hand. That's all I notice before he turns the same glare on me and it gets assessing.

"No visitors allowed," Bobby says.

"He's a contractor," Jasper says quickly.

Bobby pulls out a clipboard, flipping through the crumpled pages attached to it. He smacks his lips a few times before he says, "There's no one on the list."

Despite my insistence that coming here was our only option, my pulse is pounding in my throat.

Jasper gives an embarrassed laugh, rubbing his hand over the back of his neck. "It's kind of an emergency."

Bobby's still frowning at his clipboard. "There's nothing about an emergency on the list."

"Please, man. You'd be doing me such a favour. He's an electrician. I blew a fuse when I was here earlier. Nothing major. I was making coffee and the kettle sort of exploded. All the lights are out in the kitchen. If he can fix it fast, no one needs to know, right?" The longer he talks, his voice drops. He starts to sound like the kind of guy who ends every sentence with "bro" and doesn't know when he's the butt of the joke.

I sink back in my seat. The secondhand embarrassment is excruciating. Jasper keeps wheedling, and Bobby keeps holding up the clipboard like it's a stone tablet from Sinai. Finally, Jasper shifts, pulls out his wallet, and hands what looks like a fifty-dollar bill through the window.

"For your wife," he says. "Take her out to dinner."

Fifty bucks doesn't buy much of a fancy dinner, but maybe Bobby and his wife are nacho people like Jasper. Then again, the greedy flash in Bobby's eye as he stuffs the money in his pocket says maybe he doesn't have a wife at all. Or else he does, but she's not getting dinner out of this.

"I could get in a lot of trouble," he says, but he also punches a button that swings the gates in front of us open.

"You're the best," Jasper says, no doubt giving Bobby one of his patented lopsided golden retriever grins. Bobby doesn't deserve it.

"He's charming," I say as we drive through the gate.

The corner of Jasper's mouth quirks up. "Definitely not the personality hire. He's like a guard dog in human form."

He pulls us around to a parking spot near the front door.

"This is a bad idea," Jasper says. He still has his hands on the steering wheel like he might turn us around and head out the way we came at any second.

"We've made it this far. If we go back now, Bob will know you lied to him."

He nods grimly. "Now what?"

I study the building. While the outside is bright, the interior is very dark. Makes sense for a supposed office building after hours, but it also makes it hard to get an idea of what we're walking into.

"Cameras?" I ask.

Jasper's got his hat back on, but he itches his hair nervously through the wool. "Everywhere."

"Security?"

"Just at the front desk, but he's got a response team on call that could be here in less than five minutes if he thinks something's going down."

"Then we'll have to sell it."

He gives me an anxious once-over. "I don't think anyone's buying you as an electrician."

I could tell him he should have thought of that before he told Bobby why we were here, but it's too late for that. We have to make it convincing, and my collared shirt and slim fit sweater aren't going to do it. If either of us looks like they work in skilled trades, it's Jasper.

"Give me your flannel." I say.

His eyebrows disappear into the brim of his toque. "What?"

I hold an impatient hand out. "Give me your shirt, Jasper." I grimace at what comes next. "And your hat."

He watches me with confusion but does as he's told. As I pull my sweater over my head, he clears his throat, but he's not looking at me as I undo the buttons of my shirt.

"What am I supposed to wear?" he asks. Beneath his flannel he's wearing a faded T-shirt that stretches quite attractively over his chest. The peaks of his nipples are visible through the material in the cooling air in the vehicle.

"Take my jacket," I say as I slide out of my shirt. Goose-bumps prick up on my skin, and I slip on Jasper's shirt. It's still warm from his body. My fingers shake as I do up the button. Jasper has to lean over the console to reach toward the back seat and grab my coat, bringing him much closer to me. I inhale and my nose is filled with his sawdust scent. Or is it me? I'm in his shirt. Does that mean I'll smell like him now?

My hair itches nearly immediately after I pull the hat on, and the sleeves of my jacket are almost comically short on Jasper's long arms, but if he stuffs his hands in his pockets, it's not so bad.

"Ready?" he asks.

I lock my gaze with his. We can do this. We have to.

He nods. "The plans are in Walter's office. I know the code to get in. It won't take me long to get them. We'll be back in the car before Bobby's finished his sandwich."

We walk right up to the main security desk. A guard who might as well be Bobby's younger brother sits there. Same rattlesnake gaze, same complexion that says he's been working on his tan under the fluorescent tube lights overhead for decades.

"Leo," Jasper says, his voice deeper again.

"Jasper. What are you doing here?"

Jasper goes to point upward, but when the coat sleeve slides halfway up to his elbow, he drops his hand again and instead motions with his chin. "Electrical problem on twelve. My friend here is going to fix it."

"No one's on the list," Leo says, flipping through a clipboard of his own. What is it with these guys and lists? Not like anyone ever comes to audit a supervillain's standard operating proce-dures. Isn't the whole point *not* to have documentation of their business operations?

"We already talked to Bobby. He said it was cool. It's a quick fix."

"You won't mind if I give Mr. Wolfe a call? Any after-hours

entries have to be approved by him." Leo lifts a phone from the console he's sitting at. It's a typical security desk configuration. A bank of monitors show footage from a dozen or more security cameras. The sight of them makes my throat go dry. I can see me and Jasper standing at the desk. Our backs are to the camera currently being displayed, but when I look around, there are two more behind Leo facing directly at us.

Leo and Jasper are still haggling. I dip my chin and casually pull the hat a little lower down my forehead. While they argue, I take a small step toward the desk, making it look like I'm leaning on it while I wait for a resolution. I can't do anything about the cameras, but maybe—just maybe—I can do something to buy us a little time.

The cables running to the monitors are all bundled together with zip ties. Slowly, I wrap a hand around them. I've never had enough power to do more than short-circuit a laptop, but maybe that's all that's required here.

I have to clench my teeth as I try to focus. Leo's rattling the clipboard in Jasper's face, and Jasper's calling him a jackass. I'd tell him not to lay it on so thick, but getting my powers to work at all is like trying not to scare off an orgasm, so I can't be distracted.

There's a burning smell like, probably as I melt the coating around the wires. I cough a little too loudly, hoping no one notices. Then there's a pop and a flash as sparks shoot from the back of one of the monitors. Leo yelps and even Jasper hops away in alarm. He gives me a worried look, but I can't tell if he noticed what I did or if he's only making sure I didn't accidentally set his favourite shirt on fire.

"Oh, hell." Leo pounds at his keyboard. When I move to stand a little closer to Jasper, the monitors are all completely black.

Fortunately, Jasper sees the opportunity and slings an arm over my shoulder. We're already moving, pushing past the desk. Leo tries to catch us as we go by.

"Hey. Hey, Jasper. Where are you—"

"We'll start upstairs, then my friend here can help you with your stuff. Just make sure you try turning it off and turning it on again. Sometimes that's all it takes."

"Jasper! Wait!" Leo's flustered voice trails after us, but we're already stepping into the elevator and the door slides shut. For a moment, I lean into Jasper as relief floods me, realizing a second too late that he's dropped his arm and isn't touching me anymore. Embarrassed, I push away.

"Sorry."

"We won't have long. Leo's going to check the building systems and know there's no electrical problem. We'll go out the back before Leo can find us, but I'll need a few minutes to download the plans."

"Download?" When he said the plans were in Wolfe's office, I pictured a big roll of blueprints. Something hard copy we could grab and make a run for it. I could kick myself for not clarifying. This is why I was never going to make it as a superhero. Never mind the wimpy powers. I couldn't even think to ask what kind of plans Jasper was talking about.

He doesn't notice my upset. His gaze is on the elevator's display as it ticks upward. Eight, nine, ten. He says, "They're on his computer. He's got his own personal server where he stores his most confidential information. It was upgraded last year and can't be accessed remotely. I have to be at his desk."

"But once you're there, you'll be able to find it, right?"

"Should be." He throws me a smile that tightens too much at the corners to be truly confident. "I'm the one who set the server up for him."

The elevator dings at the fifteenth floor and the doors slide open. We don't exactly run up the hall, but we certainly don't linger either. It's only as we're ten steps away that I realize we aren't in some long office hall like I'm used to at Ziro Labs. The whole floor is glass. Walls, ceiling, even the floor is glass that looks down at the level below, which is some kind of vast white box with no furniture.

"What is this?" I ask.

"Told you he was a paranoid bastard," Jasper says. "The glass is all bulletproof, but he thinks the white room means he'll see the attackers coming before they can get to him."

"Who would attack him here?"

He winks. "That's the paranoia."

A voice in my head says it's not paranoia if someone's really out to get you. Someone's out to get me. I wish I knew who I'd pissed off enough to deserve this. Also, the white room makes the spectre of my next death feel very imminent. We need to get out of here in record time. I don't want my blood splattered on these walls.

We get to the door to the office—a giant slab of frosted glass—and Jasper puts his hand to the keypad on the wall. He says "Paleolithic" in a formal tone, then throws a look over his shoulder at me that tells me exactly how much bullshit he's playing with right now.

"Very funny," I say. My stomach is in knots.

He wrinkles his nose as he laughs. "We're not as fancy as you are." He punches in a complicated string of numbers—way longer than the code it takes to unlock my phone—and the light on the panel flashes three times before it goes green.

"How do you remember all that?" I ask.

"It's my birthday, then my dad's birthday, then the same numbers again but reversed."

"Which is coincidentally the code to get into Walter Wolfe's office?"

"It is if you're the one who programs the alarm system."

I glance over my shoulder. A camera watches us in the hallway. I'm so nervous I'm shaking.

"What exactly do you do here?" I ask as I follow Jasper into the lavishly appointed office. I guess if you work in a fortified fishbowl, you want all of it to look good from every angle.

"Officially, I'm networks and data security." He pulls back the chair from the chrome and glass desk and slides into it with ease, like he's done it before.

"Unofficially?" And how does a med student become the IT guy?

He glances up at me, lips pressed together. "I don't want to fight right now. I need to work. Watch the elevator," he says, face illuminated by the screen. "If it goes above floor five, tell me."

Great. After everything, I've become the "watch the elevator" guy.

"I can handle my own," I say.

"I'm sure you can," he says, but all his attention is on the computer. I grit my teeth because he's right that now is not the time to pick an argument, but I want to so badly. I hate being relegated to backup. It's all I've been good for my entire life. Failed superhero. Office drone. Now minion to the henchman.

I'm so busy sulking, I don't notice right away when the numbered panel over the elevator flashes, showing the car moving from the first to second floor.

"Jasper," I say.

"Yeah?" He doesn't look up from the screen.

But the elevator stops on two, stays there for a few seconds, then goes back to the lobby. I let out a slow breath. My hands move restlessly at my sides, prickling with anxiety. I struggle for a second to find something to say.

"The machine probably isn't in this building, is it?"

He glances up briefly. "Why do you say that?"

"It's like the Ziro Machine. We started building components at the lab but pretty quickly we realized if things went badly during assembly, we could crater the whole building in a millisecond. If a building that converts energy can do that, one that can reconfigure time could probably also blip us all out of existence if something breaks."

His attention is back on the monitor, but Jasper says, "Wolfe's got facilities all over town. If it turns out this really is a time machine, it would take a while to check all of them."

"How many do you think we can check between my tragic and unforeseen deaths?" I ask, going for humour, but the way Jasper's brow furrows together says I don't succeed.

"You can't think like that." He clicks the mouse a few times. I'm not sure how else I'm supposed to think. I'm on a clock no one can see.

A flicker catches my attention, and I glance at the elevator panel. Shit. Floor six.

"Jasper," I say.

His expression brightens as he looks at the screen. "Oh, found it!"

Seven. Eight.

"Jasper, someone's coming."

CHAPTER 11

Nine.

"Jasper."

He shakes his head, all his focus still on Wolfe's computer. "Shit, they're quick. I didn't think they'd move so fast."

Ten.

"Jasper!" The office is on the fifteenth floor. I whirl. We've got seconds to get out of here, and I don't even see a back door.

"Just let me . . . one second . . ." He's still got one hand on the mouse, one hand on his phone, which is plugged into the computer.

Eleven. The light moves to twelve and I hold my breath. There is no thirteen. The light goes out and flicks to fourteen. One more floor to go.

Shit. They're going to walk off that elevator in a few seconds. A few seconds after that, bullets are going to start flying.

"I need a little more time," Jasper says.

"We aren't going to have more time." I rush toward the elevator, hand extended. After the trick with the monitors below, the odds I can assemble enough power to do anything worthwhile are pretty low, but if I really concentrate, I might be able to generate enough electricity to short out the panel. If whoever is in there gets stuck between floors fourteen and fifteen, that's better than nothing.

But I come up empty. I press my palm to the buttons, and all I can gather is a tiny little pfft that might as well be a fart for all the impact it has.

The light for fourteen goes out.

"Jasper!"

"Almost there."

I believe Jasper when he says things will get ugly if they find us where we're not supposed to be, and I don't want to find out the depths of that ugliness.

I run back across the office, pulling off Jasper's hat and undoing the top few buttons of my borrowed flannel. As I come around the desk, I grab the back of Jasper's wheeled chair.

"Morgan. Morgan, wait." His phone and its cord pull free of the desktop as I drag him back.

I climb into his lap, ignoring the way the chair creaks.

"What are you doing?" His eyes are wide with surprise, and he holds his hands away from me, like he's afraid of touching me.

"We will never speak of this again," I say, cupping his adorable, scruffy face in my hands.

Then I kiss him. Hard.

He grunts in shock at exactly the same time the elevator dings to announce its arrival. I grind my lips to Jasper's desperately, hoping he'll play along. I press into him when his hands settle on my ass, squeezing.

"Jasper?" Leo's voice calls up the hall. "The monitors came back on. I called the boss. He said no one is allowed—Oh." When he stops speaking, I glance over my shoulder, feigning surprise.

"Hi." I smile, running a thumb over my hopefully kiss-swollen bottom lip. Jasper is panting, his breath hot on my chest where my shirt is undone.

Leo narrows his eyes. "You're not supposed to be up here. I thought you were fixing something in the kitchen."

I pout, pretending I don't notice the way he's got his hand on the gun at his hip. "I like it up here." Should I bat my eyelashes? No. Too much. I just push my lip out farther, hoping it makes me look like a spoiled twink and not a lying liar who lies. It's everything I can do not to lick that pouty bottom lip too. It tastes like Jasper and that is . . . My whole body makes a shuddering rippling movement I pray looks sexy, because all I can think about is the feeling of Jasper's mouth on mine. The scrape of his stubble on my mouth. Too bad we were interrupted so fast. I wouldn't have minded a few more seconds of panicked kissing.

"Listen." Leo takes a menacing step forward, but before I can say anything else, the world shifts as Jasper stands. On reflex, I wrap myself around him, arms on his shoulders, thighs at his waist, but his hands drop away from my ass—thank goodness for small mercies—and I take the hint, letting my feet fall to the floor. He gently guides me so I'm standing behind him, which is fine. Gives me an opportunity to do my clothes up again. I have to adjust myself in my pants. His palms on my backside were strong. Firm. Confident. I haven't been grabbed like that in a long time. Maybe not ever. I shiver again as I wonder what else those hands can do.

"Leo," Jasper is saying, and I recognize the tone now. He's going to charm us out of this, and I send up a silent prayer it works. "Come on. You know how it goes. We were on a date. I told him who I worked for, and he wanted the full experience. I knew Bobby wouldn't buy that, but I figured you'd be cool about it. I'm sorry, okay?"

Ugh. The whole explanation is so douchey. But we need to get out of here, so I duck under Jasper's arm, fitting it around my shoulders, and press a hand to his chest.

"It's so . . . big," I say on a breathy sigh. Obviously I'm talking about the office, but Leo snorts.

His hand slides from his gun to his belt. "You think that's impressive, wait until you see—"

"Okay, time to go," Jasper says, tugging me past Leo. "Sorry, sweetheart. We'll have to role-play at home."

"But baby . . ." I say, suppressing a different kind of shudder at the whine in my voice. "You said—"

"Not now." He bends to kiss me, and I stiffen before I remember I'm supposed to be enjoying this. I hum as I fumble for the elevator button, arching as Jasper pulls me closer. His lips stay closed, but they're insistent. We are going to kiss until the coast is clear.

So of course Leo rides the elevator down with us. And I spend fifteen floors giggling into Jasper's neck while he keeps putting his hands places that are barely an inch shy of inappropriate. I guess I could credit his consideration, but I'm too busy fighting the desire to nuzzle in farther and breathe in his scent. It's adrenaline. Stress. I'm not attracted to Jasper. I can't be. Especially not in front of his hench buddies. If I'd had any hope that maybe there was some trick—that Jasper wasn't the henchman he claimed to be—it's impossible to not let that bubble burst now. Regardless of what Bobby and Leo think about him, they know Jasper. He works for Walter Wolfe, and that means in every timeline but this one, we believe in completely opposite things.

As the elevator finally slows, I breathe a sigh of relief, and Jasper swallows it in one more kiss, muttering something against my mouth that sounds like "almost there," before he leads me out into the building's glass and chrome atrium.

"Hey, Leo," Jasper says, as we arrive at the main doors. "This can stay between us, right? The boss man doesn't have to know I sneaked up there. I was only hoping to impress my friend here. You know how it goes."

I risk a glance at Leo, who's still watching me with his viper gaze. He sneers as our eyes meet. "Sure, Jasper. Your friend. No problem, I won't say anything. But you owe me a favour."

"Whatever you want," Jasper says. "You know I'm good for it."

Then we're outside. The air on my face is cool, and my stomach twists with anxiety.

"Don't run. Don't run," Jasper says softly, as I half jog, half stumble over the pavement. I take a deep breath to centre myself, letting my stride settle back into my hips and leaning against Jasper's body again like I have nowhere else to be.

We dance for a second as I go for the driver's side before I remember Jasper's got the wheel here. As soon as the door is closed, I go to slump toward the dash, but not before I hear a "Not yet. Not yet, they're still watching."

I sit up again, glancing out the windshield at the CCTV cameras mounted at regular intervals around us.

"Paranoid bastard," I say.

Jasper laughs. "You did amazing." He holds out his hand, and I think he means to shake on a job well done, but when I grasp him, he pulls me toward him so he can kiss the back of my hand, before he flips it over and kisses my wrist. Energy crackles along my nerves like lightning, starting where his lips touch my skin and radiating to where my heart is still doing a polka inside my rib cage. When our gazes meet, I feel like I could burst into flames at any second.

Slowly, we pull out of the parking lot. We drive past the guardhouse, where Jasper shouts a cheery goodnight to Bobby like nothing is amiss even as my pulse pounds in my ears.

But as we drive away, resolve steadies my heart. Because we still don't know about the time machine, and I doubt we'll have another opportunity to get back into the building. Not tonight, anyway.

"What time is it?" I ask. The clock in this car is with the instrument cluster behind the steering wheel, and I can't see it from this angle.

"Almost eleven, why?"

I take a long slow breath, fighting back anxiety, before I say, "Can you take me home?"

"Yeah," he says slowly. "But why?"

I stare at my hands in my lap because everything about this is wrong, but if I've got all the cards, it's time to play a few of them.

"Because Indigo will be there."

To his credit, the BMW jerks violently on the deserted street as Jasper slams his foot on the brake, so at least I know he cares. "What? Why?"

"You know why," I say.

"I don't think I do," he says, though his knuckles tightening on the steering wheel says he's lying.

Still, it takes me a few tries to get the words out. "Because we have to try again, and the only way to do that is if I die."

"Try what again?" He still doesn't sound like he understands.

"The time machine plans. We should think of this like a failed experiment. We take what we learned and try again. I'm sorry I had to pull you away from the desk, but if we start over, we'll know what to look out for this time. I can distract Leo, maybe stay down on the main floor with him. We'll come up with a different reason why you're there and you'll have more time to—"

"More time to transfer the file to an off-site server where we can look at it at our leisure?"

"Yeah, something like that. Whatever you can do. If you take me back to the house and Indigo is there, then . . ." I trail off, because despite what I'm saying, I don't actually want to die. But it will be fast. Better than having Walter Wolfe pulling off my toenails. Or convincing Jasper to drive us into a wall or off a bridge. I don't think I could do that to him, regardless of how I feel. As I put a finger to my lips, it tingles where his scruff scraped over the sensitive skin there, those feelings are becoming increasingly unclear. The time loop isn't the only thing messing with my head. I really want to kiss him again, even knowing who he truly is now.

"Or we could skip the noble sacrifice part of the evening and go check out the info I downloaded and sent to an off-site server to look at in a more leisurely manner?"

I'm so focused on my inevitable meeting with Indigo that it takes a second before I understand what he's saying.

"Wait. What?"

He lifts his phone from the centre console. The screen is black, but he says, "Finished the transfer as you got in my lap. It's all waiting for us somewhere safe." He tips a mock salute to me. "So thank you very much for your kind offer, but it's not on your shoulders alone to save us. I'm pleased to report that you will not be needing to die tonight."

My whole body relaxes at his words. Clarissa's always telling me much the same thing, though obviously in less fatal terms. She says I don't need to do everything by myself. That we have a whole team of highly qualified researchers who can break down code and run models. It doesn't need to be me sitting at the lab into the darkest hours watching numbers roll over the screen until my head aches. I can lean on other people. I've never been especially good at it. For now, though, I'm going to take her advice. I close my eyes, letting the sound of the tires on the road fill my brain with static.

I must fall asleep, because the next thing I know, we're pulling into a perfectly unremarkable driveway next to an equally and perfectly unremarkable suburban house. It's a two-story home with white shutters and a detached garage.

"We're here," Jasper says.

"Where's here?"

He gives me a soft smile, less self-assured than the ones I've seen before. Something tells me even after all our dates, this is the first time we've come to this specific location, and the thought makes me apprehensive. I hate that I'm still doubting him, but how can I not?

"My place."

My sleepy brain takes a second to register what he's said, but when it does, I'm suddenly very awake. "You brought me to your house?"

"Well . . . my apartment. I live over the garage."

I glance through the windshield at the detached garage sitting silently at the end of the driveway. I don't know where I thought Jasper lived. Some hench cave somewhere, probably.

"Is it safe?" I don't know how a criminal organization's HR department works, but they have to know where he lives, right?

But Jasper doesn't seem to have any similar concerns. He gives me his lopsided grin and says, "Hide in plain sight, right? With any luck, Leo and Bobby are finishing up their shifts and are off for a few drinks at Kicks. They haven't given us any further thought."

Our luck so far has not been amazing, so I don't know why he thinks it's going to change now.

"And if they *have* given it more thought?" I'm picturing the gruesome death Jasper described earlier. Something about the way Bobby looked at me the way a predator eyes prey makes me think he'd really enjoy inflicting pain.

"We'll be quick," Jasper says, giving my hand a squeeze. I wiggle my fingers restlessly. This can't be the best plan. "I can't access the files from anywhere but my desktop setup. It's not the sort of thing you really email to yourself."

That part I understand, at least. The security protocols around information about the Ziro Machine are extensive. The five-syllable password may seem silly to Jasper, but it's only the beginning of what you have to do to have access to the plans.

We get out of the car, and when I slam my door shut, Jasper winces.

"What?"

"Just . . . try to keep it down. The neighbours are fussy about making too much noise."

Except it's not the neighbour's house that suddenly floods

the driveway with light; it's the one next to the garage. I freeze in place as the front door opens. A woman with graying hair in navy blue pajamas comes out to the porch, squinting at us.

"Jasper?" she says. "Whose car is that?"

I reach for Jasper's hand, ready to run. "Your landlady?"

Jasper sighs, squeezing my fingers gently. "That . . . would be my mom."

CHAPTER 12

S o.

Jasper lives with his mom.

Or, I guess, he lives above his mother's garage, while she lives in the main house.

With his sisters.

It's past the time of evening when most people are in bed, but Jasper's family must all be night owls, because as he and I stand frozen like deer in the driveway, three other young women appear on the porch behind their mother. They're all in their pajamas too, but they look very awake and—unfortunately— very curious at what we're doing here.

Jasper seems to be as confused as they are.

"How come you're all still up?" he says.

"We're having a girls' night!" the youngest one says. Even without being introduced, the shared traits are plain to see. They all have the same soft brown hair, same hazel green eyes, same smattering of freckles on their nose. Even their mother is cut from the same cloth. Whoever Jasper's father is—was, I remind myself he said his father died—he didn't win the genetic lottery when it came to family resemblance.

"Movie night," one of the other sisters says.

"Do you want brownies? Sierra and I made brownies," another says.

The sisters all start chattering at the same time, and Jasper throws me a nervous glance. His mom is watching me with the same expression, and finally she holds her hands up, shushing her daughters.

"I think Jasper and his . . . friend . . . might have other plans."

Oh, great. Pretending to be Jasper's boy toy at the office was one thing. Meeting his family is a whole other one.

But maybe it's the anticipation on the sisters' faces as they eye me and shoot giggling glances in their brother's direction. Or maybe it's the complete lack of judgement in Jasper's mother's eyes. Or maybe it's only because, not that long ago, I was about to walk into my home, knowing it meant death, and now I have a completely different home offering me entry and—

"Are there nuts in the brownies?" I ask. "I'm allergic."

The youngest sister smiles. "No."

"Is there mustard?" Jasper asks, which sets off a wave of howling laughter and disgust from his family as we follow them through the front door.

The house is . . . well, it's a house, exactly the way you'd expect. Worn furniture, too many shoes by the front door. The TV is on, frozen as a man and woman go in for a kiss in the rain. The den smells distinctly of popcorn, but the kitchen, as we make our way through the house, is all chocolate.

"You're late," one of the sisters says.

"We waited for you," another one follows.

"You promised you wouldn't miss movie night," the third says.

Jasper throws me a quick look. "I, uh . . . something came up."

"At the hospital?" his mother asks.

"Yes. At the hospital. We got held late after . . . uh . . ." Another glance from Jasper. This one is a clear call for help.

"Someone died."

The kitchen goes quiet as five pairs of Jackson family eyes turn to me. I shrink back into the collar of my shirt—Jasper's shirt, which is too big for me, but gives me a better place to hide—on instinct, wishing suddenly I'd pushed harder to go face down Indigo than land here.

Jasper's mother's face is stricken and she's got one hand over her heart. "That's so sad."

"She was very old," I stumble onward. "An old lady. Very sick. She was—" I finally find the off switch to my mouth when Jasper puts a gentle hand on my shoulder.

"I thought you were working in pediatrics," the oldest sister says.

"I am." Jasper smiles. "But Morgan here is, um . . . general surgery. He was on call tonight when the old lady . . . when she came in."

Great. Not awkward at all. Do they notice I'm wearing their brother's shirt? What do they think that means? I bet they can't even begin to guess.

"Who wants brownies?" Jasper's mom says, and suddenly we are all very interested in the half-empty pan sitting on the counter.

The brownies are, in fact, delicious. Dark and chocolaty and not a nut to be seen. I have two while Jasper and his family talk around me. His sisters, once they stand down from interrogation mode, are great. The oldest, Sierra, is studying to be a physiotherapist. The middle, Amelia, wants to be a teacher. And the youngest, Lexi, who looks like she's about fourteen, says she's going to be a lawyer, and the general pause that follows the statement is so short I almost don't catch it, but I do see the silent exchange between Jasper and his mom. Just a faint pursing of lips and the raising of an eyebrow, and then the room fills with laughter again. I can only assume whatever just happened has something to do with the fact Lexi is wearing a nasal canula and wheeling a small oxygen tank behind her, but I don't ask about it.

"So, Morgan," Jasper's mother says. "Are you a surgeon at the hospital with Jasper?"

Oh. I didn't realize we'd have to talk about me next. But I straighten my shoulders and put on my best face.

"Sure am." I force a smile. "Doing my residency, actually, so . . . not fully a surgeon yet. Still getting there."

Jasper's hand is on my shoulder again, and I lean into it without meaning to because it offers some small comfort in this room full of strangers. I blush as his mother looks between that hand and me and up to her son. Her scrutiny leaves me feeling vulnerable, like she'll be disappointed when it turns out her son and I aren't really together, but I won't embarrass him by shrugging away.

When Lexi starts to yawn, the whole household announces unanimously that it's very late and past everyone's bedtime. Jasper kisses his mother, teases his sisters a moment longer, then stands expectantly by the front door while I give polite goodbyes and thanks for the brownies.

"Come back anytime," Jasper's mom says. "We never meet any of Jasper's friends. If you're like him, you work too hard. Friday is pizza night, we always order too much. There would be plenty for you if you stopped by."

My throat thickens at her invitation, and I ignore the twinge of envy. I guess this is the difference between a mom and Mother. One who made brownies and has movie nights. Mine told me about the bad people in the world and how I was inadequate to fight them. In contrast, Jasper's mom calls out after us as we cross the driveway, telling Jasper not to stay up too late and me not to be shy about sneaking back into the kitchen for more brownies.

It's all so shockingly normal, and underneath my envy and relief is a current of annoyance that Jasper has chosen the life he has while his family waits at home and believes a lie. It's a privilege to have this. If he ever gets caught or hurt, they're going to be so hurt too. When they finally learn he's not a doctor, that betrayal will cut deeply. Not to mention, if Wolfe knows where Jasper lives, he has easy access to Jasper's innocent family members to use as leverage, and they won't even see it coming. Risking them like this is beyond thoughtless and selfish.

But when I open my mouth as we enter his apartment, he holds up a hand. "You don't know what you're talking about."

"What?"

"You don't get to ask about my family."

"But—"

He goes to yank his hat off his head, then must remember I'm still wearing it, so he stuffs his fingers in his hair instead, pulling on the strands in frustration.

"I'm so tired of fighting with you, Morgan. Can we stop with the judgement for a little while, at least?"

My mouth falls open. "I wasn't—"

"You were." He flops down at the edge of his bed. The apartment is a basic studio with an efficiency kitchen, a bed against one wall, a desk with an elaborate computer setup, and a door I assume leads to a bathroom. Jasper scratches at his scalp in frustration. "You were going to ask me if my mother knows about what I do when it's obvious she doesn't. I don't want to talk about it, okay?"

I have to clench my teeth not to dive right into the argument. But whether we talk about it or not, I can't reconcile the man who teased his sister in the kitchen with the man chumming it up with Bobby and Leo and builds secure servers to keep secrets for people like Walter Wolfe. And I want to, because on top of everything, I can't reconcile how much I want to kiss him again with how completely inappropriate it would be to do anything of the kind with someone like him.

I sit down next to him, even though it feels like the space

between us has never been bigger and somehow, it's always my doing. I slide off my shoes, mostly for something to do in the uncomfortable silence. Jasper stands, and my heart squeezes with worry that I really have upset him. He goes to the desk, sitting at the computer with his back to me. He types wordlessly, keys clicking, as the system boots up. I wait, quietly examining the back of his neck where his hair thins away at the nape, and the way the curve of his shoulders stretches the jersey of his T-shirt.

"So," I say, trying to sound casual. "Lexi is . . ."

He sighs. His head drops, and the clack of the keyboard falls away. But finally, he turns. He says, "It's called Emmanuel Stanley syndrome. It causes a progressive thickening in the lining of the lungs and makes it hard to get enough oxygen."

Considering how much I've thought about death—my mother's and, more recently, my own—suffocation has always terrified me. Probably because of my allergies. To slowly realize your body is going to lose the fight for more air, I can't imagine anything scarier. At least in my case, all I have to do is avoid things like murder pickles and onions. It's controllable, and as long as I'm careful, it doesn't get worse.

"Has she been sick long?" I ask.

"Pretty much her whole life." He glances over his shoulder at me, and his eyes are tired. "It's genetic. My dad had it, though he didn't get really sick until his late twenties. But Lexi had whooping cough a few times in grade school and it set her back."

I have a feeling I know where this is going. "And your dad?"

"Died when Lexi was a baby." He forces a brighter smile. "But Lexi's doing better lately. She's in a clinical trial that seems to be making a difference."

"That's good."

The conversation dies. Jasper turns back to the screen, and I'm left to pick at lint on his comforter and wonder if I've finally screwed up this thing between Jasper and me beyond the point of saving it.

After a few more minutes of silence, Jasper laughs softly to himself.

"What?" I ask.

"I took these plans, but do either of us know what the plans for a time machine would look like, even if they were sitting right in front of us?" He motions me over. On the screen is a set of diagrams. Components and directions. Notes about energy transfer and—

"I don't think that's a time machine." As I lean in toward the screen, Jasper vacates the desk chair and I slide into it. I zoom out so the whole document is visible.

"Would you know it if it was?" he asks.

"I'd have to see one to say for sure." I follow the path of couplings, but where the familiar reducer should be, something else—something labeled a *mass converter*—has been drawn in. "But it looks like the Ziro Machine. Jasper, Walter Wolfe stole our plans."

"He has your climate change machine?" Jasper bends in, shoulder brushing mine.

"Yes. But no." I point at the converter . . . "I don't know what this is, but it's not in our design. Or not all of it. Someone's made changes. "Here . . . this open chamber here? That's where the charging station is. You can't leave it open. That much power with nothing to absorb it would be highly unstable."

"So it could be a time machine?" he says.

"It could be an intergalactic popcorn maker for all I know." I squeeze my eyes shut as the glare from the screen makes my head ache. I have to call Ezekiel. Ask him more questions about that conversation he had with Wolfe. Tell him someone's broken into the system to steal the plans, or else someone who works with us has betrayed our trust. Jasper opens up other files, showing me more and more diagrams. They're all of a modified version of the Ziro Machine, but there's no clear confirmation that the changes mean it's a time machine. If it is, it leaves me with this dreadful feeling that somehow, I'm responsible for what's happening to me and Jasper. Even if time travel isn't what the Ziro Machine was built for, so much of what's in the documents is familiar.

"Did you find anything else? Any indication of where they might be building this?" My head is swimming.

"No." Jasper leans forward and closes the image. This near, I can smell him. Sawdust and earth. I go to inhale further, but he clicks off the monitor and slumps back to the bed again, yawning widely.

"I'm beat," he says.

I stare at the black screen, waiting for the strain to fade. "Uh-huh."

"Oh, wow. Hey!" Jasper's hand on my shoulder makes me jump, and he smiles as I spin. "Sorry."

"Something wrong?" On reflex, I yawn too, hiding the inhale behind my palm.

He shakes his head. "It's after midnight. That's the longest you've made it in a while."

It's faint praise and I laugh. "'Congratulations on not dying horribly' doesn't really feel like something to celebrate."

His smile fades. "We celebrate it every six months with Lexi."

Jesus. Shit. I rest my forehead on the heel of my hand. "I'm sorry."

"No. No, that one was on me. Sorry. I'm tired. Verbal filter shuts down around eleven forty-five."

"Right." I stand, stretching my arms overhead. "We should get going." But I stop halfway to the door, because where are we going to go? I feel like a video game character who's walked himself into a corner and can't figure out how to turn around. We have nothing. Plans for a machine we don't understand. No indication of if it's been built or where it might be. Jasper's family is sleeping next door, and by now Wolfe's people must know what we did in his office. We can't stay here, and yet where are we going to go? There's a supervillain at my house, and anywhere else I'm liable to get crushed by a falling anvil or drop into a pit of rattlesnakes, probably taking Jasper with me.

"Come lie down," Jasper says, patting the bed beside him.

My ears burn. "What?"

His eyes are closed, and he smiles sleepily. He looks totally relaxed. "Just for a few hours. We need some rest. I've hardly slept in the last sixtyish days."

I want to say no. Not only because arguing is what Jasper and I do best, but because sleep is scary. Vulnerable. The last time I slept, I woke up with Indigo in my house.

"I don't think that's a good idea," I say.

Of course, Jasper misunderstands. "Are you worried about your reputation? You can sleep in the apartment. I can go crash in the house."

I may not be completely comfortable with the idea of sleeping here, but I *definitely* don't want to sleep here alone. And I really am very tired. My many deaths must be catching up to me. All of me hurts and my eyelids feel like they'll never open again when I finally let them close.

"I can sleep on the floor," I say. "You don't have to go."

And I think he's going to tease me, but instead he says, "Take the bed. I'll sleep on the floor."

"Jasper."

He grabs a pillow from the bed. "Fine. You're right. We'll both sleep on the floor."

"Wait." I laugh as I grab for his wrist, but the pillow goes flying to the floor with a muffled thump.

"No, you're right. For the sake of your dignity and my virtue —" A second pillow arcs through the air.

"*Your* virtue?" My laughter gets louder. He's being funny, but there's no denying part of my giggling is from fatigue and stress. I'm so tired I'm getting punchy.

He's laughing too, and puts on a fake expression of thoughtfulness. "I've never brought a guy home before. Mom will expect us to get married in the morning, though, since you've ruined me so completely."

I leap up in front of him as he tugs on the cover, trying to pull it from the bed too. It's been a long time since I laughed like this. Played with someone. The feeling is heady. Safe.

"But she's the one who sent us up here. She's been planning for this all along." I gasp in exaggerated shock.

"She always wanted me to be a doctor, and since that's not happening, I can marry one instead." He reaches for me, and I get twisted in the comforter. I stumble forward, colliding with his chest. The cotton T-shirt is amazingly soft, but the man underneath it is not. His arms wrap around me and I tell myself he's only being polite, keeping me upright, but when I glance upward, his face has gone still.

"Morgan." His lips stay parted on the last syllable.

I want him. A lot, in fact. But we have to stay on task, so as he dips his head down, I slide away. He doesn't resist. In fact, he steps a few paces back so he can lean against the kitchenette counter. He's got his back to me, and I think we both appreciate the space, taking simultaneous deep breaths. I hold mine, watching his shoulders until he lets his out, then I exhale slowly too.

Time to be an adult.

"Look." I bend to collect the pillows from the floor and return them to the bed. "We're both exhausted. I'll be asleep in two seconds. You can sleep on the bed too. I won't even notice you're there."

He mutters something that might be "ouch," but facing away like he is, I can't say for sure. That's fine. I'm too tired to fight anymore.

I point toward the door in the back of the apartment. "Bathroom?"

"Yeah." Jasper straightens. "I think there might even be an extra toothbrush in the medicine cabinet." He rushes toward a chest of drawers. "I probably have a shirt or something in here that you could wear too if you—"

"Oh, that's—" I'm about to say I'll sleep in my boxers, but Jasper pulls the T-shirt over his head, exposing a flat stomach and broad shoulders and yeah . . . I'm going to need backup, even if it's in the form of a borrowed shirt. "Yeah, that would be great. Might take a shower too." Even though technically I showered this morning—whenever the hell that was—I feel like I've been wearing these pants forever. And the longer I'm in the flannel, the more I worry I'll smell like Jasper, and then I'll never get away from him when this is over.

We don't make eye contact as he hands me a clean towel, rumpled T-shirt, and a pair of sweatpants. I take them into the bathroom with me, and the toothbrush is exactly where Jasper said it would be, still in the packaging.

I feel strangely exposed coming out into the main apartment again. Jasper's changed while I was washing up, and he's in a different T-shirt and worn sweats with a hole above one knee. I don't like that we match, but he won't understand if I tell him.

The bed is smaller than it looked once we're both in it. Jasper's still trying to be a gentleman, so he's lying on top of the covers while I'm underneath, and his weight on the blankets leaves me feeling trapped as I try to squeeze as close to the edge of the mattress as possible to give him some room.

"Goodnight," he says, like it's no big thing.

"Goodnight," I say. "Set an alarm. We can't sleep too long."

Then I lie there as my brain goes back to spinning in dust devil circles. Because someone stole the plans for the Ziro Machine. Except that wasn't our machine. They'd modified it. And would a few modifications be enough to take it from something that stores energy to something that moves energy and life through time?

Also, the mattress has a saggy spot in the middle, and even though I try to stay away, Jasper and I are slow drifting toward each other. The weight and the heat of him are like a magnet, and they pull me away from the questions about the machine and onto questions about him, because something doesn't make sense.

"Jasper?" I say it so softly he won't hear it if he's asleep, but his "Yeah?" is nearly immediate, so he must have been awake too.

I go to roll over, but I'm trapped in the too-tight blankets, so I'm forced to stare at the wall as I say, "Who are you, really?"

CHAPTER 13

The second the question is out of my mouth, I know I shouldn't have asked, but the problem with words is they move fast.

Jasper says, "What do you mean?"

I should pretend I was talking in my sleep and deny all knowledge in the morning.

Except I don't. I yank at the covers, and he has to move away to give me some slack, and I roll so I can see him, dimly lit from an exterior light mounted on the garage.

We lie on our sides, staring at each other for a while, before I say it again. "Who are you? Really? Because you start by introducing yourself as some kind of criminal sidekick, but you seem way more interested in keeping me alive than in what might be in all of this for you. And you've got this family and they love you, and I'm pretty sure you love them too, and it's all so normal. But if it's normal, then how are you . . . how can you do what you do? You know . . . henching?" I sigh. Just one thing in my life today needs to make sense, and I really hope it's this. "I don't understand."

He rolls again, onto his back, and I follow. We stare at the ceiling, and my cheeks heat because I shouldn't have said anything.

And finally, he says, "Lexi nearly died while I was in my second year of med school. She got sick—only a cold—but then it got worse and became pneumonia and she was in the hospital and she couldn't breathe on her own. She was full of tubes and connected to all these machines. My mom couldn't stop crying. It was awful. The doctors managed to save her, but they said we'd have to be careful because her lungs wouldn't be able to take it if she got sick like that again."

"I'm so sorry." I take his hand and squeeze it.

He turns his head to look at me. "I wanted to save her. I did all the research, read all the studies. And I heard about this clinical trial that was happening, a new kind of therapy, but they wouldn't take her. They said she was too sick for their study."

My throat tightens because the strain in his voice is obvious and because I am far too familiar with the tension that comes when you're trying to talk about a loved one who is suffering— or one who died—and you couldn't do anything about it. Ezekiel needed my help those first few months after Mother died, and I was too busy with my own grief to help.

Jasper says, "So I hacked the trial."

The tightness in my throat loosens so I can gasp in surprise. "What?"

"The drug was being developed at Wolfe Tech, and I thought if I broke into their system, I could get her on the list."

"And you did?" He said she was in a trial. And she looked pretty good earlier, laughing with her family.

But he shakes his head. "I got caught. Not as talented at the keyboard as I thought I was. And Walter Wolfe himself showed up outside school when I was on my way to class one day. Told me he knew what I'd done." His gaze drops to the sheets, and I hate that he's ashamed of this. I hate that I've judged him so harshly when I didn't have even half the information.

"Jasper," I say. I've still got his hand in mine and squeeze in silent thanks.

"Wolfe said I had two choices. Either he'd tell the college what I'd done and press charges. And I'd lose any chance of ever being a doctor and probably go to jail. And Lexi would die and I wouldn't be there for her."

His words bring by a multitude of old insecurities. I know too well what it is to be powerless. You try to do good things, but it's not enough, or you wind up making it worse.

"But you didn't go to jail," I say. I know how this is going to end, but I need to hear him say it so I finally have all the pieces of the puzzle.

Jasper clears his throat, almost like he's trying as hard as I am not to cry. "Or, Wolfe said, I could come work for him. He said I'd gotten further into his networks than anyone had in a while. If I quit school and worked for him, he'd never tell anyone. And he'd get Lexi into the trial, and all I had to do was help with his security and run errands and not ask too many questions."

I close my eyes, letting the dark take me for a minute, because here is the truth. And it's been obvious from the beginning, but now I have all the pieces and they fit together so clearly.

"So, you're not really a henchman," I say, sliding my fingers between his.

He laughs. "Oh, I am. It's been two years, and I have to tell myself it's worth it. Because Lexi is doing so good, and most of the time . . ." Jasper coughs again. "Most of the time the work's not too bad. No different than working in any other office. And when it's not . . . when I see things I'd rather not, I tell myself it's worth it because my sister is okay." The last part of the sentence is a little strangled. I can't imagine what it's been like for him. Good and evil are relative terms in his world. He's only ever wanted to do good, but somehow doing it has meant doing evil too. I've rigidly stuck to my principles and judged anyone who doesn't. Knowing what your principles are and compromising them every day has to be a hundred times worse.

"And your family doesn't know?" I ask quietly.

He shakes his head. "They think I'm doing my residency at the hospital. Makes it easy to explain the weird hours I keep. I moved out here so there's less chance of me slipping up and saying the wrong thing."

I take his hand more fully into mine. It's a good hand. Strong, solid bones. It shakes a little, but he settles the longer we lie there like that.

"I'm sorry for picking fights," I say.

His thumb brushes over my knuckles. "It's okay. I'm not proud of it, but it's what my family needs. Hopefully someday I'll find a way to get out, and they won't ever have to hear what I did."

Him getting out of Wolfe's clutches sounds about as likely as us getting out of this loop. Worse, in some ways, because he'll have to do it alone. No one will know either before and after and those who do find out may never fully be able to understand, just like I didn't.

"My mother never left a lot of room for gray areas when I was growing up," I say, even though it hurts to talk about her. But I want him to understand. Maybe I want him to forgive me. "Good was good, bad was bad. There was no ambiguity, no room for things like sick sisters and tough decisions. The tough decision was following the right path, no matter the cost."

He laughs. "My best friend growing up had parents like that."

My turn to laugh. "I doubt that."

"No." He rolls so he can brush his free hand along my cheek. "You're not the first kid to grow up in some screwed-up religious family who thinks they have a monopoly on morality."

I hear his words but need another moment before I understand them. And, oh. Yeah, I guess that's one possible explanation. Why would he assume my mother fought crime and had superpowers when it's easier to assume she was some hardline Christian?

And I should tell him the truth. He's told me as much, so it's only fair. But I can't. I've held the secret of our identity my whole life. There's no gray area. No acceptable reason to share.

I can't give him that, so I give him something else, something I've been wanting too since we got here.

I kiss him. I close the last few inches between us until our lips meet, and from there it's easy. The hand on my face tips my jaw up so we fit together just right. His lips are cool under mine, and unlike before, with Leo coming up the hall, there's no hurry here, so we take our time.

"Morgan." He slides under the blankets with me. I bury my face in his neck. I really do like the way he smells, and now it's all around me. On him, on the sheets, on me, where I'm wearing his clothes.

I haven't touched anyone like this in a long time, and I'm tired. Tired of keeping secrets, tired of being strong. More than anything, I'm tired of being alone. Jasper's here and he's not the person I thought he was, and it's the best news I've heard all day.

He groans as I suck on the hinge of his jaw, and our legs tangle together. His hand goes to my hip, and I remember the feeling of it there, fingers pressing into my thighs as he held me in place as Leo stomped up the hall. I'd wanted him then, but it wasn't the right time.

Now would be okay, though.

"Morgan," he says again, his mouth chasing mine as I get to know him a little better. His fingers slide under my—his—shirt, and I jerk at the sensation. "Are you okay with this?"

"I'm not sure," I say. "I mean, yes. Yes, I'm okay with it. I'm not sure it's a good idea, but . . ."

He laughs, mouth spreading wide against mine. "If it's a bad idea, we can try again tomorrow."

I ignore the implication. We both know it's there. He's not

talking about the real tomorrow. He's talking about ours. The one where something happens—a freak tornado, or the floor gives way and I get crushed as we tumble into the garage below —and I die, and we have to start all over again.

But as Jasper runs his fingers down my spine, I think maybe we'll be okay. Maybe this is all we needed to do. If we tell each other our deepest secrets, maybe the spell will be broken?

Though if that's the case, there are some things I have to say, but it's so tempting not to and go with what we're feeling right now.

"Jasper, wait." I put a palm on his chest, and he freezes instantly.

"What? Is something wrong?"

This is a bad idea. We should stick with the kissing. But he was honest with me, and I should do the same. It's about trust, and I want to trust him so very much.

"I need to tell you," I say, "about my mother. About me. It's —" It's hard is what it is. The words are all jamming up in my throat.

"It's okay," he says, mouth coming to mine again, tongue flicking over my lower lip. "Whatever it is, you don't have to tell me now."

I don't have to, but I should.

Except then the decision is made for me when the apartment door bursts open and six men in black masks and carrying guns burst into the room.

I put my hands up in some old defensive reflex the way my mother used to when she needed to conjure up a ball of living flame and blast the bad guys. She taught me to do the same, even though nothing ever happened. No flame. No ice. For a second, I nearly feel a wave of cool power wash over me like I used to hope it would, but it's a phantom sensation and there's nothing there. Before I can make a complete fool of myself, Jasper's got one arm around me and he's pulling me behind him.

"What the hell?" he shouts, but that's all he gets to say before the men are on us and we're wrestled out of bed and down to the ground. My arms are wrenched painfully behind my back.

"Let go of me!"

"Leave him alone," Jasper says.

"Don't be a dick and this doesn't have to hurt," the man over Jasper says, planting his knee in Jasper's back.

"Leave now and you won't have to apologize later," Jasper sneers, but his words only earn him a boot to the face, clipping his chin and jerking his head back.

"No!" I shout.

Jasper spits blood on the carpet. "Another mistake. You don't know who I work for."

The man on his back laughs. "Of course we do, Jasper. Who do you think sent us?"

"What?" Jasper twists his head around, only to have it shoved back to the floor.

"You've been poking around places you shouldn't," someone says before I'm pulled to my feet. My hands have been bound behind my back, and something tight like a zip tie digs into my wrists.

Another man, taller than the others, is standing by the door. He chuckles once. "Mr. Wolfe would like a word with you and your friend here."

Then a hood is pulled over my head, and I don't see anything else for a while.

CHAPTER 14

expect to be thrown into the back of a van where we can roll helplessly, our bound hands doing nothing to protect us, but instead we're loaded into a vehicle with oddly plush leather seats. It's so well-insulated that I can barely hear the engine noise as we roll through the streets.

"This is nice," I say, twisting my body so I can pat the seats even though my hands are tied. "What is it? A Buick?" Honestly, with no more information than what I have, I wouldn't be surprised if it's a Range Rover like mine, but I refuse to think I have anything in common with henchmen. Well, with real henchmen, which these guys clearly are. Not morally conflicted and altruistic ones like Jasper. He and I were finally starting to find delicious common ground. How rude of these assholes to interrupt us.

My jibe about the Buick makes someone in the front seat chuckle softly. Beside me, Jasper hisses something that sounds distinctly like "Morgan, shut up."

I don't listen. If my true superpower is picking fights I can't win, I better go all in.

"I imagine hench money doesn't go very far, but you don't have to buy American if you don't want to. I know a guy. If you save up all your hench pennies, I could probably help you get a good deal."

The henchman laughs a little more, and I curse that we were so careless. We let fatigue and attraction distract us, and Walter Wolfe's thugs got the jump. If anyone at SPAM ever hears about this, I won't need a bus or a tainted pickle. The embarrassment will be enough to kill me on its own.

When the vehicle stops, we're led into a building. Then there's a ride in an elevator that seems to go on forever. Longer than the ride to Walter Wolfe's office. Longer than the ride to my office at Ziro Labs.

The floor as we exit is carpeted and I stumble, but firm hands on my arms keep me from falling. Just as I'm starting to feel steady, the hands give me a shove and I drop, collapsing onto what feels like a leather sofa. Jasper groans as he lands next to me.

"This is no way to treat a colleague, you guys." Obviously he's figured out what's going on too.

The hood is pulled from my head, and I squint on reflex, but the room isn't as brightly lit as I expected.

Also, the muzzle of a gun is about a foot from my face.

I jerk my head back, but the hands on my shoulders tighten, and even if I wasn't tied up, I don't think I could escape their grip.

The gun stays where it is, but since I'm still alive, I take a moment to examine my surroundings. Somehow, I thought we'd be in a warehouse. Maybe a cage at the zoo while a lion paces anxiously in the background. But we're in an apartment. A nice one. Penthouse, if the view of the city is anything to go by. The only light is a sparkling chandelier over a massive dining room table on the other side of the space.

I glance at Jasper, and his hair is mussed up—worse from the hood than his hat ever did—and he's glaring at everyone around us like they've interrupted him during the best sex of his life, which frankly, we should have been so lucky. What was about to happen was desperation sex at best and an ugly feelings sandwich at worst. Also, I was about to spill the beans on my mother, the one thing I swore I would never ever do. The zip ties are excessive, but the hench thugs saved us from ourselves.

"What the hell is this?" Jasper asks. "Dex? Carter? What the hell is going on?"

The blank-faced henchmen remain speechless. The guns, the one in front of me and the other held in front of Jasper, stay where they are.

"I think you know what's going on," a slippery voice says, before its owner appears.

Walter Wolfe. Billionaire. His tech and pharmaceutical companies employ a third of the city, either directly or indirectly. He's perpetually having his picture taken with the mayor or handing off a giant check to a homeless shelter or an after-school program. Always in a perfectly tailored suit with an equally well-pressed smile.

Today's smile is not so gracious. If we weren't already stuck on the couch, Wolfe's smile would freeze me in my tracks.

"Mr. Wolfe," Jasper says. "What's going on? I was at home, I was—" His words cut off sharply as the closest henchman swings his gun down to collide with the side of Jasper's head.

"Jasper." Wolfe is staring down at his phone. For all the interest he gives us, he might as well be ordering takeout while waiting for a conference call to start. "Don't play coy with me. We've already done that, and it ended up with you working here. I told you our agreement would only work if you stayed in line."

"And I have, Mr. Wolfe."

Wolfe shakes his head, tsking. "Don't lie, Jasper. I always know when people lie to me." He comes forward, pushing the man with the gun back. The henchman takes a position by the door. Wolfe turns his phone around, and on the screen is a black-and-white security video of Jasper and me in Wolfe's office. The resolution is shockingly clear, which means the sight of Jasper plugging in his phone into the computer tower is undeniable.

"Now," Wolfe says. "Leo and Bobby could only say that you tried to sneak your friend here into my office for shits and giggles." The way Wolfe is speaking, he may have the video of us in the office, but he doesn't have any sound. All he's got is Jasper plugging in his phone and me crawling into Jasper's lap. I could try and argue Jasper was only trying to charge his phone, but the gleam in Wolfe's eye says he won't buy that. And there were too many seconds of Jasper doing his tippy-tappy hacker thing on the keyboard for him to just be looking for a quick boost on a battery. Even if they can't say for sure what Jasper was looking for on Wolfe's computer, there must be ways to find out. Jasper said what happens next would be slow and painful. How long would they draw it out while someone tried to track Jasper's mouse clicks and keystrokes until they discover what our target was?

Though Wolfe doesn't seem inclined to wait.

"Here's how this is going to work," he says, settling into an overstuffed armchair across from us, bracketed on either side by his armed goons. "Tell me what you took, and your boyfriend lives."

The gun closest to me is cocked, and I have to bite my lip to muffle a giggle. My mother never had much tolerance for theatrics when it came to bad guys. *It's an alpha male thing*, she said. *They want to remind you they're smarter than you, even if you'll be dead before you have a chance to tell anyone.*

But I must not be quiet enough, because Wolfe's eyes narrow.

"Something funny?"

Another lesson from my mother. *Less is more. Don't speak unless it's literally the only way to save yourself. Keep your mouth shut and wait for your opportunity.*

I shake my head but get interrupted midway through the gesture when a clenched fist collides with my skull. I'd fall over, but the man behind me tightens his grip on my shoulders.

"Hey!" Jasper says. "Stop. He doesn't know anything."

"Oh, I'm sure he doesn't," Wolfe sneers. I bristle and have to force myself to relax when Jasper softly clears his throat in warning. "He wouldn't be out with someone like you if he could do better."

Well, fuck you very much. I keep my face neutral as I strain against the zip ties behind my back because I'm going to need to defend myself in very short order, but they hold fast. I close my eyes for a second, hoping they'll assume it's because of the punch to the face and not because I'm trying to centre my power. Even if it basically has the oomph of a Zippo lighter, it's better than nothing—enough to melt the plastic.

"So, Jasper, this is your last chance," Wolfe says. "And you know I've given you more chances than I would normally, because your skill set has been useful to date. So I'm going to make you an offer."

The gun barrel pressed against my forehead is cold. It's so hard to concentrate on the binding around my wrists. I keep tugging, but they won't break.

Never take the first offer. That one I didn't learn from my mother; I learned it from Ezekiel, who has turned down so many offers to buy his research and technology. But I have no way of telling Jasper that, so I jump in before he can answer.

"We were pulling records on the drug trial. My niece has the same thing Jasper's sister does. I wanted to see the results."

Jasper nods, picking up my train of thought. "I knew you'd notice if I tried to hack my way in again, but I figured if we did it from your office, I could wipe the trail."

As lies go, that one's better than most. Definitely better than me being an electrician or someone with a kink for making out in a crime lord's office. The man with the gun retreats until he's standing with his hench buddy by the door. I hold my breath as Jasper and Wolfe glare at each other and count the seconds.

Finally, Wolfe says, "You've got a soft heart. Jasper, these things are going to get you into trouble."

Jasper hangs his head in apparent shame. "I know. I'm sorry."

Wolfe puts a hand on his shoulder. "I've taken care of your family, haven't I?"

"Of course, sir. Lexi's doing great." Jasper nods quickly. Watching him grovel makes my stomach turn, and I pull at the zip ties. Do they feel warmer? Or is it only friction where my skin rubs against them?

Wolfe's eyes slide to me. "And I'll look after your friends too. We're all family here, aren't we?"

I give him a tight smile I hope looks grateful. Just what I've always wanted. My very own godfather, only more of the "I'm going to make you an offer you can't refuse" variety than the "make sure you're home by midnight" fairy kind.

When Clarissa said she had someone she wanted me to meet, I did not expect to get adopted into a crime family as a result.

"I'm sorry," Jasper says. "It won't happen again. You can trust me."

Wolfe frowns. "Can I, though?"

My chest tightens, and Jasper sits up straighter. "Of course. You've always been able to trust me."

But Wolfe strolls over to the open sliding door at the balcony. "Jasper, I think you overestimate my generosity."

"What?" He shifts, pulling at his ties, and my heart squeezes in echoing anxiety.

"I said we'd let your friend live. I didn't say anything about you. You broke into my office. Broke into my files. Him"—he glances over his shoulder at me—"I have a use for him. But you? No, I'm sorry, Jasper. Your time in my family is done."

A use for me? Is it Walter Wolfe who's been slingshotting me through time since the beginning? Somehow, I didn't think it was. It's too high tech for his usual MO. But he's got the plans, and he even told Ezekiel he had a time machine.

Jasper's got other concerns, though.

"What? Mr. Wolfe, wait." He tries to rise, but the henchman behind him holds him down. "Mr. Wolfe."

But Wolfe turns and walks back into the penthouse, through an archway and out of view. By the door, the first man with the gun takes aim.

"No. No!" For a second, I escape the henchman holding me down, and I lunge for Jasper. If I can get in front of the bullet, this all starts over.

There's a muffled pop. I squeeze my eyes tight, waiting for the pain. All I get is a spray of blood on my cheek before the thug wrestles me back into place. Beside me, Jasper slumps, gasping. Red seeps out over his T-shirt, and he looks at me with terrified eyes.

"Morgan," he wheezes.

I've been powerless my whole life. And I don't only mean the way my superness is not-so-super. When it became clear I wasn't going to follow in my mother's footsteps, I took what little zap I had and got a desk job at SPAM. A literal desk job. I made coffee and formatted slides. My mother stood her ground on the roof as Indigo broke free of her trap, and I was powerless to save her when she had spent her whole life saving everyone. I couldn't even grieve properly because I couldn't tell anyone what had truly happened. I was powerless to do anything but hide. Nothing heroic at all.

And as I'm held on a sofa, and Jasper bleeds out against me, while the goon holsters his gun and the others all look like they'd as soon start talking about sports scores, I hate it. It might even be better if they laughed at me for my failures, but they hardly even acknowledge I'm there. Like I'm nothing. Insignificant. I'm not even worth shooting. I hate myself. Hate this hollow powerless feeling and the guilt that comes with it.

I hate the people who have left me feeling like this over and over.

And I scream. I don't even know if it's out loud or not, but it doesn't matter. Because my mother died and now Jasper's died and all I can do is sit there with my hands tied behind my back and let bad powerful people hurt them and it's not fair.

I scream, focusing on the pressure of the man's hands on my shoulder. I dream of what I would do if I had even an ounce of the capabilities my mother did. I would suck the life right out of him. I would build a force field around me and Jasper and watch the rest of them wither and die. My power would follow after Walter Wolfe wherever he's gone, and it would make him hurt the way I do right now. It would be like Indigo. Painful and inescapable. They would know it was me who did it, even when I look like I can't do much of anything. I scream until the heat goes out of me, until I'm numb and shaking, and then I scream more, embracing the cold because it's better than pain and shame.

The sound echoes in my head and in the penthouse for a long time. The room has gone completely black. Except it hasn't. My eyes are closed, squeezed shut so tight I have to think about how to open them again. My throat is raw and my skin is burning.

The first thing I see is the white puff of my breath in the air.

The next is Jasper's body, the slick of blood, red and shiny. He's breathing hard, but the terror in his gaze is directed at me, not at the wound on his chest.

Then, finally, I glance around and see what I've done.

The men—the henchmen—are frozen. Icicles drip from their noses and their ears. One is still holding his gun in front of me, and when I go to knock it away, the gun—along with the hand frozen to it—shatters into a million tiny shards and falls to the glittering floor, covered in a fine layer of frost and ice like a glazed donut.

I gasp, and it sounds more like a hiccup, then I gasp again, and this one is a sob. Relief. Grief. I did this. I stopped them, but I was too late.

Beside me, Jasper groans softly.

"Oh." I reach for him. The zip ties have a second of resistance before they snap, the plastic gone brittle in the cold. I grab for

Jasper as he falls toward me. He coughs and cries out as I try to prop him up and break his ties too.

"Ow. Jesus. Fuck." He gasps and slumps against me.

"It's okay," I say, heart racing. "It's okay."

"Morgan?" His lips are coated in blood and even the few syllables of my name come out in a garbled string as his teeth chatter.

"I know. I know, I'm sorry. I didn't know that was going to happen."

"What . . . what . . ."

Jesus, of all the times for the med student among us to need help.

"It's okay." He groans again as I slide my hands under his armpits and pull him from the sofa, away from the frozen statutes of his former colleagues.

"Why is it cold?"

"It's okay." My feet skate on the floor as I drag him toward an open door that leads to a rooftop patio. Fortunately, my rage frost or whatever this is didn't make it past the threshold. Outside, the air feels comparatively warm.

"Morgan."

"Yes." I drop to my knees. It's like a reverse of the night with the bus. Only bloodier. So much bloodier. Jasper's shirt is soaked, and his breathing is shallow and wet. "Yes, I'm here."

"I'm sorry," he says.

"What for?"

"I blew it. I thought I knew what . . . I thought . . ." He coughs again, spewing blood down his chin. I lay him down on the roof. He's scarily pale, and he tries to lift his hand toward me but only gets a few inches off the ground before he has to drop it down again.

"Shh. No. It's okay," I say. "It's okay. Help. We'll get you help." I pat my pockets, looking for my phone, but I'm still in Jasper's borrowed clothes, and my cellphone is somewhere in his apartment.

Wolfe. He must have a phone. The ones on the goons will all be frozen. Wolfe wasn't in the room. If he was far enough away, maybe he didn't freeze completely.

I push to my feet. The warm evening air makes my insides thrum, like I'm recharging. I still don't know what happened in there, but I can feel it. Now that I've touched it once, it really is like a lighter, and since I've finally learned the proper way to flick the spark, I can do it again.

"Morgan," Jasper gasps.

"I'll be right back."

"Please." And his voice is so soft, he doesn't need powers to stop me where I stand. I glance over my shoulder, and he's lying there, red spreading over his clothes. His movements are sluggish, his eyes unfocused.

"No." I shake my head. "No. I can save you. I can get help, I can—" But I drop back to my knees and crawl toward him.

"It's okay," he says. "Guess we'll find out if it's just you who starts the day over."

My tears start unexpectedly. "You better come back."

He gives me a bloody, toothy smile. "I'll try. Want to see how this ends."

"I can't do this without you."

"Sure you can." His fingers brush against mine, flexing unpredictably. I think he's trying to take my hand again, so I take his instead. "You've been holding out on me. That was a pretty cool trick."

I laugh, sniffling. "You have to come back. I have to tell you. So many things. I want to tell you all about me."

His gaze is unfocused, but his smile fades, and oh fuck, he can't die. I need him. I want him. Want to tell him and to trust him.

"I'll try," he says.

"No." I'm begging now. Sobbing. All the things I never got to do for my mother. "That's not good enough. You can't just try,

Jasper. You have to come back. We have to get out of this together. Jasper."

But he's gone. His face goes slack, and he stops struggling for breath.

I close my eyes and count to ten, waiting for the air to change. The background noise. Wait for this empty penthouse on the tallest building in the city to transform into a superhero-themed diner with a painting of my mother on the wall. Wait for Jasper to come through the door so I can tell him that he's late and that his hat is hideous and that I'm so glad he's back.

But it doesn't.

I'm still on the roof with Jasper's body. He's dead, and he's staying that way. We aren't starting over.

The wind catches my hair, dragging my tears over my face, and my gaze goes to the edge of the building. It's not far. I could run. Three steps and a hop over the railing into empty air, a few seconds of gravity, and I'd be all set. Back at Wench. Jasper would be alive.

But I can't. I run straight for the patio railing, but the second my hands touch the metal, instinct kicks in and my feet come to a halt. I try twice more but the same thing happens, leaving me to scream in frustration even though no one will hear me. We have to bring Jasper back, but I can't jump. I'm afraid and I'm sad, but in the end, I'm not suicidal.

I'm going to have to do this alone.

CHAPTER 15

Walter Wolfe's phone is a block of ice. He must have been about to make a call when I went off, because the phone is in his hand, but he's frozen like everyone else. He didn't even have time to look up before he died. Whatever I did, it happened really fast. It felt endless inside me, but it must have only taken the space between one breath and the next. His death was instantaneous and painless while Jasper struggled to breathe outside. The unfairness of it chokes me.

Wolfe is in a home office. The antique desk is made of heavy wood, covered in a film of frost like the rest of the apartment. There's a small statue on one corner, a howling wolf carved out of stone. My heart races as I pick it up and swing it. I scream out loud this time as the wolf collides with Walter Wolfe's frozen head and smashes it into shards. Bits of him fly off in a wide arc. I do it a couple more times, basically smashing him to dust. This is his fault. Not mine. He's the reason Jasper was in this situation at all. In another life, I'd have gone on a date with Jasper the med student and we might have had a great night. Instead, we wasted so much time because of his debt to Wolfe, and now Jasper's gone and I can't bring him back.

When there's none of him left—and not much of the wolf sculpture either—I stand there for a second, examining my work while I wait for my breathing to settle. If I could hurt him more, I would. But I'll have to be satisfied with this. I drop the lump of smashed stone to the floor.

The penthouse has its own private elevator, so I ride down alone. But I must scare the hell out of the kid walking down the sidewalk, because he yelps and jumps out of the way as I step out of the building's revolving door. Can't blame him. My shirt is covered in blood, and I'm sure the rest of me isn't much better.

But I only have a few seconds to apologize and reassure him I'm not on some homicidal tear before a sleek black sedan pulls up to the curb and the window rolls down.

"Morgan. Get in." The authoritative order that comes from inside will not be denied, and I only have a second to catch a glimpse of horn-rimmed glasses and tightly braided cornrows before the window slides shut again.

April. Fuck. The last thing I need tonight is a run-in with SPAM's official agent liaison.

But what choice do I have? I'm not even wearing shoes or socks, much less have a phone or wallet. Not like I can call a cab. Who would pick me up, anyway, looking the way I do?

I get into the car and it's pulling back into traffic before I even have my seat belt done up.

"Looks like you've had a night," April says dryly. I don't answer. I haven't spoken to April since I left SPAM. Not that we were ever buddies. But there's a strong chance that if I try to say anything I'll burst into tears and throw myself in her lap, and we're *definitely* not close enough for that.

"How did you know to come?" I ask weakly, staring at my hands. The palms are crusted with blood. Jasper's blood.

Her laugh is a short, hard thing, like a shard of ice in my chest.

"You think we don't know where you are all the time? That you walked out of the SPAM doors and into obscurity?"

Oh, look. Here's a fight no one would blame me for having. They've been tracking me for years. That's such a gross invasion of privacy.

"It's for your own protection," she says, no doubt knowing exactly where my thoughts are leading. "You made it very clear you wanted nothing to do with us, and I can't say I blame you. But I owe it to your mother to watch out for you, and when I saw you headed to Wolfe's building tonight, I knew you wouldn't have done that on your own."

"What if I did?" I ask, bitterness creeping in my throat like ice. "Walter and I could be very close. He could have been fucking the living daylights out of me, and then you'd be pretty embarrassed right now." The very idea of being in bed with Wolfe makes my skin crawl. I want to smash him to shards all over again. Jasper is the only one whose bed I want to be in, and he's gone. Please don't let it be for too long. I send up a silent wish to whoever or whatever keeps making me do this awful day over and over that they find a sinkhole or something to plummet me and April into so I can get back to Wench ASAP.

No such luck, though. April's watching me with thin-lipped concern. I think about swinging the car door open and tumbling out into the street, but the odds of it killing me are slim, and road rash will only make this night extra painful for no reason.

"What were you really doing there?" she asks.

I should tell her. All of it. Jasper and I probably should have gone to SPAM instead of going to Ezekiel the other day. But they're sneaky, April most of all. If I showed up with a wild story about a not-so-super blind date time loop, she'd have us both shut up in a lab or protective custody. If I tell her about what happened in Wolfe's penthouse, what with the screaming and the freezing and the everyone dying, she'll never let me walk away again. That much power with no training is danger-ous. I shudder at the very thought. I've suddenly become every-thing my mother could have ever hoped for, and I don't want it. I want Jasper.

A tear runs down my cheek and I slap a hand over it, hoping to catch it before April notices.

I'm in so much trouble. More than I can handle on my own. But I can't make it SPAM's problem. The consequences are too high.

"I'm safe," I say, wiping my face. "That's what you were worried about, isn't it? That I was in some kind of trouble? Well, I'm not." I stare at my palms. The tear has wiped away some of the blood, which means it's probably smeared on my face now. Not doing a great job of convincing April I'm okay.

She watches me silently for a minute longer before she says, "I'll take you home."

"No," I say too fast. I can't go home. I can't show up looking like this and scare Ezekiel. He won't remember in this version of today. I'll have to explain it all over again and I just can't. Not tonight.

"To the office?" April says.

I shake my head. Not SPAM either. Instead, I give her an address, and pretty soon we're pulling in front of a nondescript house in a nondescript suburb.

"You can always call if you need anything," April says as I climb out of the sedan. It's probably the kindest thing she's ever said to me. When I quit, her words were much more of the "Where the hell else is someone like you going to go?" variety. We were all hurting back then.

At the last second, right before I close the sedan door, I whirl and stick my head back inside.

"Walter Wolfe is dead," I say. The immediate shock on April's face is very satisfying. "And a bunch of his crew. And . . ." I stutter over the last part. "And a friend. He was innocent. You'll find him outside on the patio. If you could . . ." The last part doesn't come out as more than a strangled gasp, but April nods. I don't want to be part of SPAM, but that doesn't mean I can't use their resources to help Jasper. I can't leave him lying out there. April will send some agents, or maybe place a discreet call to the police to take care of it.

I close the car door quietly so as not to wake the sleeping family inside the main house and walk up the stairs to the garage apartment. My clothes, phone—the battery is dead, and when I try to boost the battery, all I get is a half inch of frost on the bottom of the screen—and keys are still by Jasper's bed. I can't bring myself to use his shower again, even though I need to get clean more than I need almost anything else right now. Instead, I strip out of his bloody clothes and throw them into a backpack hung by the door. No sense leaving them here where they'll raise questions for his family. I borrow another T-shirt and slide into my pants.

The sun won't be up for a few more hours, and Jasper's mom and sisters must still be sleeping off their movie night, because the house is quiet as I climb into my SUV. As I put my foot on the brake, I glance at the empty windows behind me, and my eyes tear up. They'll wake up sooner or later, and sometime after that, they're going to wonder where he is. The lie of weird hours at the hospital might keep them from worrying for a while, but eventually they're going to start asking questions, and when Jasper's body is found with a bunch of dead mobsters, it won't give them the answers they need. But I can't face them. All I can do is add them to the list of people I've let down.

For the first time in forever, I take the day off. I'm exhausted. Numb. I shower until the water goes cold, which, given the undoubted size of the hot water tank at Ziro Hall, is a while. I try not to cry as Jasper's blood washes down the drain. No one sees me when I don't succeed.

I sleep for hours. I dream about Jasper and my mother. Mother tumbles off the roof as I rush after her, but this time she flies. She has my hand in hers, and Jasper glides along beside her. I try to explain that there's no way they'd know each other, but they don't seem worried about the logistics. Then they fly off together, leaving me on the side of the road. I think my mother tells me to take the bus, but I'm half awake by then and possibly editorializing.

When I wake up for real, the shadows are heavy outside, and my first thought is this is the longest I've ever made it, so maybe the solution was that it was Jasper who needed to die after all. The idea makes my throat tighten. I can't sit with that reality. It can't be the answer. There has to be a solution where we both survive.

Downstairs, a door slams, and I'm contemplating burying my head under my pillow when Ezekiel calls my name.

"Morgan? Morgan, are you here?"

His voice has a nervous edge to it I don't recognize, and it's enough to pull me out of bed. I put Jasper's clean T-shirt on, along with a pair of jeans.

"Ezekiel?" I say as I come down the stairs. He's standing in the front hall, still dressed from work, and his shoulders slump when he sees me.

"Oh, thank god. I was really starting to worry about you."

"I'm fine." I'm anything but fine. Even after all that sleep, I'm still exhausted. I feel stretched too thin and the sensation gets worse as I try to figure out what I can tell Ezekiel.

"You didn't come to work. You weren't answering your phone. Clarissa tried calling you too. She said you had some kind of date last night. I thought—" He frowns when I laugh.

"You thought I went on a date with an axe murderer?" It's so far from the truth and yet so close I can't help my laughter. What's the worst-case scenario most people would think of for a blind date? I guarantee it's not sixty-four straight days of death and destruction with zero explanation.

"Are you sick?" He's still watching me like I might keel over at any second, which, given my disheveled appearance and my uncontrolled giggling, is probably not an unreasonable concern.

"I'm fine," I say. "I'm fine. I—" I . . . don't have a good way to explain what's happened, but maybe it's time to stop keeping secrets. I let out a hiccupping sigh. "Jasper died."

Ezekiel frowns. "Who?"

"Jasper. The guy . . . the one from my date. You met him, remember? We came to your office."

But Ezekiel shakes his head. "When did you come to my office?"

"Last night, we—" Oh, I must still be asleep after all, because that wasn't last night. That was before. The thought that Jasper has ceased to exist in Ezekiel's version of reality is crushing. This is what Jasper meant, isn't it? That being stuck in this loop by yourself is fucking lonely. Anyone you try to explain it to will automatically assume you're off your gourd, which means it's easier to tell no one and suffer alone.

"Sorry, I didn't sleep well." I run a tired hand over my face.

As we walk to the living room, he gives me another worried glance. "Have you been asleep all day?"

"Not *all* day." I should tell him he's lucky I showered, but instead I slump to the sofa, then pop up again, because it's leather like the one at Wolfe's penthouse and I just *can't* with that.

"Morgan." He looks really worried now. If I don't pull it together, he's going to start calling reinforcements. Either Clarissa or our doctor, and neither of those will be good for me.

"No. No it's nothing. I'm okay." But I'm obviously not, because I'm pacing on the organic Afghan goat's wool rug and fluttering my hands by my face, trying to get the tears to dry before they tumble down my cheeks.

"Sit," Ezekiel reaches for me, pulling me gently back down. I perch at the edge of the cushions, ignoring the itch in my palms that says I could send the leather subzero if I wanted to. I don't know what's happening to me. Why now? There's been nothing more than a spark my whole life. What changed? And how am I going to explain it to Ezekiel?

"Sorry." I sigh, rubbing my hands together. "It's been . . . I had a long night."

Ezekiel's face is all soft compassion, and I'm having terrible déjà vu from so many conversations we had here after Mother died, but then again, my life is all déjà vu these days, so why should this be anything different?

"Something happened to your friend?" he says.

I pull on the neck of the T-shirt. A puff of Jasper's sawdust scent wafts up to my face, making it hard to breathe evenly.

"Not my friend. He . . ." Not my boyfriend either. Partner in crime? Sidekick to my sidekick? If you need henching . . . "We met a couple months ago," I say. "He was a really good person, but he was working for some bad people, and . . ." I can't say it. Not all of it. Jasper's secrets aren't mine to tell, even now. And I can't stand the thought of Ezekiel making the same wrong assumptions I did, so I skip over the details. "It caught up with him. They caught up with him. And now he's dead." On the last sentence, I pull the shirt up around my nose, inhaling slowly to keep the panic at bay. Doesn't stop the memories, though. The way Jasper gasped in my arms as he died. His uneven grin and that one annoyingly imperfect tooth that made him charming. Who am I kidding? He didn't even need the tooth. He was charming from minute one.

"Do you need to call the police?" Ezekiel asks.

I shake my head. "They can't help."

But he won't be put off. "Do we need to call our lawyer? Are you in some kind of trouble?"

Talking about this in mundane steps is comforting. Police. Lawyers. Like the world makes sense and if we follow the procedures, we'll get predictable and reproducible results.

"No. It's fine. This won't come back to me." April will make sure any possible traces of my presence in the penthouse are erased. "I miss him. He had a good heart, and I wish he'd had a chance to use it the way he wanted to."

Ezekiel puts his arm around me, letting me sag against his shoulder. He's not my father, but he's the closest thing I can ever remember having, and we've done well together.

"*You* have a good heart," he says, which only makes me

swallow back new tears. I've felt broken for such a long time, and with the power simmering beneath my skin, I feel more fractured than ever. "I know the last few years have been hard. If I could change it, I would. But you remember what I said when your mom died?"

I do. It's the thing that's kept me going. "That the best thing we could do was help the people who are still here?"

He squeezes me, and I'm getting tears and snot on his suit jacket, but he doesn't seem to care. "Exactly. And we can do that for your friend too. What was his name?"

"Jasper."

"Jasper." Ezekiel gives me a reassuring pat. "If he was a good person trying to help others, then we can do that for him too. Our work is going to change the world."

"It's going to save it," I say, heaving a big sigh as I sit up again, grounding myself in the speech we've given each other over and over.

"It is." Ezekiel smiles. "How about I order in some food and we can talk about the presentation?"

I roll my eyes. "We've been over the presentation."

"Maybe." He pulls off his jacket and loosens his tie. "But it can't hurt to look again."

"Clarissa will be pissed if we make any changes," I say. My smile feels false, but that happened after Mother died too. Eventually you get used to it.

We order sushi. We go over the slides. They're fine. The colours, the wording. I talk through my introduction, and Ezekiel paces the living room like a ringmaster, telling anyone who will listen—just me and my ghosts in this case—about how the Ziro Machine will accelerate our recovery from the effects of global warming and save at-risk communities around the world. It feels good. Normal. I applaud when he's done and he winks his appreciation.

Except I'm not normal. Somehow, only a few hours later, I'm back in bed, because it's night and that's what normal people do at night. They sleep. But I can't. Maybe it's because I slept all day. Maybe it's because my mother hardly ever slept, so our house was never quiet. Hard to fight evil if you keep nine to five hours, she'd say.

But I can fight evil now. I press a fingertip to the nightstand. At first, nothing happens, just like it always does. I think back to the penthouse, trying to recall the sequence of events. What was different that time? It was real, for one. Truly life or death. Most of the time, I'm focused on the object I touch. A laptop battery. Power cables behind a monitor. Last night I thought instead about the man touching me and somehow that meant not only could I push the energy out of me, I could channel it. Direct it. I kept it away from me and Jasper, even though the flow from the man standing above me and through my body was like an over-flowing river.

I open my eyes, and a tiny ring of frost has formed around my finger. I gasp, pulling my bottom lip between my teeth. As I imagine the river, the little ring gets wider and my pulse picks up. I have to breathe through my mouth to stay calm. If I stay focused. If I keep thinking about the man above me and Jasper's desperate gasping next to me, then—

Something like a shock zaps through me and I yelp as I pull my hand back. The frost recedes, disappearing on the mahogany veneer. My phone is lying face down next to the ring of small water droplets that remain. It's been on the charger all day, so I unplug it and turn it on. There are about a half million emails and missed calls from Ezekiel and Clarissa. They start with polite cheery requests for proof of life and get increasingly frantic the longer I don't reply.

As I clear emails, a notification pings on the screen.

New text message from unknown sender

I go to delete the text, but my thumb falters when the screen-shot of Jasper's face appears where words should be. He's the unknown sender. Of course he is. Just over twenty-four hours ago, I was waiting to meet a stranger for a blind date I was sure would be a disaster. Why would I have saved his number in my phone?

My hand shakes as I get the video to play. The shaking gets worse in the first few seconds as Jasper looks at me from the screen. He's in bed, shaggy hair in his face, head nestled in the pillow, looking relaxed and a little self-conscious.

"Hey," he says, glancing to the side for a moment before he comes back to the screen. "You're in the shower right now, so I'm hoping you can't hear me. I don't know if you'll actually ever see this since I'm going to set it to send twenty-four hours from now. If you don't, I guess it means we screwed up and the day started over. Sorry about that. Hope it didn't hurt too much. But if you do see this, then maybe we survived. That's what it would mean, right?"

My throat hurts because he can't have known how wrong he'd be.

"Anyway, there's some things I want to say to you, and if I say them to your face, you'll get flustered and pick a fight rather than hearing what I'm trying to tell you."

I wrinkle my nose, the instinct to protest strong, but he's not here for me to argue with, and aren't I proving his point anyway?

"I need to tell you that I see you. I see how hard you're trying, and how brave you think you have to be all the time. Even before you remembered our dates, I could see it. I remember, trust me." His smile softens. "I know there's things you haven't told me about who you are. And I know you don't like me and the choices I've had to make. But Morgan, I think you're amazing. You're so smart and so dedicated to what you do. I wish I stuck to what I thought was right as much as you do."

He did, though. That's the thing. He gave up everything to protect his family. That's so much more than I've done.

Jasper rolls over, the pillow wrinkling under his head. I'm still in his T-shirt, and his lumber scent makes me want to curl up in a ball and cry until I'm all dried out. Instead, I hold the phone close and listen as he says, "I can't believe I'm saying this, but I'm glad we got stuck here. Obviously not the dying part. But even when we're fighting, I'd rather fight with you than be with pretty much anyone else. There are so many things I need to tell you, and there are so many dates that I remember that you don't, and I want to tell you about those too." He sighs, running his free hand through his hair, pushing it out of his face. I have to smile because I miss his scruffy persona so much and it's only been a day. "Anyway, I'll probably be super embarrassed when you see this, but if you do see it, that means we found a way out, and that's the important part. I'll get over the embarrassment. But if we did find a way out, I hope you'll let me take you on another date. I promise it will go better than this one."

I cough on a sob that is fifty percent laughter as he grins at the screen. Jasper glances to the side again. "You turned off the water, so you're probably coming back out. I'm sure you've been thinking of ways to start an argument while you were in there, so I'm going to sign off. I'll see you soon, okay?"

Then the screen shifts, showing the blank wall next to the bed, before the video freezes.

Well, shit. I slide the phone under my pillow, like if I sleep with it there and wish hard enough, I'll wake up in the morning to find Jasper next to me. Or we'll be back at Wench. Either way is fine.

But as I stare into the darkness of my room, wishing won't cut it. It's going to take action or bust. The time for half-baked plans and trial runs is over. I'm going to figure out who is responsible for this time loop and how we escape it for good.

And then I'm going to get Jasper back.

CHAPTER 16

A day is not enough to learn everything there is to know about time travel, but I'm doing my best. I tell Ezekiel I'm taking another day off work. He looks worried, but I promise I'll be ready for the presentation, and he doesn't argue.

I think about going back to Jasper's, about making up some story as to why I need to get into his apartment so I can try to get a copy of those plans we took from Wolfe, but wasting the whole day trying to guess passwords that will open Jasper's computer doesn't seem like a good use of my time. Also, I can't bring myself to face Jasper's family. They must be devastated, and as the mysterious friend they met only hours before he was killed, my reappearance will only prompt questions, most of which I can't answer.

I think about going to work, even if I already told them I wasn't coming in. I could close my office door and no one would know I was there. But someone would figure out eventually. Clarissa, probably. I still haven't called her back. There's no time for reassurances and chitchat. I can't have any distractions. The longer Jasper stays dead, the further away he feels.

In the end, though, I wind up at Wench. The basics of the scientific method state that all variables should be kept the same as much as possible. I don't have Jasper with me, but somehow, staking out a booth at the diner feels as close to recreating the conditions as I can get.

"Second time in three days," Vee says as she comes to take my order. "To what do I owe the honor?"

I bite my lip because my instinct is to say something blunt or to ignore her friendly smile and place my order, but somehow it doesn't feel the same now that I know Jasper has seen through the armor. If he has, Vee must have ages ago too.

"Call it nostalgia," I say.

She grins, flicking her long braid over one shoulder. "You know you're welcome here any time you want."

That's probably always been true, but the awkward silence that follows fills in all the answers as to why I couldn't do it.

"So," Vee says, pulling her notepad out of her apron. "What can I get you? Peppermint tea?"

"Coffee," I say. "Black. And a tuna salad sandwich. You know what I can't have."

"Sure do. I'll look after you." She straightens proudly. The fact that even this little interaction can make her happy only leaves me feeling worse, but I don't have time for my daily dose of self-loathing.

I spend hours online. Credit to Vee, the diner has all the ambiance of an abandoned theme park, but she's got an awesome Wi-Fi signal. I start with the scientific journals, but nothing reputable publishes articles about time travel theories. So I start going through the disreputable ones because as wild as some of the theories are—they range from brain tumors to parallel dimensions—the fact remains that I lived the same day more than sixty times, and there has to be an explanation for all of it.

I read articles about alien abductions, government experiments, and homemade basement time machines that accidentally sent the inventor back to the moment of his birth and caused a paradox that meant both he and his infant self simultaneously ceased to be. It's unclear how anyone could have known about that sequence of events, given he had nullified his existence, but somehow I don't think that's the important part when the author's name links to another article about how snowflakes feel emotions. I find another article that asserts the 1980s are a myth and that's why we all feel some kind of collective nostalgia, regardless of what year we were born, for a moment in time that never actually happened.

"Oh my god." I bury my face in my hands. "This is impossible."

"Pie?" Vee asks. She's been popping by all day, sometimes with coffee refills, sometimes with small plates of allergen-friendly snacks I can munch on between paragraphs. It's a kind of caretaking I haven't felt in a long time. "Everything is better with pie. It's peach. Cooked. You can still eat those, right?"

"Will the pie replenish itself at the moment I finish it? Bring itself forward in time to help nourish me as I bang my head against the wall over this conspiracy theory bullshit?"

"I don't think peaches have any significant quantum proper-ties, though now you're making me think that a bottomless pie special might be a hit around here." Vee cocks her head. "I'll bring you a piece. With ice cream too."

I go back to my laptop, scrolling through more articles, trying to find the logic and science behind what's happening. I'm developing a headache. At least it's just stress and probably caffeine overdose, as opposed to the remnants of a concussion from a day that never stops.

I startle when the plate is set in front of me. Then a second plate lands at the seat across from mine, and Vee sits down. Along with the two empty plates, she's brought an entire pie in a pan. It only takes a few seconds before the scent of warm pastry and peaches hits my nose, and my mouth waters immediately.

"What are you doing?" I ask.

"We're having pie," she says. She cuts through the top crust and lifts slices out of the pan, setting them down on each plate. I watch, practically drooling, as she digs into hers with the side of her fork, squeezing yellow-orange goo out the sides. It glistens in the light and wow, that looks good. My stomach growls as she slides the fork between her lips and I cut a bite for myself, lifting it to my mouth with shaking hands.

"Oh my god," I say as the peaches hit my tongue. Vee is watching me, eyes crinkling at the corner in silent laughter. Her face has lines I don't remember. It's only been two years, but she's aged.

"See?" she says as she takes another bite. "Pie makes everything better."

I don't want to admit she's right, but the way I demolish my slice like it's the first thing I've eaten in a week says otherwise. Vee watches me with satisfaction as I help myself to a second slice before she's even halfway through her first.

"Good?" she asks.

"Best thing I've had since—" But the statement dies on my tongue, because they're the best thing since brownies with Jasper's family in their kitchen, and while this pie is tasty, those brownies were special. As was the company.

"What?" Vee says.

"Nothing." I shake my head.

"You got sad again."

"It's nothing." Nothing I can talk about, anyway.

"Nothing makes you sad?"

"Nothing makes me . . . " I glare at my pie like it's betrayed me.

"We both struggled after Farah died," she says after a moment, making the wrong assumption, though it's not her fault. As far as she knows, Jasper and I met once. Why would he be the one to consume my thoughts? "I should have been there for you more. But you had Ezekiel, and I could see how hard you were working, and I thought maybe it was for the best."

It had been. I was happy with my life. At least until I met Jasper. Until suddenly I was solving mysteries and tangling with criminals instead of following the steps of the neat life I'd built for myself these past few years. Now I'm grieving all over again, and it's like all that work meant nothing. It didn't protect me any more than I protected Jasper.

I can't do this alone. Not again. Ezekiel is locked away in the lab most of the time. He's as safe as anyone can be from things like time loops and Indigo. But Vee's right here, in this shrine of a diner, with people coming in and out all day. Indigo could walk through the front door, order a coffee, and zap her before she'd even finished writing his order down. Knowing she'd been out here without realizing the threat would hurt too much. I've ignored her for years and blamed her for something that was hardly her fault. I believed she failed my mother, but if the Legendary Flame couldn't stop Indigo, what hope did a mere mortal like Vee have? She didn't fail my mother, and I can't fail her now.

"If I tell you something that sounds impossible, do you promise not to laugh?" I certainly want to laugh, because the question sounds like a child asking if they can share a secret. But maybe that's what I am. Vee was always like a second mother to me. The grounded, earthly one while Mother went off on her missions and her jobs.

Vee's hand twitches, and she goes to reach across the table to touch me, but I drop my own hands to my lap because I'm not ready for that. We may be talking, but I still have two years of hurt and distance that I've been carrying around like a boulder. I can't shrug all that off in an instant because she gave me pie.

She says, "Of course. You can tell me anything."

So I tell her. Every detail. More than I told Ezekiel, because Vee was always the tactician. She listens quietly, the skin between her eyebrows pinched together in concentration. Sometimes she stops me and makes me go back, and I can sympathize with her "Wait. Was that the same day, or the day after?"

because it's so hard to keep straight, especially when you're not living it.

Finally, she pushes back in her seat, arms crossed, bottom lip between her teeth. It's her thinking face. I've known it since I was a child, and watching her process everything I've told her, I realize how much I've missed that face, along with so much else.

"So now you're . . . what?" she says. "Going to build your own time machine so you can go back and rescue him before he dies?"

I press the heels of my hands into my eyes. I shouldn't have had so much coffee. My stomach burns and my headache is worse. "I don't know. It doesn't feel fair that I'm alive and he's not."

I expect her to tell me that's normal. That we all feel that way when we're grieving. And she'd be right. But instead, she chews on her bottom lip a moment longer before she says, "Can I show you something?"

And I can't really say no, can I? Because I just dumped all of my time travelling trauma on her, so if she wants to off-load too, I'm really not in a position to refuse.

She gets up and heads toward the kitchen, and I follow, throwing a silent promise to the rest of the pie that I'll be back soon. A cook in a greasy apron watches as we pass through, but she doesn't appear too concerned by our appearance. Vee holds open a door at the back that leads to a narrow staircase going down. The smell of damp basement is apparent, and the light is dim, but I make my way, trying not to touch the walls, which look like they're coated in about an inch's worth of dust.

"I don't think the health department would approve of this," I say.

Vee laughs as she descends behind me. "That's why I don't let them come down here."

At the foot of the stairs, the walls are lined with rows of shelves, holding mundane things like boxes of toilet paper, takeout containers, and napkins. But Vee leads me past them and then down a constricted hallway where the ceiling is so low I have to bend so I don't brush my head on the bare light bulbs strung above us.

"Have you been building a secret superhero hideout down here all this time?" I ask.

Vee grins over her shoulder at me. "Something like that."

At the end is another door. This one is made of heavy metal, with a large latch, like some kind of walk-in refrigerator.

"Is this where you stash the bodies?" I ask.

Vee taps to the side of her nose with a wink. She pulls the handle and the door swings open with a groan, puffing up new clouds of dust.

Inside, the air is warmer than I expect, which is to say it's the same temperature as the rest of the basement instead of the refrigerated chill I'd anticipated. Vee turns on the overhead light by tugging on a pull chain. I blink in the brightness, only to be completely distracted by the chaos in front of me.

"Whaaat?" Where there should be shelves of food, there are walls that are covered with paper. News clippings. Maps. Lists and lists. "What is this?" Maybe my joke about a secret hideout is more on the nose than I thought.

Vee goes to stand in front of the largest map, which takes up most of the farthest wall.

"I guess I've been playing a bit of detective these last few years," she says.

I move next to her. It's a map of the city. Pushpins mark certain locations, while others have wide circles drawn around them in red.

"What are you looking for?" I ask.

"Indigo."

I choke, her answer unexpected.

"I've always known he didn't die the night when F—" She has to clear her throat as well. "When Farah was killed. The fact that you've seen him proves it, but I've been looking for signs of him every day for the last two years."

I stare at the map. Familiar places, marked in blue and red.

"What are you going to do when you find him?" I ask. Not if. Vee and I are speaking again, and together, we're going to find him.

My heartbeat quickens when she says, in a flat, matter-of-fact voice. "I'm going to rip his heart out, like he ripped out mine."

CHAPTER 17

Vee's face is determined as she stares at the map. I'm sorry for the space I've forced between us, because the suffering is evident in the way her mouth is pinched and how she keeps curling and uncurling her fists.

"There was some evidence that Indigo could use a form of teleportation," she says. "He'd show up in different places almost simultaneously. Or he'd be halfway across the world in a day. A few times, it seemed like we had him cornered, and then he'd vanish."

"So the marks on the map are where he's been spotted?" I ask.

Vee shakes her head. "No one has actually seen him since that night. Except you. But I've been looking into whether something like teleportation would even be possible."

"And?"

"He'd need to power it. You can't tear a hole in the fabric of time and space and walk through it like a door. Before Farah was killed, he seemed to be moving around the city a lot, so I built a heat map." She flips a switch on the side of the bulletin board where the map is posted, then turns out the light overhead. The board isn't quite so simple as a corkboard after all, because now it's illuminated, and the city glows behind the paper.

"What's that?" I ask, moving closer.

"It measures low-frequency energy fluctuations across the city." She taps the paper. "Took me a while. There's so much heat and noise. But once you weed it out, you find these other bursts that can't be explained by machinery and people." She points at the pushpins on the map.

"You think that's Indigo moving around? That he's been here for a while?"

She laughs. "They could be someone turning on the coffee grinder, except the locations are always weird. At the edges of the city. In parts of town where your average hipster and her cappuccino machine wouldn't show up."

I trace around one of the big red circles. "What are these?"

Vee blows out a breath. "I don't know what those are." She points at another. "But two nights ago, suddenly the whole board started lighting up like Christmas. Like tiny bombs going off all over the city."

"What are they?"

"I can't even begin to guess. They went on all night, and they were completely unpredictable. Sometimes they'd repeat in the same place over and over, then it would move around. A bunch of them were even right here, and I can guarantee Indigo didn't make an appearance. I think it must have been some kind of interference. Something's wrong."

My heart stops, and I drag my finger from the location of the diner down the familiar streets.

"This is my house," I say.

"Yeah," she says. "I was actually really relieved when you came in earlier. I was trying to figure out a way to call you without it being awkward."

But I'm already moving on to the next location.

"Kicks. Max's bar."

Vee stares at me. "You know Max?"

But I'm moving on.

"Murder pickles." My finger circles around Jasper's favourite restaurant.

"Excuse me?" Vee asks with a laugh.

I find Walter Wolfe's penthouse, but there's no red circle. Instead, there's a straight pin with a piece of blue string tied around it.

"What's this?"

Vee frowns. "That one I don't know. It happened after most of the other ones. It wasn't nearly as big, but then there was a second pulse right after it that shorted out the wiring in the board. Took me a couple hours yesterday morning to get it going again."

My heart is beating fast. I press my finger against the head of the pin until it hurts. Slowly, I exhale a fine breath as frost gently twists around the pin. The string goes stiff, and crystals create a small circle around the hole in the paper.

"That's neat," Vee says. "New trick?"

I don't even know how to explain, so I say, "That's where Jasper died. And the second pulse was me."

"You?"

I go backward, touching each of the other red circles. "Bus. Stab wound. Pickles." I trace the outline around my home. "Indigo."

Vee's eyes go wide as she studies the map. "This was you dying?"

"Think so. Except for the one with Jasper." I trail my finger over other landmarks I don't recognize. Probably the other nights. The ones I don't remember from before. I count them, then swallow hard as I lose track and have to start again.

Sixty-four. Sixty-five . . . seventy. Seventy-one.

"How many are there?" I ask. My hands are shaking, and my heart is beating so fast. Little circles of frost form anywhere I touch and I finally have to stuff my hands in my pockets.

Vee's gaze is still on the map, unaware that anything is wrong.

"I ran out of pins at a hundred and fifty, but even before that I couldn't keep up. Like I said. It went on for hours." She puts a hand on my arm and it's there. The whirlpool that would suck everything out of her if I let it. She seems to know because she hisses and pulls back. "Those were all you?"

But I can't answer. A hundred and fifty. More maybe. We've been in here for at least six months, not sixty days. I wobble with the very idea of it. I always assumed that Jasper remembered every one of our dates, but there must have been weeks or months before he started to remember.

"What is going on?" I breathe.

"I was hoping you were going to tell me," Vee says. She taps a final pin. She's drawn a circle around it, at least three times the size of any of the other markings in the city.

"That's Ziro Labs," I say, dread vying for space against panic.

Her mouth is thin as I stand. "Yeah."

"But I never died here." Not that I remember, anyway. "So what is that?"

"Your guess is as good as mine. Figured I couldn't exactly roll up to the front gate and ask you if you had a teleportation machine in the basement."

"We don't. We've been working on . . ." But my words cut off as a thought occurs to me. Or half a thought. Like a toddler that asks for attention, but you can't tell what exactly it wants. My eyes go back and forth from Wench to Kicks, the pickle restaurant to my house. I try to find the subdivision where Jasper's family lives before spinning back downtown and out again to the blank space that is the Wolfe Tech complex.

"There should be a circle here." I tap the map.

"Did you die there?"

"No, but they have a—" The toddler asks for attention again.

I told Jasper if I were building a time machine, I wouldn't set it up in my basement. Who knows what would happen if it broke down?

But Walter Wolfe had plans for the something that was almost the Ziro Machine but not quite. And Ziro Labs is pulsing like an open wound for no obvious reason.

"I have to go," I say, backing away from the board.

"What?" Vee follows. "Why?"

"I need to check something out."

"At Ziro? I'll go with you."

I stop at the bottom of the stairs, and Vee nearly collides with me. "You can't," I say. "It's dangerous."

She snorts. "You sound like your mother. Never stopped me before."

"No." I put my hands on her shoulders, holding her in place. "If there's something going on, you could get killed. If I get killed, I'll come back. I'll be right here. Literally. At the same table where this always starts. And I promise to ask for your help. Right away. I promise."

She studies me, and I ache for the years I've put between us. So instead of giving her room to argue, I pull her into a hug. She tenses for a moment before she pulls me close too, squeezing fiercely.

"Be careful," she says.

"I will."

My phone rings as I'm waiting at the crosswalk. A bus rumbles by, and I wave at the driver. I pull the phone from my coat pocket.

"Hello?"

"Morgan?" It's Ezekiel. "Where are you? I just got home and you're not here."

Shit. I glance at the time and it's later than I thought.

"I have to swing by the lab."

"The lab?"

"I forgot something."

"The presentation is the day after tomorrow. You need rest."

"I'll be back soon, I promise."

I drive faster than strictly legal across town. The sun is down, and the shadows under the lights are long as I pull into my usual parking spot at the lab. I keep my head down as I go through the lobby, waving to the security guard and making a mental note to send a gift basket to our HR team for not hiring skeevy losers like Leo and Bobby.

At the elevator, I choose the down button. The sublevels for the labs are where we developed the compressors for the Ziro Machine. The walls are ballistic-rated because the first attempts caused a few meltdowns. I bypass the first sublevel. It's where most of the day-to-day work happens. Someone would have noticed a time machine. But farther down, in the third basement level, that space has mostly been abandoned. It's where we built prototypes and where Ezekiel and I used to venture down periodically to test reconfigurations. But since the machine design was finalized late last year, I haven't been down this far.

That doesn't mean no one else has, though.

When I step off the elevator, I'm greeted by the sound of footsteps, somewhere far down the hall. I hesitate, ears straining, but the sound fades. Only the minimum number of lights for emergency exits are on. There's no evidence that anyone is or has come down here.

As I turn the corner, though, I catch a glimpse of a well-tailored suit before the man wearing it goes through the door at the end of the hall, and my stomach knots up.

Ezekiel?

But he's at home.

This is ridiculous. I'm chasing ghosts and conspiracy theories. Walter Wolfe has not built a time machine in our basement.

But then the door starts to glow.

Okay, not the door per se. But a blueish light emanates from beneath it, filling the far end of the corridor. Something hums, like the revolutions of an engine. Nothing is supposed to be down here. Could it really be a time machine?

I'm so nervous as I push open the door that I leave frosty fingerprints in my wake.

It's empty. Or at least, there are no people inside. Not Ezekiel. No techs. But something is wrong. This room should be a lab like the others, but instead it's been cleared of all the standard equipment. Benches, lockers, all gone. What remains is a skeletal and scaled-down version of the Ziro Machine. Not our prototype, but not the finished version either. Like a Ziro Machine cobbled together with spare parts and duct tape. The final version we're launching at the presentation is dense and about the size of a single-family bungalow. We had to clear out an entire wing of the lab building to make room for its assembly. The one here is about the size of a minivan, and while cables that have a circumference bigger than my arm are strung from it and lead out a door on the opposite side of the room, they're too small to be part of the Ziro Machine's transmission system.

Also, if the Ziro Machine were pulsing with light the way this machine is, we'd be declaring an emergency and evacuating the building. The light is definitely what was visible under the door, and it appears to somehow be contained, even though there are open spaces in the components that shouldn't be there.

I step forward, squinting against the glow. Slowly, a shadow becomes visible, sort of like the way shapes come back into focus if you stare into a light for too long. It's a person—a woman, actually. She's wearing something that might be a hospital gown. Her hair lifts from her shoulders like she's surrounded by static electricity.

As my eyes adapt further to the glow, shapes become more distinctive. Colours start to come through. The hospital gown is green. Her skin is so white it's translucent and her hair is—

My heart stops.

I close my eyes and turn my back on the machine and the form inside its chamber. I told Jasper that without the right parts to trap and convert collected energy, our machine could be dangerous. The void in front of me, uncontained and uncontrolled, should be getting ready to burn the building down, yet somehow, it's not. Doesn't mean I'm safe, though.

I turn back, blinking against the light. But it's fading fast, and the last of the colours are settling into place, including the deep red of my mother's hair.

She's there. Suspended. Eyes closed, but it's her, and my heart breaks and knits itself back together a million times in a single second.

"Mother?"

I stumble forward. She doesn't respond, and I'm almost glad her eyes aren't open to see how suddenly clumsy I am, my feet feeling wooden on the linoleum floor.

But she's here.

I reach for her.

And my hand goes right through her.

I gasp, jerking back. "Mom?"

Her hair floats like she's suspended in water, but when I go to brush it away from her face, my fingers slide through it too. I can almost feel . . . something. Not her. The air changes as I glide through the strands over and over. It feels thicker. Denser. But not solid, and she gives no indication that she feels me at all.

Vee. I need Vee. Or, if nothing else, Vee should be here. She should know. She thinks Mom's dead and . . . Ezekiel. He needs to know too.

A chill settles over me. I don't have to turn to know the cause. My plans and scattered thoughts all stop short because I'm no longer the only person in this room.

Like his own portable shadow, Indigo is standing behind me. His lightless shape shows off the outline of an immaculate suit. I've never been close enough to see the details, but whoever his supervillain tailor is deserves all the stars on an online review.

I don't get a chance to run, call out, or even test my fickle powers. He's already reaching for me, hand on my chest, and the burn pours in my veins as my heart stops.

I better wake up at Wench.

CHAPTER 18

Any blind date that starts with—

My brain does something like a hard reset. I have to close my eyes, which allows me to relive the last twenty-four—or is it thirty-six?—hours in reverse. My mother's floating body. The long hallway at the lab. The glowing board underneath Vee's diner. The crushing loneliness watching Jasper's sleepy face on my phone. The stickiness of his blood on my clothes. The way I held him as he died, the same way he'd held me that first night after the bus. He'd wiped my face with that awful green—

My gaze skitters to the door, half afraid of what I'll see, half afraid I won't see it.

Vee comes up to the table. "You sure you don't want something to eat? I could—"

The green hat enters and I'm already moving. I leave my laptop and my coat behind because I want my arms free to throw myself around Jasper. His stubble scrapes at my neck as he holds me close.

"I'm so glad you're back," I say.

"Me too. Dying kinda sucked." He lets me go long enough to

frame my face before he kisses me and, yes, I definitely missed this. Jasper is an excellent kisser.

I glance over my shoulder and Vee is standing by my table, hands on her hips, bemused smile on her face. Someone mutters behind us about getting a room.

Seems like solid advice.

"Wait here," I say, palms on Jasper's chest. God, I even missed this flannel shirt, but it's the only thing keeping me from groping him in public right now. I go back to my table and pack up my things.

Vee says, "Not staying?"

I hand her some money for my drink. "I'll be back. Just have to take care of something first."

She gives me a knowing wink. "So I see."

I want to stay. I want to tell her everything, but Jasper is here and it turns out I want him more.

I say, "We need to talk. I'm sorry I've been so awful."

Her smile grows. "You know where to find me."

"In the super-secret walk-in fridge lair in the basement?"

Vee's eyes get wide. I pull her into a quick hug, then hurry back to Jasper, basically dragging him out the front door.

"Are you okay?" Jasper says. I'm so impatient I nearly get us both killed and stumble to a halt at the curb as the bus goes by. Then we're moving again, Jasper trailing after me with a litany of questions. "Did Wolfe kill you too? Does it always happen like that? One second I was in his condo, and the next second I was on the street again. I guess we know now that it works both ways."

I fumble to find my car key. I'm so preoccupied I don't even look at him. "What works both ways?"

"It doesn't have to be you that dies every time. That's great, right?" His smile lights up the dusky evening around us.

Oh. There's something I hadn't thought of.

"Jasper," I say as I get into the car. "You were dead for two days."

"What?" He slides into the passenger seat his face creased with worry. God, I missed him. It has to be me who dies every time from now on, because I can't go that long without seeing him again. "No. It was . . . it felt like . . ."

I turn the motor on, then lean over the centre console. My fists tangle in Jasper's shirt and I pull him forward, kissing him hard. He grunts, but his mouth opens when I drag my tongue over his lips. He looks dazed when I pull back, which is fine by me.

"We have lots to talk about," I say. "But later." I put the car in reverse.

"Oh. Sure," Jasper says, sounding bewildered. "Where are we going now?"

"We're finishing what we started."

We drive across town. Periodically, Jasper rubs his chest, and I wonder if it hurts the way my injuries do when I come back. It doesn't seem to worry him too much, though, because he keeps rattling off questions.

"Where's Wolfe?"

Dunno. Don't care right now.

"What did you do while I was dead?"

I'll tell him later.

"Is there really a time machine?"

Maybe? I don't know? We need to return to the lab and get a better look at the machine . . . and my mother. But Indigo is there, and there are things I need to do before I let him sear my insides again.

Jasper's still going, though. "We should go back to Wolfe Tech and steal the plans again. I think I know how to disable the cameras properly. I didn't think they'd realize what I'd done so fast last time."

But halfway across the town his attention finally turns toward the streets. He frowns a little, then says, "We're going to my place."

I step on the gas. "We can't very well go to mine. Indigo

might be there, and that will sort of spoil the mood, don't you think?"

Logic tries to argue I'm being overly cautious. Indigo can't be in two places at once. He's either at the lab or at Ziro Hall. Unless Vee's right and he really can teleport. I'm not taking the chance of being interrupted again. Not a second time.

"The mood? I—" Jasper pauses, then his cheeks go a really cute shade of pink. He's trying too hard to be cool, but his smile is shy and it only makes my heart beat faster. "Oh. Oh, yeah, we can do that."

"Might as well. We've got all the time in the world." And yes, yes. There's the question of my dead mother in the basement at the lab. But she can wait, right? Two years and sixty some-odd days, plus or minus a hundred or more days Jasper and I have forgotten. What's a few more hours? I know I said sex with Jasper was either desperation or a feelings mess, but everything else is a mess too, so what do we have to lose? I've spent my entire life trying to figure out how I can be of service to other people. My mother died, and my reaction was to lock myself in a lab for two years, focused entirely on saving the world instead of looking after myself. It's time to be selfish, if only for a little bit. I'll be dead again by sunrise, and then we can get to the crime fighting.

There's no sign of Jasper's family as I park my car. They must be deep into their girls' night. I let Jasper lead the way up the stairs to his apartment. But once he closes the door, I press him up against the wall, pulling at the buttons of his shirt while I kiss him. His smell and his taste are exactly the way I remember them. It was already fading from his borrowed shirt as I worked yesterday at Wench, so to have the real thing to touch and breathe in is like winning the lottery.

"Morgan. Morgan, wait." He escapes my hungry mouth and hands.

"What? What's wrong?" I ask, breathless. "We're picking up where we left off."

He pulls his hat off, running a hand through his hair. "Is that all?"

My brain is swamped with sensation. There's no time for conversation. "What do you mean?"

Jasper blows out an annoyed breath. "I mean, are you only scratching an itch? Or you're happy to see me? Because trust me, I know that feeling, but if it's only gratitude, then maybe we're better off if we—"

"I got your video," I blurt out.

"My video?" Jasper asks.

"The one you sent the last time we were here. I was in the shower, and . . ." My face heats and I have to drop my gaze as doubts win over need. The room gets quiet for a second before his feet sound on the carpeted floor. It's hard to let him pull me to him. I liked it better when I was in charge. But his kiss is soft, and I don't feel threatened by it. I say, "I thought you wanted—"

"I wasn't asking you to pledge your undying love to me," he says. "I know you don't remember as many days as I do. You didn't get a chance to know me, so I can't expect you to say the things that I did."

I laugh. "From what you've said, I didn't give you much chance to get to know me either."

His fingers on my cheek are gentle. "No. But I liked what I saw. And I still do. But in the car . . . you said you wanted to finish what we started. If this is about checking something off a list or killing time because we have nothing else to do, then . . . I mean, I'll do it. But I want to know."

I could pull out of his arms. Maybe unbutton my shirt. Undo my fly. He'd know what my answer was.

But I missed him while he was gone. And I can't deny what I felt the instant he walked through the door, or even before. I covered it with snark and insults because I couldn't reconcile what I felt with his job. But that's not standing in the way anymore. And maybe, if we get out of this thing, I can try being honest with myself more often. In the meantime, I can try to be honest with him.

I cover his hand with mine. "There's no one I would want to get stuck on an endless blind date with more than you," I say. "And I'm sorry for the things I said before you told me about your family. I shouldn't have been so quick to judge. I know it's not as simple as black and white."

He brushes his thumb along my bottom lip, and I take a chance to clasp the tip of it between my teeth. His breath catches as he pulls his hand free, but he replaces his thumb with his mouth, and maybe I've said enough?

But he says, "I think you're being a little hard on yourself."

Hard on myself? I stare at him with wide disbelieving eyes. "I've done nothing but fight with you and belittle you. You're a nice guy, Jasper, but you don't have to be *this* nice."

He's holding me close, and I feel so safe. Almost peaceful, which is something entirely new for me. His touch is gentle when he says, "You challenge me and make me question the choices I thought only had one answer."

"Jasper," I say, aching. "My mother died. I've been so alone and angry and—" But I don't get to finish as he pulls me off my feet. Our mouths collide as he takes a few stumbling steps back, and I fall with him, until he's sitting at the edge of the bed and I get to my knees, straddling his lap.

"I'm asking you to let me in," he says. "You don't have to love me. You only have to let me be more than a henchman."

I rest my forehead against his collarbone. He's so much more than a henchman. We're past that. Past my failings too. No more sidekicks. No more regrets. And whatever that thing I saw was, it wasn't my mother. Just a mirage or a trick to keep me distracted until Indigo can find me again. The dead don't return. The future is me and Jasper.

"Partners," I say, holding out my hand to shake.

"Partners." He doesn't shake. Instead, he finally kisses me the way I've been wanting him to since he walked through the door at Wench.

Jasper's hands slide over my body and we slowly remove each other's clothes. We get to know each other in a way we haven't before. A bite on his bottom lip makes him groan. His fingers on the small of my back make me arch toward him. Jasper doesn't like it when I kiss his earlobes but makes a pleased, possessive sound when I drag my nails down his back. As I slide a hand to his groin, his lips part and his eyes flutter half shut.

"Morgan."

"Don't pass out on me here," I say.

He smiles as I keep stroking. "Wouldn't dream of it."

We do that for a while. Jasper likes it when I swipe my thumb over the crown of his erection. He explores me, tugging gently at my balls, and I moan.

He pulls me to the bed, dragging his stubble across my cheek, before he grabs hold of my hips and rolls us so he's on top. He kisses me as I laugh, and his eyes sparkle as he gazes down at me. "I can do better than that."

And oh boy, can he ever.

Jasper Jackson at my service.

It's been a while for me, and I'm immediately reminded how very little there is in this world that is truly better than a man with his head between your thighs and mouth on your skin.

I mean, revenge and vanquishing evil maybe, but other than that?

"Jasper." I gasp, fingers clutching his hair. If I'm hurting him, he doesn't seem to care. He's got one hand on my stomach, holding me down when I buck up against him. My cock is standing at full attention, and my nerve endings tingle with every swipe of his tongue as he gets closer and closer to where I need him. My toes curl in the sheets, my breath is coming in soft shallow pants, and my palms twitch with—"Jasper." I let go of his hair, horrified at the streaks of white where the strands have frozen and—"Jasper. Wait."

He glances up at me, chin on my pubic bone, breath hot on my skin. "What is it?"

"I—" I flex my palms, trying to think of somewhere I can put them that I won't regret. "I need a minute. To get some control back."

He kisses the inside of my thigh, sucking a bruise that makes me squirm. "Thought we agreed you didn't have to be in control all the time?"

"No. Wait." I push up to my elbows, wriggling free of him. "You don't understand."

He follows on his hands and knees, cock heavy between his legs, and I hate that I have to slow us down.

"I need to show you something," I say.

Jasper grumbles something I don't understand, but he lies on his side, pressed against me. He kisses my hip and runs his palm over my thigh, dipping inside to the thin skin there and—

I yelp and he freezes, expression turning concerned. I'm breathing deep, trying to hold myself together, and he seems to finally realize I'm not playing coy. He sits all the way up, leaning against the plain headboard and positioning me so I'm cradled between his thighs. It's a nice place to be. I could stay right here for a long time. He kisses my neck, but there's less heat in it now, and my breathing slows.

"Show me," he says.

I take his hand in mine, positioning us so his palm faces up and mine is face down with an inch or so between. I close my eyes, trying to find the switch that's becoming easier to connect with every time I look for it. Careful. Careful. Can't turn Jasper's apartment into a deep freeze. I breathe slowly, finding the control that means he'll feel the cold, but I won't accidentally turn his arm to a block of ice.

"What—" Jasper says, before he sucks in a breath, then

another as he pulls his hand away, hissing. "What the hell is that?"

"Call it a gift?" I say. "A special skill."

"But what is it?"

A glass of water sits on his nightstand, so I pour a small puddle into the cupped palm of my hand. As we watch, the few small drops solidify and freeze over.

"It's my birthright," I say. "From my mother."

His nose wrinkles. "You want to talk about your mother? Now?"

Oh my god. The slushy water drips over my skin as I put my palms to my own cheeks, trying to cool the flaming embarrassment there. Do I want to talk about this? No. Not right now. We're two naked guys, dicks out, and suddenly I need to talk about my dead mother? There's my usual brand of blunt and inappropriate, and there's whatever this is. Jasper's erection is deflating quickly, and I can't say I blame him. I only wanted to explain why things might get a little chilly around here as he drove me to orgasm with his too-talented tongue. But it's hard to explain what I can do—even though I still hardly understand it —without explaining who I am.

I climb up to my knees and turn to face him, kissing him so he knows I'm still here with him. With a deep breath, I say, "I need you to not freak out, okay?"

He laughs beneath my lips. "That's what people say when they know the other person is definitely going to freak out."

"Trust me when I tell you the disclaimer is necessary."

He sighs, but he lifts his hands so he can rest the back of his head against them. The swirl of brown hair in his armpits is a temptation. His flat nipples and soft hair over his chest and down his belly are an invitation. Like this, he paints such an enticing picture. I could easily skip the explanations and pick up where we left off.

But we said partners, and he needs to know.

I bunch up the sheets in my fist. My mother said never to tell anyone, but I don't want to keep doing this—to keep doing everything—alone.

Still, I can't quite meet his eyes when I say, "My mother was the Legendary Flame."

CHAPTER 19

Jasper thinks he's so smart, but the shocked expression on his face says even someone as smart as him did not see my announcement coming. I sit back on my heels to give him some space as he processes what I've said.

"The Legendary Flame," he says.

"Yes."

"Was your mother?"

"Yes."

He frowns. "Like . . . she gave birth to you?"

"I didn't hatch, Jasper." I cross my arms defensively over my body. There are some things I want to talk about with regards to my mother and some things that don't need to be discussed ever. Gory birthday details fall into the second category.

"No," he says quickly, holding out an apologetic hand. "I didn't mean it like that. But aren't superheroes supposed to, like, adopt orphans who have no idea who their parents are and mold them into the superheroes of the future?"

I tug on my earlobe. "You've got half of that right. But we look too much alike for me to have not been biological."

Jasper's gaze drifts up to the ceiling. "The Legendary Flame was your mother," he says, with something like wonder. "So, what does that make you? The Abominable Snow—"

"Don't say it." I jab a finger at him.

His grin turns playful. "But I was only—"

"Jasper. There's every chance we won't get out of the loop. If you want any hope in hell of getting laid during our time here, especially if you want it to be a repeat occurrence, you would do best to keep that name to yourself." I poke his chest and he grabs hold of my wrist, tugging me forward until I fall against him. He holds me close, and I don't fight him, letting the warmth of his body seep under my skin. It's nice here. I could learn to like it here.

"The Legendary Flame," he says again. "That's wild. So, you're a superhero?"

I shrug. "Subpar hero. I failed super puberty or something. Until now." I'm trailing my fingers up and down his arm and as I inhale, the heat of his skin leaches into my fingertips, making the hairs on his forearm stand on end. He shivers, and I pull my hand away.

"Like right now?"

I roll my eyes. "Yes, Jasper. This very moment. I was so wowed by your magic sex powers that suddenly I can suck the heat out of the room."

His laughter makes me shake against him, but I don't sit up. The vibration is soothing. Fucking would be better, but this is pretty good too.

"Magic sex powers? You know what I mean," he says, voice a rumble beneath my ear. He runs a hand over my back and I want to purr like a cat, though animal noises are still Clarissa's field of expertise, not mine. "When did you learn to do that?"

"When you died." The words are hard to get out. Slowly, I tell him about the scene in the penthouse. He remembers parts of it, but what with the bullet in his chest, he missed out on some of the important things, like me turning the whole place into a freezer.

"Entropy versus enthalpy," he says, nodding like it makes perfect sense.

"What?"

"You said you focused on the man holding you down. Basically sucked the life out of him."

"I'm a superhero, not a vampire." I squirm, trying to sit up, but he holds me tight. We don't fight anymore. That's what we said. Also, the term *superhero* on my tongue feels weird. I've never felt like my abilities—or inabilities, really—were something to be proud of, but Jasper's heart pumps an excited rhythm in his chest and mine beats in time.

"Flame, like your mom, is energy outward. It creates heat. Entropy. What you're describing is enthalpy. You don't release energy, you take it in. Consume it to power something else."

My instinct is to snap that I understand the difference between entropy and enthalpy. That it's the foundation of the Ziro Machine's technology. I know the terms, but I'd never thought about superpowers in that way. Flame, frost, speed, strength. They are their own discrete things. The tie to physics suddenly seems so obvious. It's what I've studied for years. But I never saw it like that before. Maybe because I was too busy thinking about my lack of power. I swallow my reflexive words down and take a moment to consider what he's saying in the context of myself and what it means. Maybe I'm not broken. Maybe I haven't been a failure all this time. We never understood how my powers were supposed to work.

The mood thoroughly deflated, Jasper and I lie like that for a while. Legs tangled together. My cheek on his chest. His fingers trace small circles on my skin. It would be easy to let the heat fade completely. We might even fall asleep and I'd probably enjoy that too, but I still want him.

I brush a thumb over one of his nipples. With each pass, I leave a trail of condensation on his skin. He watches me with a heavy gaze, and when I blow over the area, his nostrils flare.

"What are you doing?" he asks.

"Playing." I circle the nipple again, making it stand up from his chest. The skin around is cold.

"Jesus, it's like an ice cube."

I drag my tongue over the chilled nipple, then cover it with my mouth.

Jasper groans. "God. Your mouth. So hot."

We play like that for a while. Hot and cold. Energy back and forth. He's so responsive, and the sounds he makes are amazing. We have nothing but time. No gangsters coming for us. No one at work waiting for me. No one even knows we're here. Jasper said I had to give up control, but I don't think I would get tired of toying with him like this. After a lifetime of hiding pieces of myself and being a disappointment in other facets, when I look at Jasper, there's nothing left hiding between us. No lies, no omissions, no misunderstandings. The vulnerability of it is terrifying, but along with it is a sense of security I don't think I've ever felt before.

Finally, though, he rolls me over onto my back, covering my body with his once more. I spread my legs open so he falls between them, trapping our cocks between us as they lengthen all over again.

"Morgan," he says.

"Want you," I say.

"I've wanted you for months." He lifts long enough to grasp our shafts, stroking gently. The velvet hardness of him against me makes my eyes roll back in my head and my hips rock all on their own. Months. He's known me for months. I've known him for what? A week? Sort of. And he thinks it's only been two months when I know it's longer. But these are thoughts for later. Another day. Another loop. One where we have our clothes on.

He lets go and slides down, and his soft eyes lock on mine as he runs his tongue over his lower lip, then licks the head of my dick. It's a beautiful sight, and it gets better when he takes me into his mouth. The suction is bliss and he works fast. I lie still, focusing on controlling the power that keeps trying to break free.

But when he tugs on my balls, the heat at the base of my spine goes cold as something entirely different tries to burst forth.

"Jasper," I say. "Fuck me."

He pops off me like he's been waiting. The spit on my dick dries in the warm air of the bedroom, and I'm so sensitive all it would take is a couple fast strokes and I'd be done. So close. I was so close. But I didn't want to. Not yet. We're only getting started.

Jasper pulls lube and some condoms from his bedside drawer. He holds the condom between two fingers, looking at me with an arched eyebrow.

"I haven't had an STI test in a while," he says, "but it was negative the last time I did."

My laugh is bleak. "Not like it's an issue anyway. Hard to share STIs if I'm going to die before infection becomes a problem."

As soon as I say it, I realize I'm doing it again. Killing the mood. Jasper's smile droops and his fingers tighten on the condom.

"Fuck. Sorry. Forget I said anything. But we can skip the condom." I rise up, pulling his head down to mine and kissing him hard. He resists for a moment, but when I pull his bottom lip between my teeth, Jasper cups the back of my head in his strong hand, holding me close so he can devour my mouth and I let him, going soft and liquid against him.

Well . . . mostly soft. My dick aches and leaks in my hand. I might still come if he doesn't get inside me soon. I let go of myself and take him instead, stroking my thumb over the flared head and pressing against the slit, rubbing the bead of liquid that forms there in slow circles.

"Morgan," he says. One more circle is all I get before he lets go of me, flipping me over so I'm face down on the mattress. I only have a second to adjust so my dick is flat against my belly before the cold shock of lube on my ass has me jerking. It's followed immediately by the hot sting of Jasper's palm on one cheek, and the cry that leaps from my throat is unexpected and raw.

"Hold still," Jasper says as he soothes what is undoubtedly going to be a bright palm print on my ass. The thought makes me flush, and I'm so caught up in the idea of Jasper marking me as his, even temporarily, that I'm not prepared when the first lube-slick finger presses against my anus, making me yelp.

"Sorry," he says, his voice hoarse.

"Keep going." I wiggle my ass, letting him know how much I want him. The tip of my cock drags over his sheets, leaving a smear of wet precome. The nice thing about living the same day over and over is you don't have to do laundry, so I rut shamelessly against the bed while he works me open. The room fills with the sound of my needy moans.

"You're good. Doing so good," Jasper says, and the praise makes me harder.

"Soon. Please. Jasper. I'm ready." I'm already basically fucking his fingers. Please tell me his dick isn't far behind.

Finally, he pulls his hand free. He wraps an arm around my chest and lifts me to my knees. The blunt head of his cock is ready at my entrance, and all it takes is a long breath as I lean back and take him in. When my ass collides with his hips, we both groan, and his arm across my torso holds me tight to him so I can't move. All I can do is feel. The pressure of him as he stretches me open the last fraction of an inch. The wet heat of his breath on my neck. The steady thump of his heart where he's pressed against my back.

"Jasper." I reach behind me, threading my fingers in his hair while he mouths against my throat. He bites and sucks and I can't help the way I imagine the marks he's leaving. So blatant. So temporary. I don't want temporary, but unless we escape it's all we have.

When he finally thrusts up, he bumps against my prostate. It's a good thing he lives out here in the garage apartment because there's no way his mom and sisters wouldn't hear me scream otherwise.

"Jasper."

He's still holding me so tightly I can barely move, and I grope desperately for my dick. It's rock hard and leaking a steady trickle down the shaft, but when I go to stroke, Jasper finds me and stills my hand while he rocks inside me.

"Wait," he says.

"I don't think I can."

"I waited for you for sixty days. Just give me a few more minutes."

How can I say no to that? I lean back, tilting my head against his shoulder. He croons, telling me how good I am while he pumps inside me. Since I've gone pliant against him, he lets go of me, letting my weight keep me where he wants me while he grips my hips, lifting me up and down on his cock while my own dick bobs mindlessly in front of us. Every thrust feels so damn good. We're warm, even unclothed, and sweat slides against our skin where his front and my back are pressed together.

I'm trying to wait. I really am. But every time he hits my prostate, my insides coil tighter and tighter. The sensation is overwhelming and I'm not going to last.

"Jasper," I gasp. "Hurry. I'm going to come."

In one motion he bends forward, pushing me down so my ass is in the air and my face is squished into a pillow. I have to turn to the side to breathe, but all the air seems to have gone out of the room. I gasp as he slaps against my ass. His fingers on my hips are so tight he'll probably bruise me and I don't care. His. If it's like this every time, I'm so his.

With one last thrust, he sends me over the edge. The orgasm shoots out of me in a rush. The strangled cry scrapes against my throat, and my hands go cold. It's all I can do not to let the feeling wash over me completely, but I'm not sure I'd be able to stop it right now once I let go. Behind me, Jasper groans and has a chance for one final thrust before he loses the rhythm, and the hot splash inside me says he's coming too. I've never had sex without a condom before, and the pulse of his dick in my ass sends off little aftershocks from my own dick, leaving me to drip helplessly onto his sheets.

When he pulls out of me, I collapse like a broken doll. The wet spot on my belly is ick, but not so much that I want to do anything about it. I may never move again, actually. The best way to escape the time loop is to stay here in Jasper's bed and let him fuck me senseless whenever he wants.

He falls beside me, flopping onto his back with a contented sigh. His lips curl up in a sleepy, happy smile. I could stay here forever.

"That was nice," he says.

"Just nice?" Immediately, the drowsy feeling evaporates. I roll toward him. "It was *nice*?"

But he laughs and pulls me until I'm on top of him again. He wraps his arms around me, holding me still.

"No more fighting," he says. His voice is already thick with sleep. I squirm a little more, mostly to prove the point, but he only hums and kisses the top of my head. "You're cute when you're mad."

"I am not cute." I stab a finger at his sternum and I expect him to laugh, but he grimaces, tensing with pain. "What is it?"

"I don't know. I—" He pushes me up so I'm braced over him. A bruise the size of a palm print has settled in the middle of his chest.

"How long has that been there?" I ask.

"What?" Jasper also rises up on his elbows. His brows crease in concern as he looks down at his chest, then he rolls out of bed, rushing toward the bathroom. I follow after him. We're both naked, but no one's worried about that. Jasper stares at his reflection in the mirror, fingers tracing the outline of the angry mark on his skin.

"This wasn't here before," he says.

"Definitely not." I was pretty focused on getting laid as we stumbled into the apartment, but I'd have noticed if he'd been banged up like this while I showed off my spiffy chilly nipple trick. "Does it hurt?"

"Like a son of a bitch. Do you think this is from getting shot?"

My blood goes cold in my veins. I wrap my arms around him, careful not to press too hard on his bruise. The position is eerily familiar, like the way I held him while he died. My palm on his chest is in the same place it was as I tried to hold his blood inside him.

"Does it usually hurt for you?" Jasper asks as he turns in my arms.

A sick feeling settles in the pit of my stomach. I can practically see it spreading beneath his skin.

"I can't remember ever being shot. But that wasn't there before, and usually my aches and pains get better, not worse when the day starts over."

We stay there for a few minutes, quiet as our thoughts whirl around us. I'm almost afraid to touch him, like any contact will damage him further. Finally, he takes my hand in his and leads me back to the main room and the bed.

"Sleep," he says. "Everything is better with sleep."

He's right, but that doesn't mean relaxing is easy. My post-coital stupor is long gone, and I toss restlessly in bed. Jasper stays still so long I think he's managed to drift off, but after a few minutes he says, "We had a few dates that went really great, you know."

I stop rolling. "We did?"

"Yeah." Jasper takes my hand in the dark. "Once, I showed up and told you who I was—or who I should have been, I guess. A med student. I was about to start my residency and was specializing in pediatrics. I told you all about Lexi. We talked about saving the world." Even in the dark, I can see the glint of his teeth as he smiles. "It was a really fun time."

"Sounds like it." I snuggle deeper into my pillow, ignoring the pang of annoyance that Jasper gets to remember that date and I don't.

"But it wasn't real, regardless of what story I told you and whether you liked me or not. And we went our separate ways at the end of the night, and sometime later, you died and we started all over again. So even if we had fun, it didn't mean anything." He lets out a heavy sigh, and I can't help myself when I squeeze him tighter. How frustrating it must have been to be stuck with me over and over without me ever remembering who he was. "I got angry. I avoided you for a few days after. And the next time, I showed up and told you who I really was, and you didn't give me the time of day."

I laugh. My body is relaxing as he talks.

"If you need henching," I say.

"Yeah. That one."

I'm so close to sleep that it takes me a minute to realize what he's saying.

"You mean . . ."

"I only told you what I really did once. And that was the day you started remembering."

Ugh. Would it have been better if we'd gone through this with me believing his lie? If I'd remembered earlier and thought he was a doctor on a mission to help people like I was?

I wake up enough to make my muscles work, squeezing his hand.

"I'm sorry it took so long for me to see who you really are."

"You know now." He dips his head down to kiss my lip and I snuggle into him. I fall asleep in his arms and think about how many more nights I could be this lucky.

A crash wakes me. My heart pounds as I wait for the hands to grab me and yank me out of bed again, but they don't come. I lie still, waiting for my nerves to settle. I don't know how long I've been asleep, but it feels like a while. Light pours out of the bathroom, making me squint. The rest of the bed is empty.

Another crash comes, followed by a groan.

"Jasper?" But I'm already moving before he can reply.

He's on the floor in the bathroom, crumpled on the tile.

"Jasper!" I drop to my knees. He groans again, then lets out a choking cough that makes my heart squeeze. "Jasper." I roll him over, and bright red blood glistens on the tile floor. His skin is the colour of the ceramic beneath him, and his forehead shines with sweat.

The bruise on his chest has gone from being the size of my palm to the size of a plate. I can practically see where the blood is dripping inside of him.

"What's going on?" I ask.

He puts his hand to his chest. "Hurts to breathe." He coughs again, and the blood on his lips is crimson.

"Was someone here?"

He winces. "No. I woke up and it was hurting. You said it hurt."

"Not like this." I pull a towel off the rack and wipe his mouth before I grab a second towel and place it under his head. "Stay here. I'm calling an ambulance."

He's dying. Again. I can't watch him go all over again.

"Morgan," he wheezes. "It's okay. You know what to do. If I stay dead this time, I—"

"No." I put my fingers over his lips. "No, don't say it. I'll get you back."

"Morgan."

But I'm not having this conversation. Not watching him die again. Partners. That's what we agreed.

I lie down next to him. He groans when I roll him to face me.

"What are you doing?"

"I'll see you soon," I say.

"What?" But he coughs, cutting off the rest of his question. I put my hand to his chest, over the wound that has opened up and started bleeding inside him again. I'm so afraid this won't work I almost can't find my powers, but once I find the thread, it's easy enough to bring it to the surface.

Jasper jerks as the cold moves over the bruise. "Morgan."

"It's okay," I say. "It's going to be okay. It's energy. Enthalpy. Freezing is like going to sleep. And when you wake up, I'll be there with you."

"Morgan." But the cold is seeping over him and his muscles spasm and twitch, trying to keep him warm, even though he's lost too much blood for his body to function properly, even on reflex.

"It's okay." I kiss his forehead. His shivering stops, and his lips are slowly turning blue.

I'm not doing this without him again.

Last time, I protected us. Built a force field so that the bad guys around us froze into hench statues while Jasper and I stayed safe. This time, I don't. I imagine the whole little bathroom being consumed with ice. It's like a wave, creeping down one wall to the floor. It covers the tile until they glisten with frost. I open my eyes, and my breath is coming in soft condensed puffs between my lips. Beside me, Jasper's eyelashes have little snowflakes on them. His breathing is shallow, and he doesn't protest when I pull him close. I squeeze my eyes shut.

"Just like falling asleep," I say. Or like falling in love. I didn't have to do anything. One look at Jasper's scruffy face and artless grin and I was done for.

My teeth chatter, and still I let the power run free. No more need for control. No need to hold on. The cold envelops me. My joints are stiff, and I'm not sure I can actually feel Jasper against me so much as I know he's there.

"It's okay," I say, though Jasper can't hear me anymore. "It's okay."

When the shivering stops, a heavy warmth settles around me, until it's all I can feel. I hold on to the mental image of the two of us slowly being covered in ice. Maybe in a few thousand years someone will excavate us and wonder what our story was.

Or in a second I'll open my eyes and find myself staring up at my mother's judgement from the ceiling at Wench. Oh boy do I hope it's that option. I don't want the two of us to be some archaeological myth. Two men found embracing on the bathroom floor of an early twenty-first century residence. What happened? Were they lovers? Friends? No, wait! Brothers! They were definitely brothers. That's the only possible explanation. No one would ever be able to guess.

Tomorrow. Please let it be tomorrow.

"I'll see you soon."

CHAPTER 20

Any date that begins with—

I don't even stay at my table. Vee's about to ask me if she can't make me something, but I don't stop to talk as I rush for the door. When the green cap comes around the corner, I take off running down the sidewalk. Jasper is deep in thought and doesn't even look up until I'm ten feet away. His eyes widen in surprise as I launch myself into his arms.

"Oof." He stumbles back as he catches me. "What did you do? How long was I gone?"

"No time. No time. I couldn't. I couldn't do it without—" My words are all punctuated with giddy kisses and he laughs.

"Morgan."

"Are you okay?" I barely have my feet on the ground and I'm pulling at his shirt, fumbling with buttons.

"You're going to strip me right here on the street?" He's still laughing, but he grabs for my trembling fingers, trying to keep me from undressing him entirely.

But I won't be dissuaded so quickly. "The . . . your chest. The wound. Are you—" When I brush over the spot where the ugly bruise was the night before, he yelps.

"Ow. Shit." Then he freezes. "What . . . why does it still hurt? It never hurts the day after for you, does it?"

I pull him across the street. If he won't take off his shirt in public, the next best option is my car. He tugs both the flannel and T-shirt over his head, groaning as he does it. I hope his modesty will survive as I turn on the overhead dome light, though I hardly need it. The bruise on his chest is ugly and purple.

"Why? It's bigger now than it was before." He brushes the edges with his fingertips. "Why is it like that? You don't have any scars or anything, do you?"

I shake my head. Jasper's stomach growls.

"Oh, for fuck's sake," I say between clenched teeth.

"What?" He grins sheepishly. "I may be dying, but doesn't mean I'm not hungry. I deserve a last meal."

That's decidedly unfunny. Now is not the time for humour. "I'm not going to let you die."

He grimaces, rubbing his chest. "Not sure you get a choice." Without warning, he coughs. The sound is already wet. We don't have much time.

"Jasper." My voice wobbles.

"It's okay." He takes my hand, kissing the knuckles. When he looks up, dark circles are forming under his eyes.

I shake my head furiously. "It's not. I have a plan. My powers. I can restart the day. Whenever we need to. It doesn't hurt."

"And what?" he asks. He hasn't let go of my hand and he runs his thumb over the back of it. It's meant to be comforting, though his words are anything but. "We go on our first date forever and ever?"

"We'll make progress," I say. His gaze is steady, but there's sadness in his eyes. Resignation. It's like the first night again, when he thought he'd be alone forever, only now he believes it's me who's going to be left here by myself. "Don't worry. This isn't the end. When you . . ." I clear my throat. "When you . . . we'll start over."

Jasper doesn't say anything. He shivers as he pulls his shirt on, covering the internal wound that's slowly killing him. Again. I don't understand it as I run my hand over my own body, feeling all the places where aches and pains have healed. If I were like Jasper, after two months or even more, I shouldn't be able to walk—or breathe or speak or anything. The bus alone should have left me a crumpled mess.

I lean across the car and kiss his cheek. "We'll go to the lab," I say. "See about the machine in the basement. If that's as far as we get today, that's fine."

"The lab? What lab?"

Did I not tell him about that? Was I so horny that the topic of the apparition of my dead mother slipped my mind? It certainly wasn't enough that I didn't—

I gasp and cover my mouth with my hands.

"What? What is it?" Jasper pulls my wrists.

The horror is unthinkable. Oh god. I seriously consider freezing us both solid in my car to avoid the conversation, but it's not like he won't remember if we start again. The only way out of this is through it.

Still. Asking the question is agony.

"Did I really interrupt you midsex to tell you about my dead mother?"

He blinks a few times. Clearly, he was expecting a different, more earth-shattering crisis, though I really don't see what could be worse than this. But then he wrinkles his nose like it's the funniest thing he's heard all day, and when he laughs, I know it's going to be okay.

"Technically, it was midforeplay. And it seemed kind of important."

I put my hands to my cheeks, trying to cool my burning face. "But not so important that I remembered to tell you I saw her."

His smile vanishes. "What?"

"At the lab. Right before the last time I died." Not including giving myself hypothermia on the bathroom floor. "Well . . . the other last time."

He whirls, like she might appear in the car. "You saw her? Your mother? You saw the Legendary Flame and jumping my bones seemed more important?"

"I didn't jump your bones, Jasper. I seduced you."

He looks appalled. "You didn't even buy me dinner first."

I gape. "Now who's fighting?"

He's laughing once again. Jasper always seems to be laughing. But suddenly he winces, putting a hand to his chest. His face contorts in pain. We're running out of time.

"We have to go to the lab," I say.

"Your mother is at the lab?"

I don't even know who's at the lab. Indigo, yes. Something that looks like my mother but has all the substance of a mirage. So many questions, and if we don't hurry up, Jasper will be dead again before we get there.

Jasper coughs a few times as we drive, and each one ratchets up my nerves. I have no idea how long he has. If we go by yesterday, then at least four or five hours still, but I would have noticed the bruise on his chest while we were having sex, wouldn't I? So it's accelerating, making today's timeline uncertain.

We go in through the back door, and Jasper doesn't make a dig about my "Prestidigitator" password, which makes me even more nervous, as does the way he's moving slower than normal. I lead him to the elevator, and when the door opens to the subbasement, I hesitate for a moment. Maybe this is the wrong choice. Maybe, instead of dragging Jasper around town, we should go somewhere quiet. Somewhere private. Enjoy the time we have.

Inside, though, I'm afraid I won't be able to save him. I can't survive this alone. I mean, I probably can. Sooner or later, I'll figure out what's going on. But I won't. I refuse to escape only to spend the rest of my life grieving Jasper and the fact I couldn't save him. There was ultimately nothing I could have done for my mother, and it's nearly wrecked me. Losing Jasper in here would be my fault, and it isn't something I'd ever recover from.

"Now where?" Jasper asks behind me, jolting me into motion, and I lead him down the hall.

The door at the end isn't glowing, and I'm torn between the fear that the room will be empty and that it isn't. When I push the door open, the space inside is dim.

But the machine is there, and so is my mother.

"Woah," Jasper says as he walks past me. He stares at my mom. "She looks like you."

Everyone always said so. I never could see it. I reach out to run my fingers through her hair, then gasp when my fingers tangle in the strands. My mind reels. How is that possible? Last time, she might as well have been a hologram or projection. Now she's here. Solid. What's different? There's two of us here now. And Indigo isn't. Jasper and I have both died again.

I stare at my hand in awe. It's barely enough information to form a hypothesis, much less a conclusion.

"What's wrong?" Jasper asks.

"She's—" I reach for her again, but this time my fingers slip through her like they did the previous day, and with it, all my fractured ideas go floating away.

Wishful thinking.

Jasper coughs, long and wet. I spin, expecting to find him on the floor, but he's staring at the dials on the machine. "What do you think it does?"

Ugh. Despite my previous confidence, we're never getting out of here, are we? So many questions still unanswered.

But at least Indigo isn't here? Suddenly, being in control of my own death is a far more comfortable thought than waiting for him to pop up.

"Let's go to my office," I say.

"Your office?"

"There's something I want to look at."

"What about . . . what about her?" He glances up at my mom, still floating in her light-up cocoon.

I drag a finger through the glow, making it ripple. She blurs, like there's a lag in a signal somewhere, before she seems to recombine, more solid than before. I'm not brave enough to try to touch her again, but my heart seems to beat in time with the gentle pulse of the light around her.

"She's not really here," I say, taking his hand. "But if we can figure out who built the machine, maybe we can figure out what it does and if it's related to the loop."

He holds my hand all the way up the elevator.

"If Clarissa or Ezekiel asks, our date has been one for the record books."

"No way to avoid them?" His face is the colour of the elevator walls. I would do anything not to see them with him in such bad shape, but time is a cruel mistress.

"They were both here last time, so we have to assume . . ."

The end of the sentence freezes on the tip of my tongue and sends the rest of me subzero.

"Oh," Jasper says with a cough. "Because of the data breach. I helped him fix that last time."

"What time is it?"

"Just before eight, why?"

I stab at the panel, pressing every button I can until the elevator stops, one floor below my office.

"Get off," I say.

"What? Why?" But he does as I say. Jasper stands, bewildered, as the elevator doors close without us on it. "What's going on?"

But my head is racing as I do the math. I stab at the elevator's down button, waiting impatiently for a new door to open and return us to the lobby. I want to take the stairs, but I don't think Jasper can make it. When we finally get back on the elevator, he leans heavily against the rail. I need to help him, and the best way to do that is to solve the riddle of how we got stuck here and a piece—a really unnerving piece if I'm right—has finally clicked into place.

On every date, Jasper and I were supposed to meet at Wench at seven. He was a few minutes late. The second time I remember, I was so out of it after getting hit by the bus I basically fled the moment he arrived. We argued—because that's what we do best, or is it second-best, now?—on the street for a bit. Then I drove home. It's at least twenty minutes from downtown out to the house. So no later than seven thirty, I was at home and Ezekiel was leaving because he'd gotten a call about the data breach. He was on his way back to the lab, which is another fifteen minutes from the house if there's no traffic, and you don't catch every red light between there and here.

But today, we were here at the lab by seven fifteen, and his car was in the lot.

"Morgan." Jasper follows as I shove through the back door, rushing toward my car. "What's wrong?"

"I forgot my laptop," I lie, getting into the car. My hands shake as I release the lock on the other side. This can't be it. This can't be the answer. "We don't need to go to my office. We can check at home . . . at your home."

"My house? It's kinda far from here." Jasper's got a hand on his chest and he's gone very pale. "Are you sure—"

"My place, then." Anywhere that Ezekiel is not, so I can think.

I put the car in reverse and wheel around toward the exit like I'm getting ready for the demolition derby.

The house is quiet when we pull into the driveway. In a fit of what I pray is needless paranoia, I don't park in the garage, instead going around to park by what was originally servant's quarters and is now a guesthouse—not that we have many guests.

Jasper is wheezing audibly behind me as I push open the guesthouse door. The space is significantly bigger than Jasper's cozy apartment. The front room smells like dust. For a while after Mother died, I thought about moving over here, but Ezekiel convinced me to throw myself into work instead.

"Keep those off," I hiss when Jasper flips a light on.

"Why?" But he shuts it off and doesn't argue further when I glare at him. "Okay, okay. What's with the spy act?"

"I need to see something." I squint as my laptop turns on. Jasper slumps next to me, kicking up a cloud of dust and fluff from the disused sofa. His whole body strains with every inhale.

"I'll try to be quick. I need to get into the lab security system."

"Do you want me to—" He wiggles his fingers. I pretend I don't notice the way they tremble. Jasper can barely hold his hands up.

"It's fine," I say, logging into Ziro Lab's security system. "Being the boss's stepson does have some perks. I have remote access. No hacking required."

Fortunately, what I'm looking for is security camera footage from this evening, so it doesn't take long to find.

Unfortunately, what I see is exactly what I was afraid of. Ezekiel's car, parked in his spot. In fact, it doesn't even leave. It's been there since seven this morning, when we both arrived for the workday.

"Well, shit." I slump back in my chair.

"What?" Jasper coughs into his sleeve, and the flannel comes away bloody.

"Ezekiel is outside the loop."

"What?" This one is shouted, then punctuated by more coughing that doesn't stop. His chest gurgles as he gasps.

I stare at the screen where the BMW sits unmoving in the parking lot. "Ezekiel should have gone home and come back like the first time. But instead, he spent all day at the office."

"Maybe something changed." Jasper's sweating. "Like something happened that meant he had to stay at work?"

"No." I stare at the black-and-white image of Ezekiel's BMW

on my screen. "If we're the only ones who affect the loop, and he was at the house before, then he should be here, unless I do something to change it."

His brow creases. "But when we went to see him, he said he didn't know anything about the loop."

And here is the part that makes my stomach turn. "He lied to us."

"Maybe he—" Jasper groans and slumps over, spitting blood onto the dusty floor.

"Morgan, I can't—"

He may not be scared, but I can't stop my heart from pounding in my chest, even as he coughs his life away.

"It's okay," I say, helping him lie down completely. I crouch on the floor so we're eye to eye. "It's okay. We've got this."

He smiles at me with bloody teeth, and I wonder if this is how he felt all those times he had to watch me die on a sidewalk. Because it really sucks.

"It's okay," I say again.

"I'm ready," he says. Panic bubbles inside me and I shake my head, but he holds my hand. "We agreed. Start again. It'll be fine."

I take a long breath. His heat is already leaching into me, even as I breathe out puffs of condensed air.

"I'll see you soon," I say. This will be easy. Just like last night in the bathroom. Like falling asleep. I put my hand on his chest. He groans, and I whisper apologies as I reach inside myself and find the tip of frost that is already becoming familiar.

Jasper is cold all the way through when I finally let go, but somehow knowing that I'll be at Wench waiting for him soon doesn't make the whole thing any better.

I glance at the laptop and the image of Ezekiel's car. It doesn't make sense. Why would he lie to me? And more than once?

The minutes tick by. I should get on with it. Back to Wench. But I can't help myself when I go back to the computer. I watch the motionless car for a long time before finally clicking through other feeds.

There are no cameras in the room in the basement, but there are in the hall. The footage is so uneventful that I set it at high speed. I scan through days of footage before the first person appears. A janitor mops the floor. I wait for him to scrawl a hidden message on the wall or drag a body through one of the doors, but he finishes mopping and goes back to the elevator.

I go back further. Lots of emptiness. Then a man in a suit. I expect it to be Indigo, but as he's about to step through the door, he glances back once, and my heart stops.

Ezekiel.

He's there a lot. Up and down the hall. Through the door to the last room and back. He's always alone. The timestamp I'm looking at is months after we moved to the primary assembly wing. But he can't have built what's behind that door by himself. I never see him carrying anything. So where did all those parts come from?

Questions for another day. Another attempt. Jasper's waiting for me. Next time, we won't leave the diner. Travelling takes too much time. Hopefully Vee has a cord to charge my laptop. No wonder I was never able to manage more than a little spark. It wasn't my power at all. Like trying to run batteries in the wrong alignment.

Just as I'm about to close my eyes, though, a beam of light passes over me, shining through the window, before it arcs away. A car turns into the driveway, heading toward the main house. On instinct, I duck, but the car is already pulling into the garage.

"Jasper?" I say, though he can't hear me. "Someone's here."

Ezekiel. Ezekiel is here. I glance at the time. Just after nine. On the first day, I was still awake, tweaking slides I'm starting to think I'll never get to present. Ezekiel should still be at the office.

Is he Indigo? He couldn't have betrayed my mother like that. Why would he have helped her and Vee build the light box to trap Indigo if it meant trapping himself? Unless he's the reason it failed? Maybe the box was never going to work but would give him deniability when Indigo killed my mother? But that's impossible. There were too many times where Indigo was across the world and Ezekiel was here. There were witnesses. Business meetings. There's no way he could be both of them.

After this is all over, I hope I stay dead the final time long enough to at least get a decent nap out of the deal.

Lights come on in the house. My pulse pounds. I promised Jasper we'd do this together, but all my intuition says that something is wrong and that I need to know what Ezekiel is up to. I've spent the last two years working by his side, and to my knowledge he's never lied to me. Why he'd start now, at the same time everything else goes haywire, feels all kinds of wrong.

I mutter an apologetic promise to Jasper and leave the guesthouse.

Sneaking across your own front yard like you're trying to break into the house is weird. Even weirder is picking your way through the dogwood underneath the windows, hoping no one notices you being a creep.

Ezekiel is in his study, illuminated by the brass lamp on his desk. He's on the phone, and I can't hear what he's saying, but he looks relaxed, with his tie loosened around his neck and the top button of his shirt undone. Is he checking in with some henchman of his own to see if I've died yet? Whoever he's talking to, the conversation doesn't seem very urgent. He might as well be confirming travel plans, a busy philanthropist squeezing in a few more hours of productivity at home after a long day at the office.

I'm being paranoid. Too many attempts at the same day have gone to my head. Watching my boyfriend die three times in a row—facilitating that death twice—is a big ask. I'm seeing things that don't exist. What does Ezekiel gain from my death? We've essentially been brothers in arms—stepfather and stepson in arms sounds awkward—for the last two years. What does betraying me now get him?

Ezekiel's presence at home must be explained by some kind of butterfly effect, like Jasper said. Every time Jasper and I behave differently, tiny ripples cause other things to happen. I don't get hit by a bus, which means one of the passengers makes it home on time. I don't call Clarissa to whine about my date, so she has time to call Ezekiel earlier to tell him about the data breach. Maybe tonight there's no data breach at all and Ezekiel was able to come home early.

I should get back to Jasper. We can go see Ezekiel at the office together and ask him what he knows. If he says nothing, we can trust that, right?

My foot slips on a rock in the garden. Tumbling forward, I put my hands out and bang against the window frame before I drop to the ground.

Smooth. Very smooth. I glance up at the window, and the light has gone out. Great. Ezekiel will be out here to investigate any minute now and find me lurking in the bushes. I keep my head low as I get back up, risking one last peek through the window. What I see has my foot slipping again.

The light isn't out. The glow is still visible on the far wall. But none of it shines toward me, obliterated by the shadowless void that is Indigo.

He's standing at the desk where Ezekiel was a moment before. Panic washes over me like an icy wave. No, not panic. Power. The tiny dogwood at my feet has turned to brittle ice as I gathered energy on reflex. Indigo. I may have to fight Indigo to save Ezekiel. Unless he's already dead? It could happen that quickly.

I hold still, hoping Indigo can't see me beneath the windowsill. The closest exterior light is by the driveway, so I shouldn't be visible through the window, especially with Indigo blocking the light at the desk.

Slowly though, he raises a hand. I flinch, because if he's seen me, I'll be dead—and painfully—in the snap of a finger. But instead, he claps his hands together, and suddenly the room gets brighter again.

Indigo is gone. If I'd hoped to avoid the truth, it's too late for me now. My reasoning has failed because, once again, Ezekiel is standing at his desk, while the traces of black-hole shadows swirl around him and slowly evaporate. He turns, and our gazes meet through the window. His eyes flicker with surprise for the barest of seconds. I can only guess what he sees on my face, but it's not good. There's no way to hide what I know.

My heart hammers at the truth I can't avoid anymore. Because Ezekiel is Indigo.

He rushes to the window, and even through the glass, I can hear him shout my name. My heart is pounding so hard in my chest I'm dizzy. Ezekiel rushes toward the window, trails of inky smoke following in his wake. My ears are ringing. He shakes his head, like he's trying to deny what I've seen with my own eyes, and reaches out to me.

But as his hand presses against the glass, he disappears, and Indigo replaces him, a void in the warm light and sumptuous surrounding of Ezekiel's study. I swallow hard, waiting for the click of his fingers and the rush as my body shuts down, but it doesn't come.

My hand is not my own, though, as I raise my arm and touch the window, my palm pressed where Ezekiel's, where Indigo's is. I stare where his eyes should be. What would I see if he wants an empty nothingness? Still the same regret? Shame? Derision that I couldn't see what was in front of me the whole time?

Cold purpose settles over me and I open myself up. Instead of taking Jasper's hurt, I imagine taking Indigo. Saving Ezekiel. Maybe if I can separate them, then—

I realize my mistake immediately. It should have been plain from the start. Because the second Indigo's energy slips inside me, every part of me shrinks away. I'm a split second away from the most unimaginable pain, and I yank my hand back, breaking the connection. But it's not enough. My insides turn sour, and I can practically feel them rotting. I'm contaminated. Even that tiny moment of contact—and even with the separation of the glass—leaves me feeling polluted. I choke on it as I tumble backward to the grass. As I fall, Indigo vanishes and Ezekiel is there again. The expression on his face is fearful.

Sucks to be him, but it sucks to be me more.

Because now he knows I know.

I don't know what will happen if I stay here, letting the virus of Indigo spread inside me, but I don't intend to find out. I hold Ezekiel's gaze as I imagine the ice taking me. It forms a hard case around the tainted parts of me that Indigo has touched, then I push it outward, over my organs, my muscles and bones. My heart slows, and I lie back, already planning next steps.

When Jasper and I start again, we're going to have to act quickly.

CHAPTER 21

He's late.

And we're running out of time.

My heart is beating so fast I feel shaky. I glance anxiously at the mural overhead, but this time, instead of avoiding eye contact with my mother, I look directly at Indigo.

Did she know?

She couldn't have.

Indigo's chin is tilted back from the impact of a punch that happened a split second before the painter captured the moment. Is it really Ezekiel in all those shadows? Have I been staring up at a marital dispute this whole time? Mother would have been livid if she'd known. She'd have done more than punch him.

"You sure I can't—"

"Not now!" I shout, making Vee jump back. Heads turn toward me. She looks alarmed, and I can't blame her.

"Sorry," I say. "Sorry, just nervous. About my date. Whatever you want to make will be great."

She gives me a look that says she doesn't appreciate my outburst in her place of work. I go to apologize again but catch myself. There isn't time to explain what I've seen. Jasper will be here soon, he'll be dead again not much longer after that, and it turns out the stepfather who has been my rock for the last two years killed my mother and is probably responsible for my and Jasper's deaths too.

When he finally comes in the door, he looks awful. Even his hat is worse than usual.

"You look terrible," he says as he sits down. I can't possibly look worse than he does, but I smooth down my shirt and sweater, wrinkling my nose. Technically I only put them on this morning, and fortunately every time the day resets, whatever stains are on the material vanish. But equally as technically I've been wearing the same thing for an eternity. If we ever get out of here, I'm going to burn this outfit.

But never mind my wardrobe. We have more important issues to contend with right now.

"Indigo is Ezekiel."

Jasper rubs his chest. "I think I'm getting worse. It hurts more this time."

"Did you hear me?" I ask. Maybe I didn't speak. The words keep yelling themselves over and over in my head.

"Hmm?" Jasper says. His eyes are ringed in dark purple-like bruises, and even his cheeks look sunken.

"I said, Indigo is Ezekiel." I half shout it, trying to quiet the noise in my brain.

Jasper pales further when I didn't think that was possible. "What?"

"Indigo is who?" Vee has returned to the table and is staring at us with undisguised shock. The table descends into awkward silence as I wrestle with what to say, but you know what? Fuck it. My stepfather is a supervillain, and my boyfriend is dying with alarming frequency. I need all the help I can get.

"Indigo and Ezekiel are the same person."

Jasper frowns. Vee gasps.

"How do you know?" she asks.

Oh, that might be a reason to not tell her, because there's not enough time to cover that whole backstory.

"I saw him," I say, abbreviating. "In his office. He snapped his fingers and suddenly he was . . ." I wave my hands. "Empty."

"So what do we do?"

"We?" Jasper says. "Aren't you a waitress?"

My toes curl in my shoes as my ears go flaming hot. So much backstory. For everyone.

"Vee and my mom were . . . they knew each other."

Vee jerks a thumb at Jasper. "Who's this?"

"He's my . . . partner . . . boyfriend. Uh . . . we're on a blind date for the sixty-seventh time. Maybe more. You're going to need more pins for the board in your freezer tonight, by the way."

"Feels like I'm missing some details here," Vee says. "And how do you know about the board?"

Jasper laughs, which quickly turns into a consumptive cough. The effort doubles him over. He appears to be shrinking inside his flannel.

"We don't really have time for that," I say, pushing up from my chair.

"Does he need an ambulance?" Vee asks.

"More like a miracle," I say. People are watching from their tables. My mother is watching from overhead, and I can't think like this. "Can we go downstairs and talk? We need help."

Vee doesn't hesitate. Jasper stumbles. I put an arm around him to help guide him between tables. Getting down the stairs to the basement is trickier, but we manage. Jasper's breathing hard by the time we're all tucked away in the freezer.

"Wow," he says as Vee helps him sit down on an old leather desk chair with cracked arms. "This is pretty cool."

It is. The maps. The lighting. There are fewer pins on the board than there were the last time I was here, but as I watch, they begin lighting up. Tiny explosions that start at the diner begin radiating outward.

Silently, I count. One, two, three. I lose track somewhere around thirty when Vee goes, "What the hell is that?"

I don't need to count to mentally tick the number going up higher and higher.

"It's me," I say on a sigh.

She looks me up and down. "What do you mean?"

I pinch the bridge of my nose. It would be so helpful if just one person could remember what was happening here so I didn't have to explain every time.

The phone in my pocket starts to ring. When I pull it out, my heart drops so fast, little ridges of frost form on the screen around my fingertips.

Incoming call from

Ezekiel Ziro

Okay, someone other than Ezekiel. I put the phone back in my pocket, fighting for breath. He doesn't know where we are. Doesn't know about this place beneath the diner. Does he?

Vee, of course, has been watching over my shoulder and says, "You're not going to get that?"

"Not really feeling like talking to him right now." I can't. I can't even begin to think of what to say. Because Ezekiel is Indigo. He killed my mother. He killed *me*. More than once. He's living a life outside the confines of the time loop, and all of that put together means he must be the one behind it, and the very idea makes me want to throw up. Betrayal is the worst kind of grief.

"He's not really Indigo, though?" Vee asks. "You didn't mean what you said upstairs?"

I nod. "I don't understand either."

"But that's impossible. I was there. Your mom and me and Ezekiel. He was in the room when Indigo killed people on the other side of the world. He can't be two people at the same time."

I had the same thought. But I can't deny what I saw in the window at the house.

My phone rings again. Still Ezekiel. My throat goes dry just looking at the name. If I'm right, the implications are overwhelming. What does it mean for me? My mother and Vee? What does it mean for all the work I've put in over the last two years?

"Morgan," Jasper says. He's staring at the board with wide eyes. The lights are still flickering.

"What is it?"

His lips are moving, and I realize while Vee and I have been talking, he's been counting.

"It's a lot," he says, voice wavering. "Maybe a thousand? I dunno. I keep losing track, but I've crossed two hundred a few times."

We stare at each other. My knees threaten to give out from under me. A thousand. That's what, three years? How? How could we have been in the loop for that long? And if it's true, what changed that we finally started to remember?

The phone rings in my hand again. Jasper coughs, doubling over with the effort. He lifts his shirt as he straightens and the space between his nipples is mottled with bruising. Blues, purples and red. It's modern art. Or something trying to burst out of his chest.

"What the hell is that?" Vee asks him, looking alarmed.

"Morgan," he gasps. "I don't think . . ." But he gets cut off again in another spasm of coughing.

I answer the phone. "What the hell did you do to us?"

"Morgan," Ezekiel says. The relief in his voice makes me angrier. "What are you doing? I never wanted you to kill yourself. What were you thinking?"

What was I thinking? How can he even ask that?

"Answer me," I say. "Why are you doing this?"

"I know. I know." He sounds absolutely wrecked, and a flicker of sympathy sparks inside me, but one glance at Jasper's flagging frame is all I need to bolster my conviction. "I'm sorry. I can explain everything. Where are you? I can come to you."

"Like hell." There's no way I'm letting him within a mile of Jasper and Vee.

"Please, Morgan. I'm so sorry. I never meant for it to go this far." He sounds genuinely sorry, and I want so much to believe him. I know him. Have known him for years and even more so while we worked together on the Ziro Machine. But if everything has been a lie from the beginning, I'm not sure how I'll survive that.

"How long has it been?" I ask, because if he'll admit that much, maybe I've misread everything. He must have a reason. "How long have we been in the loop?"

The phone gets quiet. Jasper coughs. If he gets any paler, he'll be translucent.

"Four years," Ezekiel says softly, and the answer offers exactly zero reassurance.

"Why?" My voice wobbles with tears.

"I had to," he says, sounding almost as distressed. "Please. Please tell me where you are, and I'll explain everything."

"And you'll bring Indigo with you to finish us off?"

I expect him to deny it, but all he says is, "I can control him. You don't have to worry."

Worry? I glance at Jasper. He doesn't have much time left. Vee's watching us both with deep concern, and I regret not getting her involved sooner. Like four years ago, apparently. I was so caught up in grief and Ezekiel's lies that we were going to change the world that I didn't notice when my blind date turned into an Olympic event. Vee would have smelled a rat from the beginning.

"I'll come to you," I say. "Meet me at the lab. With Mother."

That he doesn't ask for more information or feign shock says exactly how much he really knows. All he says is, "Yes. Yes, thank you. Please come. I'll see you there soon."

My hands shake as I hang up.

"What do you mean, 'with Mother'?" Vee asks.

I bury my face in my hands. How is this my life? I thought it was bad before when I was somehow both an epic failure and a guardian for one of the most powerful secrets in the world. This is a zillion times worse.

Jasper staggers up his chair, though he has to hold on to the back for support.

"Let's go," he says.

I shake my head. "No. You stay here with Vee."

They both protest, but they're not going to change my mind.

"Jasper, you're dying. Again."

"What do you mean 'again'?" Vee asks, voice echoing off the freezer walls with frustration. "What's with all the cryptic covert bullshit? Will one of you please tell me what's going on?"

"Jasper can," I say, but he stumbles forward, grabbing at my wrist.

"You can't go see him. What if it's a trap?"

"Oh, it's a hundred percent a trap," I say, giving him a rueful smile. "But what's he going to do? Kill me for the twelve-hundredth night in a row?"

Vee makes a truly aggravated noise. If I survive, I'll be apologizing to her for a long time.

But Jasper only holds on tighter. "If Ezekiel is responsible for the loop, that means he also knows how to stop it. He could kill you and then . . ." He trails off, but the fear in his eyes is clear, and I don't need to hear the words to know where he was going. This could be it. Ezekiel could trap me, stop the loop, kill me one last time, and that would be the end. No more dates. No more arguments. No more Jasper.

I kiss him. I try to put every feeling, every promise, every apology into it. We wasted so much time, most of it without ever knowing what was happening. I chose bickering over being with him. If this is all we have, I want this last moment to be everything we could have been.

"Don't forget about me," I say, resting my cheek against his.

He holds me close. His breathing is raspy on my neck. "I love you."

"I love you too," he says desperately. "Whatever happens, I'll be waiting for you. Come find me."

I will. Whether it's at Wench or the big diner in the sky, we are owed some time to ourselves.

Vee walks me back upstairs and to the door.

"I can go with you," she says. "Your mom would be pissed that you're going alone."

I shake her hand, letting a little frost build up between us. She gasps as she stares down.

"I'm not as defenseless as I used to be," I say, giving her what I hope is a confident smile, even though I feel anything but. "And this is how it works, right? The hero and the villain, facing off one last time." I was never much of a hero, but I know how the game is played.

She hugs me, her embrace tighter than Jasper's.

"Farah would have been so proud."

I don't know if that's true or not, but now is not the time to dwell on old hurts.

When I step outside, I look both ways and cross the street to my car alone.

CHAPTER 22

The parking lot is completely empty as I drive up to Ziro Labs. If this really is going to be some kind of showdown, Ezekiel clearly doesn't want an audience. Even the security guard at the desk is gone. My footsteps echo in the hallway. I've been inside this building every day for the last two years—I refuse to think of it as longer—but suddenly the clean white walls and the squeak of my shoes on the tiles aren't familiar. The silence around me is ominous, and I have a moment of panic as the elevator doors shut. Too late now. I descend to the subbasement.

The hallway is as vacant as the main floor, but the glow from the last door beckons me. When I open it, everything is nearly the same as it was last time. The machine. My mother. Except now Ezekiel is there, and he's holding her hand.

"Look," he says with an elated smile as I walk in. He lifts my mother's hand triumphantly. "Isn't she perfect?"

I can't make myself approach. She may be solid, but she's not awake. Whatever is happening, that's not really my mother.

"What did you do?" I ask, trying to keep my voice from trembling.

"I brought her back. I told you we were going to save the

world." Ezekiel's gaze is glassy and unfocused. He might know I'm here, but I don't think he's actually speaking to me.

Something like an inky black tendril slithers out from one of his shirtsleeves, winding its way toward his hand . . . and my mother's.

Indigo.

Ezekiel's eyes widen as he looks down at their joined hands, and at least he has the sense to pull away. He laughs as he adjusts his cuffs. The black apparition slides back inside like a creature returning to its den.

"You see?" he asks. I really wish he'd stop smiling. "I told you I could control him."

A million questions collide together in a traffic jam at the back of my throat. What does he mean by control? How long has he been Indigo? Is that really my mother? If so, how did he get her here? And what does that have to do with me and Jasper?

Finally, his focus sharpens, and his smile turns kind instead of feverish as he looks at me from across the room.

"I owe you some explanations," he says, and for a second, I can see my stepfather. My colleague. He would never let me get hurt, if only because he loved my mother too much to let it happen. But as I glance at her still form glowing in the machine, an uneasy voice in the back of my head asks if maybe that's exactly the problem. He loved her too much.

"Were you always Indigo?" I can't help the way my hands clench into fists as I speak. "Were you always going to betray us?"

His expression changes to surprise and he shakes his head adamantly. "No. No of course not. I'm not Indigo. I'm only working with him for a little while."

"Like you're working with Walter Wolfe?" I half expected to find him here, gun at the ready while he issued threats. But it's only me and Ezekiel, who snorts at my question.

"Wolfe has nothing to do with this. His vision is too small. He started bragging about a time machine, but he didn't understand its potential. Thought he'd use it to steal crown jewels and buy stocks for public companies that hadn't hit it big yet. I knew it could do so much more." He's back to staring down at my mother, and I want to scream at him to get away from her. Whether he's himself or Indigo or something in between, I can't have him corrupting her.

"So, the plans?" I ask. "The ones in his office?"

"Stole them. It wasn't hard. We weren't making progress fast enough, and Farah kept getting further and further away. Indigo could only provide so much support. I'm sorry for sending you on a wild goose chase, but I needed more time. Your mother wasn't ready yet."

The confession leaves a bitter taste at the back of my throat. His sketch. The one that jump-started the machine design. Jasper and I believed Wolfe had stolen the Ziro Machine plans, but it was the other way around the whole time. And when he says he needed more time, somehow I know he means he needed me to die some more, though I don't understand the connection yet.

"This isn't really about climate change, is it?" I ask. All of me is poised to run. Not that I can outrun Indigo if he makes a full appearance. But there's something almost as menacing about Ezekiel's mannerisms right now. Like if I ask the wrong question or upset him, he'll leave me dead on the floor and waltz out of here with my mother to finish up whatever experiment this is somewhere else.

"It can be," he says, looking up at the machine. "After we bring your mother back, we can do anything we want. Everything is energy, in the end. Indigo explained it to me. I found him after he . . ." He has to clear his throat before he keeps speaking. "After your mother died. I went to the building looking for her body, even though the authorities said it was hopeless. I found him instead. He was weak. Nearly dead himself. But he said . . . he promised me . . ." His tears catch me off guard as they spill down his cheeks. "I failed her, Morgan. I told her the light box would work. That we could trap him and no one would get hurt. But she did. The box failed, and she died, and it was my fault."

I stumble back. The pain in his voice hurts almost as much as my heart stopping, because I know it so well. I've felt it, as the voices in my head tell me that it was my fault. That I was never good enough, and if I'd only found a way to be as super as she was, I might have been able to save her.

"But partnering with Indigo? That was the only solution?" I ask.

He wipes his nose with his sleeve. It's a decidedly un-Ezekiel gesture. Indigo's inky coils try to slip free of the cuff again.

"He said he'd tell me how to do it. All I had to do was give him somewhere to recover. I didn't realize at the time he meant inside me, but we all have to make sacrifices. For the greater good. And what could help humanity more than bringing her back? When she's alive again, she'll be able to stop him," Ezekiel says, taking her hand again. The Indigo wisps wrap around her too, spiraling quickly up her arm. The intrusion makes her ripple, like she's reverting to her intangible form. She won't be able to stop anything the way she is right now.

"Ezekiel!" I point, and he finally seems to notice the threat, letting go of her and shaking his arm like it's on fire. His face contorts as Indigo realizes his intrusion has failed and turns itself back on Ezekiel. For a second, his eyes go completely black, like the pupils have consumed everything else. He flickers, becoming negative space where the light around him continues to shine, but his silhouette blocks it from passing through, before he returns to his normal, human form. Though I'm starting to wonder how much humanity is really left in him.

"See?" he says, like nothing at all weird has happened.

"So you're in charge? Except for the times he showed up at the house and here to kill me on the spot?"

"An accident. I was distracted, and he gets impatient sometimes. Your deaths are inevitable now. Nature is always about balance. Once it happened the first time, it was always going to happen again. But if it takes too long, sometimes he slips his leash to speed things along. Every reset makes him a little stronger, I think, just like her, but I'm still in charge. I can reel him back in. Nothing to worry about."

I am so, so worried. What does he mean my deaths were inevitable? My fingers prickle with power, with the desire to freeze him to the floor and smash him like I did Walter Wolfe. But he's talking for a change instead of feigning care and ignorance like he has since I started remembering. If I think of this as a data-gathering mission, not a suicide one, maybe I can finally get the answers I need.

"What about us? Me and Jasper. What do we have to do with anything?"

"It's all energy," he says, like it's the simplest explanation in history. "All of it. Climate. Storms. Travel is moving your molecules through and around others that stay in place. Life and death. She was still there, Morgan. We couldn't see her, but you don't cease to exist in death. Your energy only goes somewhere else. All I had to do was find it, anchor it to something compatible, and bring her back."

I have a sinking feeling. "Compatible?"

His smile is once again compassionate. Fatherly. "She loved you a lot. You're so similar. Stubborn. Brave. She would be so proud of how hard you've worked. So who else could I have used to call her back? Once we had the machine assembled, it was easy."

"Easy as me dying?" Like I've become some kind of super-hero homing beacon. The last few years have been filled with so much purpose, but it was all a sham. Lies to keep me from guessing what was really going on.

Ezekiel moves toward me, reaching out like he might comfort me. Slim chance of that. I can already see Indigo trying to creep out from Ezekiel's sleeves again, as well as from the neck of the fine collared shirt he's wearing. The ink swirls around Ezekiel's throat, and he doesn't seem to know.

"It's a balance. Death releases so much energy," he says. "How could she not come back for that? Of course, her energy returned in very small amounts every time, but that's why you weren't supposed to remember. Our minds aren't built to understand the repetition of time. We want so much to see it as linear. But I needed more of it, so I built the loop."

And trapped us for years. Over and over without our knowledge or consent. I don't think I can ever forgive him for that. For what he's done to Jasper. And what he's describing goes beyond finding a needle in the cosmic haystack. Even if that's how death worked, it's not the same as finding change on the sidewalk. You can't vacuum her up, sort through the bits, and reassemble her puzzle pieces to make a living, breathing human being.

Though as I look down at her, floating in the machine's radiant embrace, I have to admit somehow, he seems to have done it. But at what cost?

"If we keep going in this timeline, Jasper will die," I say, trying to appeal to any shred of humanity he has left.

He nods, making me hope he understands, until he says, "I'm sorry about your friend. I didn't consider what the long-term effects might be. Without powers or a legacy like you and your mother have, it was inevitable he would die. Every reset scrambles things a little. I can't believe he lasted as long as he has, to be honest. But I thought you might enjoy spending time with him. That's why I picked tonight to repeat. I saw it when we were working. You were so isolated. I figured if we needed to buy time until your mother came back, at least you could have some company. You seemed comfortable enough with him when you came to see me at the office. Didn't you like him?"

The mental gymnastics going on inside my head better win me a medal when this is done. He's saying that our date was some kind of matchmaking distraction. Poor oblivious Morgan won't notice he's died a thousand times because he'll be too busy gazing into Jasper's speckled eyes. And worse, that Jasper is only collateral damage. That my mother's life matters more than his. Why? Because she might save people and he won't? Only because he never had a chance. He could have helped so many people as a doctor if he hadn't been caught up in Walter Wolfe's traps . . . and Ezekiel's.

I look up at the machine. The thick wires dangle from the ceiling, out of reach.

"Turn it off," I say.

Ezekiel blinks, looking confused. "What?"

"The machine. Turn it off. The experiment is over." I reach for the closest cord. No idea what it does. It might electrocute me with the voltage of a small power station or make me burst into a ball of flames. Doesn't matter. I'm sorry Ezekiel's grief has pulled him so far under, but that doesn't justify what he's done. Who's to say he'd only use it this one time? He might get my mother back and decide to resurrect other great heroes from the past. Or he's vastly overestimated his control over Indigo. If Indigo wins, he might trap so many people and their deaths in the machine for his own profit. Even in a world with powerful heroes and villains, there are limits to what can be allowed.

"Stop." Ezekiel grabs me. The glow in the room gets brighter. My emotions are rising and my control is slipping. If I could get a hand on the components inside, I could freeze them enough the whole thing would probably short-circuit. Even the most powerful flow of energy stops if you drop the temperature enough. I'll sink this place to absolute zero if I have to.

For a split second, my gaze drops to my mother. I think her eyelids might flicker, like she's dreaming. If she is real and actually here, I hope she can't hear what Ezekiel's done. He may think it's justified, but I don't think she would ever forgive him.

"I love you," I whisper. "I'm sorry."

I twist, breaking Ezekiel's hold and plunge my hand into the glowing field until my fingers tangle with my mother's. Then I find the switch inside me. I flip it, focusing on the not-quite-alive weight of her hand in mine. There's something there. Ezekiel is right. She's so close to coming back. I don't know how he did it. Better if I never know. The sacrifice is too high.

So instead, I close my eyes and focus on pulling the something inside of her out.

Absorbing it.

Making it mine.

It's a lot. I expect her to go cold. Turn icy like the thugs in the penthouse. Maybe she's close enough to living that she's fighting me. My hand is freezing and hers is burning hot. I frown as I take the heat, letting it slip inside me. It's like frost thawing on a windshield. The warmth wins the battle, travelling up my arm, lighting my heart on fire.

Around me, the sounds of the machine and Ezekiel's protests vanish. There is only me and my mother. For a second, she opens her eyes.

"Morgan," she says.

"I'm sorry. I'm sorry."

The fire and the ice twist and dance and consume us both as the basement room comes back into focus.

"What are you—" Ezekiel asks, but he's too late. "Stop!" He collides with me, knocking me off my feet and ripping me away from my mother's still form. His eyes are fully black as he snarls. "What did you do?"

The room around us is so bright it hurts, and the machine's noise shakes the floor, like some part of the gears is off balance.

When the light clears, my mother is gone. Vanished. There's no body on the floor, or in the air, or anywhere. But it's not over. The only way to finish this is to destroy the supervillain roaring in my face. Ezekiel's eyes are still black, and his face is contorted with rage. His hand is on my throat, and I mirror the gesture, squeezing tight just beneath his jaw. He said it was all energy. Me, him. Even Indigo. And it turns out, now that I know how, I am *very* good at moving energy from one place to another.

I close my eyes and open up. I hardly even need to flip the switch. A long exhale while I focus on Indigo's power clashing up against mine is all it takes. Unlike at the window at Ziro Hall, I don't fight it now. I let it in, even as it makes me gag. It's not like the others. It's so much more. Bigger. Uglier. His is a poison meant to kill.

"What are you doing?" His voice is a snarl. It hardly sounds like Ezekiel anymore.

Honestly, I'm not sure. It hasn't even been a week since I learned how to do this. Not really. But all I know is Ezekiel has to be stopped. Why couldn't he have grieved like the rest of us? There's throwing yourself into your work and then there's ripping through the fabric of time and mortality.

"I'm sorry," I say. I am. But my whole childhood was spent being told that it was our responsibility to make the hard decisions. That we had to keep people safe, even when the personal cost was too high. And I could never do it. I couldn't be the person I'd been told from the beginning I was destined to be. Until now. I'm not afraid of the pain. Not even afraid of dying. I've done it so many times now, that kind of fear is a distant memory.

I let it in. All of it. The darkness. The rage and despair.

Indigo is like venom. I choke on it, but when he tries to pull away, I tighten my grip on him, using both hands to hold him— and Ezekiel's body—in place. The inky darkness is erasing the features I knew, dissolving it all into shadow. For a second, I panic. I can't hold on to shadows. I try to pull Indigo in faster before he escapes. Then the shell of Ezekiel is gone, and my fingers slip through the emptiness. I scramble backward. Indigo follows, swelling to consume the light in the room.

No, he's not following. I'm taking him with me. It's like we're connected, and even as he seems to get bigger and bigger around me, I can sense more and more of him inside me, writhing like an animal in a trap. I can practically taste him in the back of my throat and feel him in my veins. I know how it happened. How Ezekiel let Indigo and his sadness win, taking him to places no hero ever would. It takes all my effort to hold on to Indigo. I am the trap, like the light box two years ago, and just like the box, I'm breaking apart. Ezekiel would never have been able to fully withstand him.

I stumble toward the machine. The floor shudders beneath me. The empty chamber where my mother was is still glowing. The blue light shimmers and blinks, flashing like a warning.

Energy has to go somewhere. Ezekiel has poured four years of death and grief into this experiment, and now it needs to be contained.

The machine sounds like a monster demanding to be fed as Indigo makes one last bid for freedom, but I don't think we could untangle ourselves now even if I wanted to. We're going in together.

Stepping into the machine is like stepping into a cheese grater. The connection with Indigo is torn apart, leaving me with the sensation that my chest has been ripped open. The inky black swirls away down some kind of cosmic drain. I'm left alone, watching as lights and colours spin around me. For a minute, I can see it all. Every day. Every night. Jasper's lopsided grin, and the stain of his blood on my hands. The flash of bus lights. Then further back. My mother's funeral. Her with Ezekiel, sitting together like they're settling in for a night of television. I'm not even sure that ever happened. Maybe it's what I wished for them, if their lives hadn't been so defined by ambition and obligation to a greater purpose.

"Are you coming?" a voice that sounds like Jasper's asks over my shoulder. "You didn't forget, did you?"

He smiles as I turn. I take his hand. He looks like the first time I saw him. Charming. Handsome. Optimistic. This is the Jasper I want. He has to survive so we can be like this together.

"I would never forget you."

The world blasts into shards of infinite blue and white, taking us with it.

CHAPTER 23

wake up in a white room. Feels like I've been hit by a transdimensional bus. Maybe a few of them. I run my tongue over my cracked lips and taste blood. When I stretch, my muscles feel like piano wires, and several joints pop audibly.

"Take it easy," a voice says. It crackles worse than my joints. I need to blink several times before the face to my left comes into focus. Dark lashes, fire engine–red hair streaked with black. Red cat-eye glasses. But it's the way Clarissa cringes in the corner, whining softly like a frightened cocker spaniel, that gives me the confirmation I need.

"April," I say, swallowing a few times, trying to find some spit to lubricate my throat. "I'm at SPAM."

"You'd rather be at City General?" she asks with an arched eyebrow. "I'm sure there are police there right now looking for anyone who was in the building when your lab spontaneously exploded last night."

Individually, I understand the words she's used. But the whole picture is a completely different story.

"The lab?"

"Ezekiel," Clarissa says, rushing forward. "They only found two of you when they started digging. Did you see Ezekiel?"

The last time I saw Ezekiel, he was trying to kill me. I shudder at the memory. There is still the feeling of Indigo inside me, like it's stuck to my cell walls, polluting me.

I'm going to throw up. I push onto my elbows as nausea swamps me. April and Clarissa scurry to respond, and I close my eyes, fighting to maintain a little dignity. At the last second, there's a pop and a sizzle, and when I open my eyes, the hospital room is dark and my sheets are stiff like they've been hung out to dry on a cold day. At least I haven't vomited.

But I've put my hands out like I was warding off an attack, and now, in front of my palm, is a tiny ball of fire, hung in the air waiting for me to direct it.

"Wow," I breathe. I haven't seen fire like that since . . . not since my mother fell from the roof and died.

"That is . . ." Clarissa's cell phone light flashes on. She's looking up at the ceiling, which is basically gone. Not like the panels have burned or cracked to reveal the wiring and duct-work above. The whole thing is gone, leaving a black void like nothing has ever existed in that space. Who knows where it leads.

"I'll get someone to check on the offices upstairs," April says without looking away from the ceiling. But Clarissa's gaze turns to me and I hold it, daring her to ask for an explanation. Not that I can give her one.

"Wait," I say as Clarissa's previous question comes back to me. "What do you mean there were two of us under the building? If it wasn't Ezekiel, who was it?"

Even April looks uncomfortable as she and Clarissa exchange a glance. Oh, this is going to be bad. Maybe they found two of me and would like an explanation as to how that's possible.

"It's your mom," Clarissa says, earning a sharp glare from April.

"My mom? Mother? She's alive? Awake?"

"She's—" April starts to say, but her answer doesn't really matter. If SPAM found my mother's body under Ziro Labs, they wouldn't have left her there. Which means she's here. I swing my legs over the side of the bed, yanking at the IV in the back of my hand. "Stop!"

"I don't work for you," I say as my feet hit the cold floor. The hospital gown barely covers my knees and my ass might be on display for everyone to see. Doesn't matter.

"Morgan!" April calls after me as I hurry into the hall.

"You should be in bed," Clarissa says, but she takes my elbow, leading me through a heavy door and to a glass wall. She slows, and I'm about to protest until I catch sight of my mother's red hair on the pillow.

"What—" I say, though I don't know how to finish that sentence. It's my mother. Here, and very solid, if the way Vee—dressed in a hazmat suit complete with a breathing apparatus—holds her hand as she sits by the bed is any indication.

"You can't go in there," Clarissa says. "It's an isolation room until the doctors figure out . . ." She waves her hand. "Everything."

"But Vee's in there."

"She was very insistent," April says as she catches up to us. "Forceful, even." She winces, and I notice the bruise forming on her cheek for the first time. I whistle softly. It takes a lot of woman to dare to punch April.

"Did someone call her?" I ask.

"She was at the lab when the emergency vehicles showed up," Clarissa says. "I don't know why. She's refused to talk to anyone. All she does is sit with your mom."

I watch them for a minute. My mother is unconscious. Vee's holding on to her hand, rubbing one thumb back and forth over her knuckles. It reminds me of the way Ezekiel held her hand. They both loved her so much, in their own way. Though hopefully Vee's way doesn't include breaking laws of physics and murder. What would be the sentence for killing someone a thousand times? We'd have to rebuild the machine for Ezekiel to live long enough to serve it. Assuming he's even alive now.

I tap on the glass. Clarissa shushes me, and even April jumps, but Vee looks up and when our gazes meet, something like surprise passes over her face. She sets my mother's hand down and rises.

It takes a few moments for her to get through several air locks and take the suit off.

"You made it," she says, like she's been waiting for me.

"What happened?" I ask.

She thins her lips and glances at April and Clarissa. After a moment of awkward silence, April nods and steps back. Clarissa says something about checking on the excavation and disappears up the hall.

"You've got some explaining to do," Vee says.

"So do you. I thought I told you to stay at the diner."

"I did," she says. "For a while, anyway. Until the board lit up so bright at the lab, I'm still seeing spots. After that, I don't care what noble intentions you had. You needed backup. And since Jasper was—"

"Jasper?" I practically shout it. "Is he—where—"

Her expression softens and my stomach drops. I shake my head. No. He can't be dead. Not after everything. I may or may not have a supervillain living inside me. Maybe some of my mother's powers too. Surely that's enough price to pay.

"I don't know," Vee says. "He told me to go. He was worried about you too. But Morgan, I wouldn't get my hopes up. He didn't look good. I'm so sorry. I should have checked on him, but your mother was—"

I don't wait to hear the rest. We can sort out questions of my mother's resurrection and everything else later.

"Clarissa!" I call as I run down the hall. April's wandered off to do something officially SPAMmy—maybe to see if any of the agents who worked above my ceiling hole were transported to another dimension—but Clarissa's head pops out of an open office door. "Where are my clothes?"

My clothes were taken for analysis, apparently, though

Clarissa can't say what they're being analyzed for. God only knows what residue is on them after years of time travel and whatever may have been present when I passed through the machine. I did say I was going to burn them, so it's no great loss, aside from wasting time I could use to find Jasper instead of trying to find a fresh set of something other than a hospital gown.

My phone has also disappeared, so Clarissa calls me a ride. Driving to Wench feels absurdly normal, but the driver has barely come to a stop before I'm stumbling out onto the street and through the diner's front door. Vee gave me the keys. The inside is dark, like everyone has gone home.

"Jasper?" I shout. My gaze is on the kitchen door, and my heart is already halfway down the stairs. I dread the thought of finding Jasper dead on the floor. This can't be it. We can't be over.

A flash of green catches my attention on a table in one of the booths by the wall. Jasper's toque. Beside it, his feet stick out, motionless on one of the benches.

No.

"You're late."

I trip over my feet as a dry voice comes deeper inside the booth. Then Jasper sits up, bracing between the table and the wall. His hair is askew and the buttons of his flannel are undone, but I don't care. I practically sprint across the room and throw myself at him.

"You're here," I say. "You're here. Are you okay? Are you—"

"I'm fine. I'm fine. Morgan. It's okay." He doesn't fight when I push up his T-shirt and inspect every inch of his chest. No sign of bleeding. No pain when I press my hands to his skin. He tangles his fingers in my hair to hold me in place while he kisses me long and hard. "I'm okay," he says.

"What happened?" I ask.

"Don't know. I don't remember a lot. Vee left. I was cold. So cold. But there was this flash, and when it cleared, I was sitting here."

I laugh, wiping my nose with the back of my hand. "The day reset? Just for you? How?"

His grin is perfectly uneven. I love him so much. "You're asking me? You're the scientist, Morgan. I'm only a lowly hench-man." His stomach growls, and he flushes. "Sorry. I'm still hungry. I'm always hungry here."

That requires more kisses. "You're way more than a hench-man. Partners. That's what we said."

"What happened?" he asks, gasping against my onslaught. "With Ezekiel?"

"My mother," I say. "She stayed. After the flash, she was still there."

I tell him what I know about Mother, which isn't much. About Ezekiel, which is more.

"You're okay?" he asks.

"Mostly." I wriggle my fingers. "Aside from the fact I have no idea what day it is. Or how my mother is back. And I may or may not be sharing my body with a supervillain." One of my feet is falling asleep, and I regretfully crawl back so I can sit across from him. I take the opportunity to groan as I bang my forehead on the table. "Guess I'm back to working for SPAM again. There's no way April's letting me out in public until we know exactly what the Ziro Machine did to me." I trace a finger over the tabletop, leaving a trail of frost on the veneer.

"And me? Did Ezekiel tell why we started remembering?"

I shake my head as I pull his hand across the table. "I'm sorry. I let him talk as much as he wanted, but he didn't say anything about that." I give him what I hope is a roguish smile. "Maybe you were so swayed by my charm you transcended the bounds of reality and time travel. We were fated, Jasper, and even a time loop couldn't stop us."

We stare at each other. His hazel gaze is endless. The circles around his eyes are gone. He looks exactly like the first time I remember seeing him. Healthy. Charming. So far out of my league.

He bursts out laughing. "Fated? That's the most out there thing I've ever heard you say. You believe in fate?"

I didn't use to. But I also didn't believe you could live the same day over and over or get a second chance to make a first impression. I was wrong about a lot of things.

I'm still holding his hand, but I let it go long enough to hold mine out to shake. He grins as he takes it.

"Hi," I say.

His smile is bemused. "Hi?"

"I'm Morgan Murray."

His grin grows exponentially as he stands, still holding my hand. "Jasper Jackson, at your service." We both come around the table until we're standing face-to-face.

"Nice to meet you, Jasper. Clarissa's told me a lot about you."

"You too. Alyssa said you were really cute, but I can tell we're going to have lots to talk about besides that."

I can't think of anyone I'd rather have a conversation with.

"What do you do?" I ask.

He straightens, eyeing me carefully. "I work IT and security for Walter Wolfe. I was studying to be a doctor, but life got in the way. Maybe someday . . ."

Someday soon. My new catalogue of powers means I'll be able to look out for the people I care about, including Jasper and his family. If Wolfe thinks he can keep blackmailing Jasper about the drug trial, I'll make him wish he'd stayed a block of ice up in the penthouse.

"You said you were hungry?" I ask.

He winks. "Starving."

"Great. Looks like they closed up this place, but I know somewhere else we can go. They make the best deep-fried pickles."

Jasper laughs as he leads me toward the door. "Oh yeah?"

"Yeah. They have mustard in them, though, so I can't eat them. Allergic."

"Oh, that sucks."

"I'll survive. Want to give it a try? You can tell me if they're as good as everyone says."

He pushes open the door as a bus rumbles by. "I'm sure they're great, but is that really what you want to do on a first date? Just pickles?"

I slide my hand into his. "We'll start there. After that, who knows? I've got all night."

"That's great! So do I!" Jasper smiles. I can't believe a guy like him is smiling at me. He probably thinks I'm some kind of fussy lab nerd. Wait until he hears I've got superpowers. But I can tell him about that later. Tomorrow, even.

We've got all the time in the world.

Thank you! For details on upcoming new releases, sales, and the occasional picture of my dog, sign up to receive The A-List, my monthly newsletter.

If you need more Subparheroes in your life, check out the whole series on Amazon, and don't forget to order the next book in the series, An Ex-Hero's Guide to Axe Handling by Jenn Burke.

ABOUT THE AUTHOR

Allison lives in Toronto with her very patient husband and the world's cutest team of rescue pets. She tries to split her time between writing, exploring Toronto's parks, and traveling anywhere that has good wine. Tragically, this leaves no time to clean the house.

ROMANCES BY ALLISON TEMPLE

Out & About

Work-Love Balance

Honeymoon Sweet

The Seacroft Series

Top Shelf

Cold Pressed

Hot Potato

Shared Series

Puppuccino (part of Bold Brew)

Under Her Roof (part of Accidentally Undercover)

My Not-So-Super Blind Date (part of Subparheroes)

Standalone

Up North

Boyfriend With Benefits

The Pick Up

The Neighbourly Thing

LGBTQ+ FANTASY BY ALLI TEMPLE

Afterlife Incorporated

Only Mostly Dead (coming soon)

The Pirate & Her Princess

Uncharted

Unbroken

Unleashed